HOPE

A Story of Devotion

HOPE

A Story of Devotion

Anthony Morena

TATE PUBLISHING
AND ENTERPRISES, LLC

Published by Tate Publishing & Enterprises, LLC
127 E. Trade Center Terrace | Mustang, Oklahoma 73064 USA
1.888.361.9473 | www.tatepublishing.com

Tate Publishing is committed to excellence in the publishing industry. The company reflects the philosophy established by the founders, based on Psalm 68:11,
"The Lord gave the word and great was the company of those who published it."

Published in the United States of America

ISBN: 978-1-63063-301-1
1. Fiction / Literary
2. Fiction / Christian / General
14.08.22

This book is dedicated to my parents; it is their example that motivates me and without whom I would not have the confidence necessary to write.

Chapter 1

Dr. Nancy Glacieux walks slowly down the corridor. She clutches her clipboard to her chest in an unconscious desire to keep her emotions bottled up inside. Her heels click along the linoleum with the regularity of her heartbeat. She focuses on the slight echo of the sound they make on the cold, polished floor. The effect extends beyond the initial rap, ricocheting off the walls, to the end of the corridor and back again to the inner canal of her ear. The echo of sound reminds her of the ringlets created when a stone is dropped into a pond, the waves go on and on, past when one can hear or see them. She feels her life is like that, like a weight has been dropped into it and its mark is continual and disruptive.

She is pulled back to reality by the sound of voices approaching from the other side of the nearing set of doors. Through the small spaces between the doors and the frame the sounds pierce the quiet and overshadow her thoughts. She can clearly discern two types; a man and a woman. As the door swings open, in the few seconds it takes to pass through the frame, she knows and understands their struggle. Although she dares not look at their faces, she hears the soft sobbing of the woman. The man has his one arm placed protectively over her shoulder and with the other holds the door open both for her and Nancy as they cross paths. She catches a few words that resonate deeply,

"It's going to be all right, honey," he says.

Nancy continues her measured pace, and as the doors swing closed and they continue in opposite directions, she still hears him but can no longer distinguish his words.

Dr. Glacieux falls back into her own thoughts as if the distraught couple never existed. She glances at her watch. It is nearly 9:00 p.m. and she hasn't had dinner. Today, as like many days, she survives on the late afternoon extra-large coffee and whatever looked least stale in the hospital cafeteria. This evening, like many others, she dejectedly makes her way to the parking lot and plops herself into the soft leather seat, exhausted by the stress and length of the day. Not finding the answer she seeks she is nagged by the thought that she is running out of time.

Fifty-two-years-old and perceived to be at the top of her profession. On the outside all shined, polished, and in order. She glances into the vanity mirror and sees looking back mysterious, deep, dark eyes, set a bit wide apart, exposing not a hint of age. She tilts her head ever so slightly and the light from a car behind shines on a cheek revealing a still smooth, almost teenage-like freshness to her skin. Her nose is not what one would call dainty, yet its shape fits her face, and its narrow, somewhat pointed look does not distract, but rather adds to her beauty. Her mouth is natural, she distains lipstick; doesn't like how it feels on her skin nor does she wish to attract more attention. Surrounded primarily by men with drive, men who are accustomed to getting what they want, when they want it, forces her to maintain a most impersonal veneer. She learned very early in what was even more "a man's world" back when she was in med school, that she needed to remain guarded and aloof. Over the years, men have become an almost unnecessary evil. She struggles momentarily with control. The sleek, imported automobile drifts on the curved ramp that leads to the expressway and the monotonous ride home, its tires rolling noisily over the designed bumps in the pavement. The noise spooks her out of the daydream and she sways, with the car, back on to its path. Once again in control, she enters the highway, quickly merges, accelerates, and slides into the left-hand lane.

With no traffic at this hour, within twenty minutes she is nearly home. She loves the North Shore, especially at night. The local roads are quiet. The distinguished houses are illuminated against the night, become as paintings. The scene uniquely pastoral, a mere mile or two from the overused highway, is a sanctuary to her. She turns into the driveway of number seven and the garage door rises to meet her. As she nestles the car into its normal spot, the door reverses itself, and by the time she exits, it is snug against the ground and she is safe. Although she doesn't like to acknowledge it, even here, one needs to be cautious. Safe is a relative word; you think you are safe and yet you read about others who also thought they were safe but were not. Only a few months ago, back in the spring, she read about a home not far from here that was invaded by armed, masked men. They tied up the homeowners, an older couple, and kept them in the basement for most of a day as they methodically went through the house. Alternately, they would untie and bring one up into the house. Then they would beat and threaten until they were sure there was no safe in the house, no hidden spot with gold or jewels. They left them to die, bound and gagged, in the basement.

Three days later an employee from the water company came to read the meter. As was her custom, she circled over to the left side of the house to access the external meter-reading device. She completed this quick task and had turned to leave when she caught a glimpse of something odd and looked back. She had serviced this route for nearly two years and had become familiar with many of the houses, some of the owners, and certain charms about them. She knew who had a dog and who did not. She was conscious of the landscaping, being especially careful with those that had bulbs planted for the spring, or flowers in season, and knew where the sprinkler heads were located.

Funny, how our lives intersect and how even the smallest occurrence can alter our fate; this particular water meter reader had hopes and dreams of her own. She had an eye and a certain amount of flair for decorating. She loved fabrics, tapestry, and how these could be used to enhance the look and feel of a home. In short, her modest desire was to open a shop that would focus on window treatments. This particular house had some of the nicest curtains and accoutrements. She had become aware of it on the very first visit. The lady that lived here had been sitting on the swinging chair that hung from the overhang on the front porch. Behind her were two huge windows and the chair was centered between them. She recalled how the woman greeted her by asking, "How are you, dear?" Her initial thought was how pleasant the tone of the woman was. She had the feeling that the woman really wanted to know how she was doing. When she raised her eyes to see who had spoken to her, her mind was immediately taken by what she saw. It was as if it was a picture from a magazine. The woman that spoke was evidently older. She had a neat cut of all-white hair and rocked ever so gently in the chair, her ankles crossed, a pair of knitting needles moving steadily with some finished work rumpled up on her lap, a plain house dress adorned with a butterfly pin set on her right shoulder, and a delicate set of pearls encircled her neck. The two windows open with the sheerest linen blowing out towards the front yard from the breeze. She could see the heavier material that folded itself vertically around the left and right side of each window, and the valance that arced along the top of each. It was a momentary feeling, a bit surreal to her; it was as if she had seen a vision. She and the woman exchanged a few kind words. She inquired what she was knitting. It was a child's sweater, destined for an orphanage in Romania – "The poor little ones have nothing there," she said.

At each subsequent visit during her rounds she checked the swing on the porch to see if the old woman might be sitting there. From that time until now, she had not appeared again. What she had noticed though, as she remembered that initial picturesque setting, was how particular the old woman was about her windows. There were four more across the upper floor and two more on the mid-level on the left side (where the meter was), and two additional small ones closer to the ground on that side, which let some light into the basement. Each was nicely framed and seemed to give the house a warm, inviting look. It was how she imagined she might have a home of her own someday, and how she hoped to help others with her business in the future. But whom was she kidding with this dream of hers? She could barely pay the bills with what she made. She could never save what was needed to make that happen.

On this particular day, she looked back at the basement window and noticed that it was covered with a dark plastic. She looked to the other that was set a bit more to the back of the house and it too, was darkened as if to keep out the light. She thought that was strange. It wasn't as if the windows were broken. They were not. She could not describe her feeling but she couldn't imagine the lady she had met, the lady that took such care of her home, would put plastic up over her windows. She went to the front and rang the doorbell. After a half-minute she was almost glad when no one came to the door. What would she have said? Maybe it's best, she thought, I wouldn't want to get myself in any trouble; what was I thinking? She started off to the left, figuring to dart quickly across the lawn and to the next house to try to make up for lost time. She looked at the darkened basement windows one more time and shook her head, thinking, "Something is not right." This time she pressed her eyes against the glass, blocking the sunlight with her cupped hand and peered into the darkness. She gasped and jumped back a bit as she thought she heard an eerie sound coming from within. Then she pressed her right ear against the glass and blotted out all other noise by covering her exposed ear with her left hand, held her breath, and listened deeply.

It is hard to imagine a pair of novice thieves that would be so cold as to take what a couple had and not care whether they lived or died. They easily overcame the elderly couple, not that they tried to put up a fight, they did not; they were quite willing to give the bandits what they came for. The intruders raged on regardless. First the tying up in the basement, later the interrogation and the beating that they had learned would loosen even the tightest lips. In reality they were weak, not strong. The couple pleaded for their lives. The husband offered himself as the victim in a vain attempt to protect his wife. He offered to take them to the bank, to help them take whatever he had, no questions asked, and still they refused. He did not know what was worse, to be beaten or to hear her being tossed about upstairs by the

11

attackers. When they returned her to the basement he could not see her due to the tape put across his eyes, but he heard her muffled moaning through the tape that had been set across her mouth. He wept.

Although time had lost its meaning, in what must have been days, he had given up hope of discovery. When the doorbell rang he came to consciousness, and the keen desire to live rose up within him. He called out from behind the tape and was able to make a muffled shriek in hope it would be heard. He felt like one stranded on a desert island that hears a passing plane and looking up sees that it is much too high to notice him and yet still waves his arms and regardless calls out, "I'm here. I'm over here." Of course, the plane passes and continues on, oblivious of the dire situation below. The bell did not ring a second time. There was no breaking down of the door, no noise, only the silence of his despair. He realized his wife had made no sound. "She must be dead," he thought. This was the point that grief overwhelmed him. It really didn't matter to him if they even found him now. The groan came not from his vocal cords but from someplace deeper. It began rather meekly, as if from one that had given up. Its intensity grew like a wave that rises just before it comes crashing to the shore. The strange utterance increased in force, exploding from within, and the sound of his agony reverberated in the small confines.

It was at that time, when Nancy read about what happened to the elderly couple, whose home had been invaded, that she was glad that she had listened to Harry and had the security system installed.

Chapter 2

Back at her office at the research center the next day, Nancy taps the desk impatiently with her pencil. Karl, her assistant, normally pranced about outside the sleek, modern vestibule of the 'open office' construction. Her interior designer had convinced her that this was the way it was being done these days; convinced her that she would "get used to it." She had not. So instead of some quiet calm behind her own door, within the walls of a sealed office, she tolerates the antics of Karl beyond the partition they now call an office; an office without a door. Her impatience increases as she stares down at the blueberry muffin she grabbed from the kitchen counter as she flew out the door this morning. It isn't really the muffin, or Karl that makes her so impatient; she is hungry. This will be breakfast if only he would get here with her coffee. Dammit, is it too much to ask for a hot cup of coffee so I can get my day started? What is taking him so long? She bounces the pencil eraser more firmly and more frequent. How can I start without my coffee? It's as if her brain is in suspended animation, trying to think, yet caught in a freezing stupor. She senses the inertia created from the lack of caffeine, an impatience growing from a dearth of food. It isn't her stomach so much that reminds her of her privation, it is her bloodstream. It needs the sugar boost. It craves the as yet to arrive caffeine. Where the hell is he with my coffee?

If it is something the world needs it's a competent assistant. Now that would be a breakthrough. That would be something that the medical profession would stand up and take notice of. Shit, that's something that would change the world, she thinks as she taps and her mind whirls devilishly in this 'I must have my breakfast now' mindset she finds herself in. She should fire his ass. If he doesn't get here in the next thirty seconds I'm going to just fire his ass. She watches the digital clock on her desk that is supposed to keep accurate time to the hundredth of a second of the 'real' time. Nine, ten, eleven seconds tick by. She keeps her eyes riveted to the clock. She eyes the muffin, taps the pencil. Sixteen, seventeen, eighteen, I swear, I'll fire him if he doesn't get here with my damn coffee. He is probably flirting near the elevator as my coffee gets cold and he causes his own demise. Twenty-four, twenty-five, twenty-six, . . . He turns quickly around the frame of the modular office, lets out an exaggerated sigh, with exaggerated quickness, and apologizes for the line at the cafeteria.

"I swear," he says, "I can't believe they can't get a competent cashier down there. The line was horrendous!"

Her icy stare shifts from the clock to her coffee, never looking up at him. She exhales deeply not having noticed she had held her breath during the last few seconds of the countdown. She can't even pretend it doesn't matter to her. He sets the coffee down in its usually place and turns to go. She manages an insincere "thank you," addressed to his back as he stomps out of her space.

****

I should just quit, he thinks. She treats me like some common flunky. She doesn't appreciate what I do around here. Sends me for her coffee for God's sake. Errrr….

Although he must admit, it does give him another chance to see that smooth skinned creature down in the cafeteria. Once in the morning when he arrives, just fashionably after nine (not that she would be here to notice); and again when she arrives and usually just announces 'coffee.' Just the one word, 'coffee.' Not please get me a cup of coffee, just 'coffee' and he is supposed to jump to attention and do her bidding. God forbid he isn't at his desk to take the order, or even if he is on the phone, she marches past, announces her wish, and he is supposed to end the conversation and jump to attention. It's like the freakin military.

It wasn't like that initially. He remembered back to his first day, how she seemed almost apologetic about sending him on this errand. She asked if he wouldn't mind, he said, "Of course not, I'd be glad to get you a cup of coffee in the morning."

She smiled sweetly and seemed generally pleased that it was not an issue for him, "Feel free to get something for you as well," she added. But he never did.

****

She sips the hot elixir, allows it to warm her mouth, her throat, feels its presence down her chest and imagines it now dispersing its medicine throughout her blood stream. Why can't the cure she seeks with her research be this easy? Take this pill; watch it work in a matter of minutes. It's not just the science part that's complicated. It's getting the funding. Finding the donors and convincing them that her research and methods can bear fruit. It's the dog and pony show she detests. It's the cajoling, and once signed up, it's the follow-up requests. She hates asking people for money. She feels like a prostitute, and depending upon how one looks at it, perhaps even is. She has something that people want, or at least what they think they want, takes their money, and gives them the illusion of satisfying their strongest desire at the moment. Through it all she is willing to sacrifice herself so she can get the money. She takes another sip of the dark potion and pushes back the thought she has rationalized away many, many times in the past few years.

She takes a bite of the underside of the muffin. Already at her laptop she is careful to not get any crumbs in the keypad. Stray crumbs and loose fragments, would not be good. She works at the muffin with her left hand and allows her right hand to continue to punch the letters and numbers, to scroll and click single-handily. Meticulous to a fault, she is careful to not let even the grease stained left hand finger tips touch any part of the computer.

She works with the one clean hand and it reminds her of being on a plane and sitting next to a clean cut young man who, like herself at this moment, worked ferociously at his laptop. It was during the one long

15

trip she took to her husband's homeland. He had the food tray down and although the set-up was tight, seemed determined to get some work done. What stood out about this particular young man was that he worked with only his right hand. His left gone, and she too polite to ask how it happened, even though she wanted to know. His right hand seemed to make up for any deficiency. Its fingers flew across the keypad with incredible speed. From time to time the hand would rise in an awkward and apparent need to perform a function not normally ascribed to that hand, a function that would have been much easier if the left hand and fingers were still attached. What was amazing was the agility with which he completed his task. He was much faster than many people are with two hands. It was this ability - the ability for the human body and mind to compensate for an unexpected area of lack - that was her hope. The body adapts and the mind helps it, or rather, can help it. Sometimes it appears that the mind does the opposite, it hinders. This is part of her struggle. She attempts to get the body and mind to work together in such a way as to maximize the benefit. This young man had an advantage; he knew what the handicap was. He had a left hand, lost it in some freak military accident (she presumed), and knew he needed to rely on the remaining right hand so much more. Being young, being positive, and having the proper motivation, his mind was able to coordinate the two parts of his being to function. It appeared his remaining right hand functioned at a much higher level than it likely would ever have if it hadn't become necessary to do so. So, she reasoned, the ability to perform above and beyond what can normally be expected is a realistic expectation when the body is tasked with something outside of what it was designed to do in its normal state. She is convinced that is part of the key.

Nancy has only the muffin top left. It is her favorite part and she often leaves it for last. Sometimes she immediately separates it from the base and leaves it to the side. Other times, like today, she eats away the stem to be left with only the crown she desires. Her mental wanderings have caused the heat to dissipate from the cup. She glances out and sees that Karl is not at his desk so she wearily rises,

16

cup in hand and saunters over to the little kitchenette area she had set up for them. It has a small, dorm style frig, a toaster oven, and a microwave, all set on one cart with the multiple plugs all jammed into a strip. This will probably burn the place down someday from the overload. If not that, than the burnt crumbs on the bottom of the oven will catch fire when left unattended or more likely from Karl's frozen, calorie reduced lunch overflowing onto the hot grates while he flits about the office compound. She pops open the door of the microwave and thrust the cup onto the exact center of the base and hits 25 on the timer. She grew accustomed to hot coffee very early in her residency. Then she often had only a few minutes to quaff a quick cup between tasks and she was exhausted enough to know that she needed to recharge in whatever way possible. She learned to drink it hot. Even now, many years later, it is still her preference. Only now she has to reheat a cup two or three times before she finishes it off. This is especially true when she is by herself.

In the quiet of her own mind, surrounded by her thoughts or absorbed in her work the clock moves too rapidly. The seconds tick off into short minutes and large chunks of her life seem to whisk away from her as if caught in a current. Fifty-two, fifty-two! Jeez, how did this happen to her? She is getting old. Too wise, she realizes that the external shell, still nearly perfect, will only mask the inevitable corruption on the inside for so long. The internal, more serious, will begin to reflect on the outside. It's just a matter of time. She knows it is simply a fact of life.

She has been blessed with near perfect health. From an early age, after the mandatory shots and the precautionary physicals, she hadn't even seen her family doctor. The occasional cold would touch her but her immune system fought those off without difficulty. Aside from the last time she drank too much she could not even remember when she last vomited purely from being sick. Teeth straight and white, no cavities; no abnormalities that could be seen with a test; no deformity of shape, or distinctive mark marred her frame. Even her mind is clear, although not untroubled. She possesses the increasingly rare

17

knowledge of who she is and with intense self-examination she understands her own traits, and has come to terms with her deficiencies. She does not struggle as many do with who they are. No false personalities can worm their way through the defenses she has built. She knows the issues she has she brought to bear on herself. She would not sit back and dismiss the world and her place in it. Her struggle is not one of confusion but one of fairness.

How is it fair that she escaped the pain she saw all around her? The elderly sick don't trouble her much; that is simply the inevitable consequence of advanced age. It is the children, the ones she works with, that tear at her. Early in her career she found herself sobbing at times when she allowed something she saw to touch her. She never allowed a tear to form in front of the children or the families, nor in front of the nurses and doctors around her. Once, after she thought herself immune, she nearly exposed her true self. She had been speaking to a young patient, a boy who had just turned five. He shared her brother's name, David, which is why she remembered it from among the many others. But that wasn't it, that wasn't why she remembered him or why she had cried so terribly hard. It was his face. It was perfect. Looking back she described it as angelic. It was lit and the cheeks round and full. It had a glow she would expect from a healthy child that had just come in from running around in the first snowfall of the year. The wrap about his head looked like a woolen cap to keep him warm. Beside herself, she thought of nothing to say, so as if in the setting she envisioned him, she offered to get him a cup of hot chocolate. It was his smile and the life that jumped into his eyes upon that suggestion that shook her.

He said weakly, "Yes, please. That is just what I was wishing for."

Doctor Nancy Glacieux left the room, turned the corner into the hall, and found a small supply closet unlocked. She entered, shut the door, and fell sobbing onto the floor. When she composed herself she wiped her eyes, stood and straightened herself up, placed the stethoscope neatly around her neck, took a deep breath and re-entered the hall. Her world back in order, she walked crisply to the nurse's station, found someone she knew was competent and asked her to make sure David got a cup of hot chocolate with marshmallows right away. The nurse, knowing Nancy well enough, quickly rose to follow through on this request. Not normally part of her duties, it was the slight extra emphasis on the "right away" that made her know she meant "do it now."

Nancy did not go back to David's room that day, and he passed during the night. She did not see him or conduct any additional tests as she normally did when a child she was working with died.

Chapter 3

In high school she always seemed to get stuck with pricks. It took a long time for her to figure out exactly why that was. In the early years, she remained hurt and confused. Her young mind, advanced in many ways, was still adolescent in others. She developed slower physically than many of her girlfriends. Nancy was long and lean with a nearly flat chest well past the time when others had bloomed. She was painfully aware of the difference and evidently the boys were too. She saw who got the attention of the males in her class, and noticed how they acted to keep it. She secretly hated one particular girl. A girl that seemed to move with ease in the world of boys; a world Nancy was excluded from. Her parents sensed the hurt. They were aware when the giggles of little girls turned into the nervous laughter over an infatuation with a boy when her friends gathered at the house; the startlingly quick transition from dolls to boys; from playing house to the not-so-secret game of who likes whom. There were dances that were missed. Junior high dances, those initial forced social events thrust upon the young by their well-meaning educators. It was sheer terror to her. Plainly put, the circumstance required a date. Children placed into an artificial circumstance where one needs to have a date to be considered successful in one's own mind and by one's peers. Forced into shy handholding and the inevitable teasing that children participate in when placed in a competition for which they are ill prepared. Her father would make an attempt to cheer her up if he happened to notice her altered demeanor. Her mom, more in tune to what was happening, would tell him when she missed something she had hoped to participate in. He often called her "daddy's little girl" when she was a child, but now she couldn't remember the last time she had heard that from him. He would call her that and sit next to her on the couch and watch whatever silly show she had on. Never mentioning the dance itself yet providing the warmth she unknowingly yearned. He would pull her towards him and kiss her gently on the side of her head and say, "Nobody loves you like your daddy." She knew that was true. She was comforted by that thought and now, years later, still is.

Later on, when she moved from exclusion to painful inclusion, when her body responded to the forces of nature and genetics, it was still awkward for her. A bit older, a bit wiser to the ways of her tribe, she nevertheless found herself with minimal opportunities to date. There were times she secretly cried and sobbed under the covers as she fought visions of the good times others were having, and she, left at home, alone. A bit more aware and of a more appropriate age, she was hurt more deeply than she was during those pre-pubescent times. She had breasts now, those boy magnets were evident. They stood tall and proud. It was around this time that she came to understand her own beauty. Never before separating herself from the pack, she came to realize she was attractive. While obvious to others from the time she was a child, it suddenly became obvious to her. As a child she thought as a child and figured the adults she met through her parents were just being nice. Older and wiser, a full-grown teenager, she would hear comments somewhat less spontaneous, especially from men. Even her father's friends would turn to him, in a lowered voice presuming secrecy, albeit loud enough to flatter them both, "She is a looker, George. You better keep your eye on her. You'll have to beat the boys off with a stick." She thought that was a strange saying, and in high school, it was never quite like that.

In high school, she often had no date. At the time she never fully made sense of it. She didn't yet understand the male psyche. She was beautiful; beautiful and smart. That is an intimidating combination. How many men, never mind a teenage boy, will even consider going out with a girl that they think is smarter than they are? Aside from

21

that, how many guys, young or old, have the confidence to approach a woman so endowed? There are really only two types that make the attempt. The first are too dim to know that the woman they desire has a superior intellect and that she will quickly become bored with their antics despite any stature they might bring to the relationship – she had a few of those; they ended quickly. The second, so full of themselves that they view her only as a trophy, not unlike the ones they earn with athletic feats on the ball fields of their youth. Neither type had much appeal to Nancy. The few that would dare to approach her were either summarily dismissed or discarded once their true nature became apparent to her. As a result, she didn't date much.

Her reputation, built upon by the rejected suitors, quickly created a bigger chasm. In their youthful judgment, with its limited expression, she was simply "a bitch." Those words, not too subtly expressed at times, left scars. Every scar she has ever seen has a story behind it. Sometimes that story revolves around pure chance, other times around an inevitable incident, but all of them involve pain; pain, the healing process, and the scar that remains.

One such incident determined for Nancy that she would join the medical profession. She was twelve, her brother was ten. It is his pain, his scar, which helped shape her destiny. What would she be doing now if she hadn't become a doctor, she wondered? Her brother was playing with a friend in the basement. Their parents had gone out on a short trip to a nearby store. Nancy was always mature for her age and was trusted to mind her brother in their absence. She liked being left in charge.

Shortly after her parents left there was a knock at the door and she raced to get to it prior to her brother. She got there just before him and reminded him that she was in charge and that they were not to open the door when mom and dad were out. The Thompson children were taught to be careful in that regard. The door was nearly always locked, but especially when their parents were out. The cars were generally locked when they sat in the driveway, and the emergency numbers (grandma, the neighbor, fire, police), posted by the phone.

It was a friend of her brother, the neighbor's kid. He wanted David to come out and play. Her brother begged to go out but Nancy stood firm and held to their parents' wishes. They were not allowed out when their parents were not home. Her brother whined and complained and carried on so. At least let him come inside and play, he wailed. Finally, she acquiesced, breaking a rule, but nonetheless, allowed the boy to come in and play with her brother. After all, she reasoned, he couldn't go out, that was too dangerous. And the neighbor always came over and played with her brother; and he had been bothering her so. This would divert his attention and give her some peace. They would go down to the basement, like they had many times before, and amuse each other for hours playing army with little plastic figures or fighting evil in the world with various cartoon inspired creations. What harm could come of that?

They rambled down the stairs in little boy joy and quickly immersed themselves in imaginary play. Relieved to be left to her own devices, Nancy pushed any thought of wrong out of her mind. She worked diligently on the puzzle set up on the dining room table – this was the best place to do a puzzle. The table had natural light from the window that, during the day, allowed for noticing color differentiation, and even at night it was usable due to the strength of the overhead fixture, although not as well. It could be left out, undisturbed, over several days or sometimes even weeks (the small family ate in the kitchen, the four of them fitting easily around the table each night), if she became distracted by other pursuits and ignored it.

She liked how the shapes forced her mind to think. She approached the task in a methodical fashion. First the edge pieces, easiest because the straight portions could be picked out from the rubble. Then she worked in sections, usually some distinct part of the whole. Examining each opening and its subtle differences she could often pick out a piece amongst hundreds. Other times it was the color that gave away the hints that allowed her to narrow down the possibilities from the remaining tiny individual sections. It was something that the others in her family could pitch in with. Her dad, in particular, would look over her shoulder, and sometimes within just a few seconds, pick up a piece and place it in an area that she struggled to complete. Typically, that was followed with another, and another in rapid succession until the flower or basket or tree that she was beginning to think was impossible, was nearly complete. It was at times like those that she was glad to have her father looking over her shoulder to help get her over the difficult patches. He would smile and comment on how well she was doing and how difficult this particular puzzle was. He was secretly pleased that she had some of his characteristics. Without her realizing it, she was like her father, and it was that realization which made him smile.

****

Her research is not unlike this. She has a puzzle in front of her and has to figure out where the pieces go. This puzzle is the most difficult she has ever attempted; at times she feels it is too hard. The pieces are nearly all alike; the colors blend in too subtle shades to discern their differences even in the light of the day. She wishes her father would look over her shoulder now and place a few key pieces in their place. She cannot recall a single puzzle that she ever gave up on. She finished every one she had ever started and is determined to see this one through. Actually, she is more than determined; she is committed to the completion of the task. She will not - cannot - fail. There are lives depending upon this. It is non-negotiable. She will continue to do whatever she needs to until it is done. Besides, at this point, there is no turning back.

Her peaceful contemplation of the picture was burst by a shriek from the basement. Nancy broke from the table and bounded down the first flight of stairs, made the turn and took the second set that led to the basement in two quick strides. Her brother clung to his left hand and howled in agony. There was blood, actually quite a bit of blood, streaming down his wrist from under his grasp. "What happened?" she cried out as she surveyed the scene.

"I cut myself," he said between clenched teeth. "I was trying to get the guys off the plaque so we could play with them."

On the floor was the rectangular plaque she had seen with baseball figures set on it. Two of the guys were already freed from their fixed positions. The plaque with the remaining three ball players was thrown to the side, and like nearly everything else, had blood on them. Their dad's sharp scraper, with the bare blade protruding from its sheath was also on the floor. The neighbor's kid was off to the side, cowering and weeping in the corner in a near fetal position.

"Stay right there," she shouted at David, worried about the blood staining the beige rug upstairs, and bounded back up the steps, turned left this time and into the utility bathroom. She threw open the medicine chest and grabbed a box of bandages and some antiseptic. Then she reached down, swung open the vanity, and grabbed the roll of paper towels her mom kept there for cleaning. Nancy bolted back down to the basement. Her brother, immobile with fear, had even more blood showing between his fingers. The neighbor's kid, still with his arm over his head, was useless, but at least not making any noise. He rocked himself just a bit. "Jesus," she thought, and shook her head in contempt.

Without thinking, she took control. "Sit here, Dave, under the light, so I can see." She led him gently by the arm to a small, wooden chair that they kept down there from when they were younger. "It's going to be OK," she said. "Let me wipe up some of this blood so I can take a look." She ripped off a few sheets of paper towel and covered the blood-covered hand, grasping the damaged one. Then she wiped the left wrist as it too had blood streaming down it from the wound. She threw the soaked piece to the ground and ripped off a few more pieces, wrapped the clean ones around the wrist to catch any continuing flow, grabbed a few pieces for herself and said to him, "Now let me see it." The firmness in her voice commanded him and he obeyed, slowing releasing the left hand. She placed the paper towels in her hands close, anticipating the need to catch some more blood. Her brother jerked his hand away as upon release the blood spurt from the wound like a small geyser. His girlish shriek awakened the neighbor from his now nearly calm, yet still rocking clutch. The blood shot up and as David moved it left a trail along the workbench and some of it struck Nancy on the shoulder and she felt a warm drop, not unlike the feeling of tears, on her cheek. The neighbor, did not look, but heard the commotion and moaned louder and rocked faster in a ball in the corner of the room. She grabbed Dave's left arm above the wrist and held it tightly. She forced the paper towels she held back over the laceration and stemmed the flow of blood.

"Hold still," she commanded, and again he obeyed, not that he had much choice as she had a firm grip on his arm. She pressed his wounded hand with her own. Within a second or two she realized they would need better supplies. She told Dave the plan, "We need to clean this and I need to get the first-aid kit. We must go up to the bathroom. Walk with me and keep this towel on the cut. It's important. We need to control the bleeding. Do you understand me?" He nodded his head and looked into this sister's eyes. She was calm and confident, nodded back, indicating agreement. He knew she would help him through this. They left the neighbor in the basement and walked carefully up the stairs together, into the bathroom. Nancy instructed her brother to hold the towel against the wound like she was doing and she would run to the second-floor bathroom the first aid kit that their dad kept in the house for emergencies.

It was only now, while fetching the first aid kit, that she had a few seconds to think about how angry her parents were going to be when they got back. Oh well, I can't worry about that now, she thought, as she grabbed the kit from its place and bolted back down the stairs with huge, athletic strides. Although a bit shaken, she instinctively knew that this was not life threatening. Dave had lost a bit of blood, and the spurting was a bit of a shock, but she knew what to do. Keep pressure on it until the flow lessens, then clean, re-new pressure, and finally wrap tightly with clean gauze and bandage.

When she finished wrapping the wound and David was calm, sitting with his wrapped hand raised up, and the neighbor, reassured out of his cocoon, was sent back home, she contemplated what had transpired. Though startled, she kept the situation from getting out of control. Her normally resistive brother followed her directions without question. The blood, particularly the quantity, was new to her, and yet she did not flinch. Calmly wiping and catching it, seeing it smear and drip heavily like dark red paint spots, trailing on the floor, her mind stayed clear and focused. The view, inside the slit of the hand, intrigued her. It was as if she could visualize the layers of skin and tissue in her mind's eye, the capillaries carrying the blood, severed. Although she could not actually see it as the wound was not deep enough, she knew just below the laceration was the bone that gave the hand its shape, and oddly she sensed a desire, a wish as it were, to have had actually seen it. It was partially this knowledge, the fact that the physical aspects of this distress, even of someone from her own family, did not trouble her which made her consider for the first time how she might fit in this world. Even at a young age, she felt a need to make some sense of the world and her place in it.

For days after, no, it was more like weeks or perhaps even months, she was haunted by the emotional reaction of the kid next door. Moaning and curled into a fetal position, it was that which continued to trouble her. She could not understand. The reaction was so far from what she felt. It made her uncomfortable. Over the next few days Nancy could not bear to see this boy, shying away from him when he came over. It wasn't that she disliked him or was mad that he was no help to Dave in his time of need. It was how he made her feel. She re-saw the emotion each time she laid eyes on him. It was the noticeable lack of any such feeling within her that made her pull away. Seeing him forced her to look at herself and her total void of reaction scared her. She was just twelve. She never told anyone.

Chapter 4

Her brother now viewed her in a new light. She was no longer the ogre placed in his life just to torment him and make him feel small. Now she was a wise and benevolent protector. Dave wanted to give her something as a way to thank her for taking care of him. He swore to his parents that he would never touch one of Dad's sharp tools again, and, at the time, he meant it. Isn't that the way of youth? Some event happens and they cross their heart and hope to die or swear an oath without knowing what that really means and not capable of keeping it. Not that most adults are any better.

Still, how he felt about what Nancy did for him needed to be recognized. He had some money but didn't really know what to buy her that would appropriately show his gratitude. It had to be something special, he thought. He looked around his room for something of his that he could give to her. His eyes rested upon the now empty spot on the shelf where the plaque with the baseball figures glued to it had stood. Lying flat near the spot was one of his most prized possessions. It was a sturdy stick, shaped like a baseball bat, actually a replica of the one his favorite ballplayer uses. His dad bought it for him. It had the player's signature on it, Moose, a nickname because of how strong he was and how far the ball traveled when he hit it. That was it, as an expression of his gratitude. He had to give her what he valued most. This was the item most dear to him at ten.

He approached her while she sat in the den quietly reading.

"Nance, I want to give you something for helping me."

He held the miniaturized weapon in front of him with both hands extended. It was presented as if he was a high priest bringing some treasured gift to a deity or a queen. He was so solemn that she had to suppress a smile. Nancy took the replica Dave offered her with graciousness. The moment caused her eyes to mist just a bit and as she blinked that away, she extended both her hands and he placed it gently into hers. She had time to say nothing. He darted quickly away, and she sat there, still holding it gently in both her hands with her palms pointed upward. She smiled knowing that this idol was dear to David. With that thought, she went to her room and found a place of honor to keep it, a place prominent and visible. David would be able to see it from the doorway (little brother was not allowed in her room) when he passed by and know that she valued it too. To her friends the bat was out of place, surrounded by fluffy stuffed items in various shades of pink, yellow, and red; delicate figurines of precious moments; tall, perfect in every way, yet lifeless porcelain; but she didn't care. When all the others were left behind this was the one item that followed her, first to college, then medical school, and she still had it. How many years has it been? Then it was purely sentimental, a symbol of a connection to her brother and a reminder of what they shared. Now it was more than that. Now she knew it was something she would always keep. Someday when she is old, or perhaps when she is gone, she hopes her child will find it amongst her belongings and wonder at what a strange thing her crazy mother kept.

Nancy's mother, Helen Thompson, was not crazy. At least Nancy didn't think so. Helen Thompson was a hard-working woman and a loving wife, mother, and friend to all that knew her. If accused of being a little strange it would be from the fact that she was open about her faith. Perhaps open is a bit weak. Helen Thompson took seriously the admonition that if one is ashamed of God then He would be ashamed of them on the Day of Judgment. She also believed that "you can't hide your light under a bushel," along with numerous other admonitions that she was likely to bring up at an inopportune moment. Helen Thompson looked at every situation through a prism of spiritual faith. Nancy's friends were, at times, quite open about saying, "Your mom is weird." Nancy knew there were some friends that avoided their house because of this and there were others that seemed to be drawn to it. For all the forwardness no one could ever say they were mistreated in the Thompson household. Both her parents always welcomed their friends, treated them respectfully, and provided a safe, warm environment at all times. As she and Dave grew older and experienced other households and other families the contrast became more apparent.

Helen Thompson took the primary responsibility for the daily child rearing and the creating of a home. At a time when society would suggest she sacrificed too much to do so, she relished and was fulfilled by the role she willingly chose. She knew that David and Nancy were gifts, given to her and her husband for just a short time and that she was bound to raise them to the best of her ability. She understood the possible reasons, but could not fathom how a mother could hand her child over to be attended to by others for much of their waking hours, particularly during their formative years. It was not a matter of sacrifice, although the Thompson's did sacrifice, it was a matter of love and responsibility. She and her husband were responsible for the two little ones that God had blessed them with. Lest anyone characterize her as harsh or judgmental, they would be wrong. Helen Thompson would reach out to the single parents she came in contact with; she was apt to volunteer to help in any way she could for any number of causes - one of the first to provide the support that is so desperately needed at times for those that find themselves in need of a helping hand.

There was a time during Nancy's senior year in high school that one of the girls Nancy and her friends knew became pregnant. While sitting over a tray of brownies that Mrs. Thompson had baked, the young girls chatted around the kitchen table about the news. Helen overheard the topic of their conversation and listened a bit harder from where she sat in the next room.

The four young women - Nancy and her three friends - had just found out earlier that day in school. One version of the story they heard was that Ruth Meyerson was in Civics class and one of the boys started making fun of her, calling her babyphat. Ruth's attempt to ignore him only encouraged the boy to intensify the teasing. Soon another chimed in, followed by a third. The teacher was unable to correct the troublemakers and maintain control of the classroom. As Ruth shrank under their scrutiny and sat with her hands gently under the small bulge protruding from her abdomen one of the nearby girls gasped, covered her mouth with her hand, and said, "Oh my god, are you pregnant?" And that was that, the secret was out.

Later, as the gossip mill took over, it became known that Ruth was five months along, intended on having the baby, and would be in full bloom by graduation, which was just another fourteen weeks down the road! The halls were filled that day with laughter, speculation, and scorn. Helen Thompson's heart went out to the young girl and her family and she said a silent prayer for them for strength, wisdom, and health for the baby in her womb.

The girls meanwhile, wondered at the identity of the father; expressed disbelief that Ruth would be so stupid, she couldn't be.

"What if it was 'date-rape.' You know how common that is," one of them said.

They were even more incredulous that she would continue in school, watch her belly grow ever larger, and planned on putting her life on hold to care for a baby. They knew her, she was like them, had dreams of college and a future; and now this! There was something unsaid in the room and all the girls knew it. One ventured gingerly into the dark abyss. Nancy and her friends were what people would call 'good girls.' They were smart and came from respectable families.

"I don't know what I would do," one of them sighed.

That statement hung in the air, pregnant with meaning. Innocently it could have intimated any number of things. Perhaps the girl simply meant she would drop out of school before anyone knew; or perhaps go live with an aunt in a distant state; or expose the young fellow that dropped his seed so carelessly; or any number of contrived scenarios that one thinks about when in the dark and the thoughts of fear and uncertainty come. Helen Thompson's ears perked up. After only a short pause, a second stab into the mystery of decision was proffered.

"Well, I'm not sure I could go through with it," said a second. Quickly, she covered the apparent meaning with a plea to her conscience and to her friends. "I mean, what would I do? Have a baby?!?" as if that was justification, then turned the focus from herself and said, "What is Ruth going to do? Her life is ruined."

It quenched the spirit of the young women at the table and they were silent, eyes averted, with thoughts searching within themselves.

Helen Thompson wanted to jump out of the chair and chastise the girls for their indecision. She checked herself, remembering what she had read that morning – "Let no corrupt communication come out of your mouth." She also remembered an argument she had with Nancy in the recent past about her butting in on conversations that were "none of her business" – as Nancy put it.

It wasn't silent long. A group of girlfriends never seem to let the stage remain quiet for long. Generally an awkward silence like the one that encapsulated the Thompson kitchen would be broken by some diverting, simplistic suggestion or shriek coupled with storytelling, leaving the unspoken thoughts to be swallowed beneath consciousness.

"I'm proud of her." The remaining three looked up at their friend. "She is doing the right thing." A quick sideways glance, moving clockwise and fastening ever so briefly on each of the eyes of the three gave Nancy the assurance to continue. There was a slight, gentle nodding of each head, and a resolution that became evident in a firm lipped, countenance of agreement. "We need to be there for her. You know how cruel some kids can be. She's going to need all the friends she can get; true friends, not phonies." It was done. The young ladies decided to keep Ruth under their wing. They would include her in their activities, watch out for her, and make sure she knew that her friends cared about her. And, they made a pact that they would never allow themselves to get into this kind of trouble.

Helen's eyes moistened and she reached for a tissue. It would not be forgivable if she embarrassed Nancy in front of her friends. Even so, she could not be more proud of her daughter than at that moment. She wanted to run to her, pick her up under her arms like she did when she was a toddler, twirl her around the room until they both laugh so hard and become so dizzy that they tumble to the ground amid panting and giggles. Life was simple then, she thought. It was easy to care for her and to protect her. One of her biggest fears was not always knowing where she was, who she was with, and what temptations had come her way. The newspapers didn't help, there always seemed to be some story of a young person getting wrapped up in danger. Drinking, car crashes, drugs, sex or some predator; it is as if the deck is stacked against this generation. She didn't remember it being quite so hard when she was young. Sure, there had been a rough crowd at her high school, and she was sure there had always been such groups going back to the beginning of time – after all, Cain killed Abel. But now it's different, it's as if the atmosphere is changed and just walking amidst the culture taints the young people. She heard the criticism, "You can't isolate them, Helen," as she sought to be sure they were in as good an environment as humanly possible. She knew they couldn't be isolated, as a matter of fact, didn't want that for them. However, she did desire to see them insulated. "Be in the world but not of the world," she recited to herself.

Some months later, Helen and Nancy were in the mall looking for a prom dress for her and had a chance meeting with Ruth. It had become known that the young father of Ruth's child would have no part in its life. The unknown story was much more disturbing. Nancy had followed through on her pledge to keep Ruth close and to make sure she was a friend to her. They did things together, and even arranged sleepovers, lately just the two of them. Nancy's friends started off the pact with enthusiasm but, like Ruth's boyfriend, had little staying power. It seemed they had other places to go or people to be with. Activities and cares, perceptions and judgments got in the way of their pure design, and so their interest and resolve waned. Ruth kept an upbeat and cheerful disposition despite the difficulty she found herself in. There were times, however, that the mark she wore brought out the worst in people. The whisperings of strangers and the gossip common in high school would occasionally win the battle over her will and she would get mad at the world, mad at God, and perhaps most of all, mad at herself. It was during one of these times she confided in Nancy about what had happened.

Ruth never really had a boyfriend; it was one of the things Nancy could relate to. She was not beautiful and had a thin, almost lank frame; not un-pretty, albeit plain. It was exciting to her when the young man began showing interest in her. The bulk of their relationship was of an electronic nature; he living in a nearby town and they just happened to cross paths. In the romanticized notion of a hardly noticed young girl it was as if their meeting was destiny. Why they could have easily missed each other by only a few seconds, or she could have been 'away' having dinner or some other such nonsense when he first sent that initial text greeting.

They bantered back and forth online, shared pictures and personal conversations apart from the world and generally seemed to be kindred spirits. At some point, they discussed meeting. They didn't live too far apart, only a short bus ride across town. They decided they should meet, and they did. From there things progressed rapidly. She was eager to please him and he seemed attentive and adoring. So it was that they found themselves meeting in a quiet place. Furtively, as if they did not want the world to see them, somehow embarrassed at what this meant about them or unsure of whom they wished to see them together. They met, laughed, flirted, and touched. The first rendezvous ended with a long kiss. A kiss accompanied by the groping passion of youth and a desire that Ruth had never felt in quite that way. It appeared perfect. Over the next forty-eight hours they continued to say sweet things to one another in their normal way and arranged a second meeting for the following day - a meeting Ruth could not wait to take place. She could not sleep. She could not think of any other subject than him. She eventually fell asleep that night after a time of fitful fascination.

The following day she readied herself for the rendezvous, added a little color, a little scent, a bit of gloss with a shirt open and what would have been plunging if she had the wares. Preparing to leave the house she planned her excuse should someone be home to question where she was going. She looked in the mirror before she left and briefly cautioned herself about what this meant. Timing a slip out of the house, she left unnoticed as she had hoped, avoiding have to answer a question with what surely would have been a lie. She was walking to the meeting place when she got a text from him, he had been able to borrow a car and would pick her up rather than have to take the bus across town and walk to the park where they planned to meet. A car, how exciting she thought, she didn't even have her license yet. He pulled up along the curb beside her as she walked, called out and she got in. "You look great," he said as they sped off.

"Where are we going?"

He grinned back, and told her not to worry. He knew a great place to hang out. He passed her a brown bag that contained a glass bottle with brown liquid in it. He noticed her hesitation but quickly encouraged her. "Just take a sip. A sip isn't going to hurt you. Haven't you ever had a drink?" With that, she dutifully complied. The brown liquid stung her throat when it hit it, she almost lost her breath for a second and then it felt warm as it went down. She giggled and took another quick sip, more prepared this time. It went down easier. She passed the bottle back. They carried on this way a few miles until the car took a path Ruth wasn't aware of, not that she was paying close attention to where they were. He pulled up to a small alcove, cut out from the surrounding woods, another car sat off to the left.

"Nice place, right?" he said. "Couples come here all the time."

She liked that he referred to them as a couple. They kissed, and as they moved closer it became apparent that the center console was fixed as a barrier between them.

"Come on, let's get in the back." Without waiting he took her hand, opened his door, and led her. She stepped over the console and was in his arms briefly as he forced the seat forward and guided her into the back. They kissed. They had been thinking of each other since they last touched a few days before. She felt at ease and was easily maneuvered to a nearly prone position. He pressed against her, touched her, and she let him. She had never been this close to another person in all her life. He was on top of her and for a moment was scared as she realized she could not move with his weight on top of her. He forced her legs apart and she was surprised at her own comfort in this.

"I need you," is all he said, and with that, she pulled him even closer.

The rest was a blur. He awkwardly and frantically opened his own pants. His hand was again on her hips. Her pants, already low riding, did not have far to slide as he opened the button that held them. He was on a mission. A mission he was committed to as much as any soldier ever set his mind to accomplish. Stronger, and in a superior position, he was in control and with one quick shift of weight and agility, his chest pressing forcefully on her chest, pinning her down, with both hands took her pants down to just below her knees, settling quickly back on top of her and forcing her legs apart. Ruth came to her senses, feeling him now even nearer to her, feeling flesh on flesh. She pushed back on his shoulders and tried to squirm from under him but there was nowhere to go and he resisted.

Nancy reached out and held Ruth's hand as she continued.

"Wait!" I cried out. "Wait, I'm not ready for this."

Neatly positioned he continued to press his advantage. A short burst of pain, some blood, and her virginity was gone. Gone in the back seat of a car to a boy she hardly knew. A few thrusts of his hips and he was gone too.

Nancy, listening to her friend tell the story, not of how she became pregnant, but how some man forced himself on her, made another pact, this one with herself; she would never let that happen to her.

36

Chapter 5

For a few years Ruth and Nancy kept in touch and would occasionally meet when Nancy was home from college. The child, conceived in the back seat of a borrowed car, the seed of a stranger, was a joy to the Meyerson household. Ruth's mom helped her a lot, and Ruth was able to work and go to the local community college. Then, as life became busy and distance became a handicap the two girl's lives separated, as many do. Nancy's mom met Mrs. Meyerson in the grocery store a few years after that and she shared with her how Ruth had met a nice young man and that she was married now and had a second child with him. Nancy was glad to hear that she was happy and that she and the child are part of a family. All the statistics say that kids have the best chance in a home with both a mother and a father. A story like Ruth's doesn't always work out so nicely. Nancy couldn't help but think about that discussion she and her friends had at her mom's table when they first heard about the pregnancy and debated her decision to have the baby. Ruth had no regrets. As a matter of fact she couldn't imagine not having that child in her life.

Nancy contemplated this bond of parent and child. She thought about war and how when it struck Europe parents sent their children away, in many cases likely never to see them again, because they wished them to be safe and to live. She thought of the story of Ishmael and how God heard the cry of Hagar and saved the boy, providing water to live. But mostly she considered all the parents she had worked with, parents with very sick children. Ruth's child was perfect, a joy to be around, and one might think that the irreplaceable bond was the result of that goodness or that particular child. But that hadn't been

Nancy's experience; the parents she met revere the time and cherish the contact with their children. Immaterial things about the child, like if they have freckles or disappoint in some way, don't appear to matter to them. Perhaps it is more obvious when the child is sick. The parents give all they have, try every avenue to help. They believe beyond the facts that are staring them in the face, even until the very end.

It is this that troubles Nancy most. She knows the child brought to her will die. She cannot even say with certainty that the regime she requires will help any individual child. There is remission, there are cases of limited success, and some of the little ones are resilient and yet there creeps a thought that she is a charlatan, an ancient medicine man, a peddler hawking an elixir that preys on the hope within the breasts of these desperate ones. She is torn with believing she can help heal and knowing the control is not hers. She often ponders the question if it is more the hope within the little patient or the faith of the parent that keeps them on this side of the sphere. Their existence balanced as it were between life and death - clinging to life - groping for a lifeline which she throws out to them. What for? To what end? A life extended even though the end result is the same?

Karl pops his head in and announces Mr. and Mrs. Randolph are here for their 10 o'clock. She puts the pencil down, unaware that she is still incessantly drumming. "OK, give me a few minutes," she says and sifts through a pile of legal size folders until she comes across the one with 'Randolph' written in bold, neat letters across the exposed tab. Nancy reviews the bio first, Karl has stapled it to the inside cover. The staples, one on each corner, each perfectly aligned, in the near exact spot as the ones before, each parallel and equidistant to the edge of the page, as he always does. There are things about him she likes. When he does work he is conscientious. He is reliable. What she appreciates most of all is she knows he is trustworthy and loyal. That alone makes him invaluable to her.

She glances at the address and knows Thomas and Cecilia Randolph live in a modest suburb of the city. He is an auditor for the

Internal Revenue Service (written out, small and neat, not abbreviated IRS as generally seen, all in the too small box called Occupation); she is listed as a Homemaker. The form is filled out in one hand, even the portions that refer to her, and each box has precise information, with neat accurate letters and numbers, the contents of which never cross the line, but fit, no matter the length of the answer, the only variable being the size of the lettering. Both parents sign at the bottom of the page. He the obvious author and she merely given the document to sign after he has done the due diligence. It's amazing what you can tell about a person from the way they complete a form. Nancy gives a cursory glance to the remaining personal information; they own their home (or at least the bank does) and even though he has what most would describe as good federal health benefits with no lifetime or annual limits to what it might pay, she knows already that her regime will soon draw a flag from the carriers that oversee and scrutinize the billing once the treatments hit a certain number. She sympathizes with her colleagues that moan about how little they are forced to accept for an "office visit" by the mammoth health care industry. And yet, she knows she will be able to collect handsomely, but only for a little while. Once the administrators, who have been instructed by the bean counters to stop payment for her kind of services do their job, the gravy train will come to a screeching halt and Mr. and Mrs. Randolph will have no way to pay. She turns to the various doctor's reports, sees the cause scrawled in the imperfect, irreverent penmanship of one of her colleagues – PML: Progressive Multifocal Leukoencephalopathy. In short, the boy has a rare brain infection - prognosis terminal.

The patient is male; seven years old; three feet six inches tall; weight forty-two pounds; name - Christopher. He'll be eight in six months, if he lasts that long.

Karl ushers the tense couple into her office. Each puts on a pretend smile while greeting and mention their name with hand extended.

"Cecilia Randolph."

"Ted Randolph."

"Dr. Nancy Glacieux. Please sit. Would you like coffee . . . or tea?" The brief awkwardness of silence is broken as Nancy shuffles the papers in the file and informs them, "I've been reviewing your son's file." Her quick glance up finds what she has come to expect; two pairs of eyes looking deeply, directly at her, imploring her to say something positive about the case. She looks back down as if still reading and says, "Your son is very sick." There is a new pause and her next glance sees the same pair of eyes, she locks on the mother's and now the mixture shows fear, the father's displays a frown. "Has Dr. Barter given you a diagnosis and explained to you your son's condition?" she proffers.

They both give an almost imperceptive nod and the mother begins to say, "He has progressive multi . . . multifocal Leuko . . . Leuko . . ."

"He has an infection in his brain," the dad interrupts with a glint of irritability.

All three fall back into an awkward silence. "But he says there is a chance. He said you were the best. That you had some success with cases like Christopher's . . ." her voices trails off as her husband gently places his hand on her forearm. Nancy knows the drill, knows what she must say to this anxious couple. She has learned that brief is better at this time. She no longer goes into the medical complexity, or the treatment regiment, or the thinking behind the effect on the tainted cells. Unless pressed she will not even give a hard percentage of cases that go into remission.

"I have treated patients with your son's condition," she begins. "They are difficult and complicated cases. At this point in time there is no cure," and she looks at the effect of these words in their eyes, "However, there has been limited success in stalling the progressive nature of this disease. There have been some children that have experienced periods of . . . 'normalcy' during their illness. I cannot give you any guarantee whatsoever that the treatments I provide will allow for complete recovery, or for that matter, that they will cause the illness to go into remission . . . even for a season. Each child and each condition is unique. The results are . . . unpredictable at this time."

With that Nancy stops and gives the parents a chance to respond.

"So, you can help?" the mother says. "You will accept Christopher as a patient and begin treatment right away?"

Without giving her a chance to respond the father interjects, "Will the treatment hurt much, I mean will Chris be in pain all the time?" This was quickly followed up with, "I have insurance. It's listed on the form there. Will that cover the treatments?" The mother, who had not taken her eyes off Nancy since they sat down, shoots him a quick, sharp glance at that last question. He was sorry he asked it almost before he said it but it just came out of his mouth and he is more sorry upon seeing the glance thrown at him from his wife.

They look again to her with the same imploring eyes as if willing her to respond in the positive to their inquiry. It may be only that which causes her to frame her answer with as hopeful a response as she can muster.

"I'm fairly certain I can treat your son. There are a few tests I must do first, but we can start right away. Can you bring him to the clinic tomorrow morning?" Upon receiving the nods in the affirmative she goes on. "I expect he will be in no more pain than he currently is, and I'm hopeful that his condition will lighten, at least initially. A fair number of children seem to respond positively within a few days to a week of treatment beginning. As I said, there is no guarantee. Each child is unique and the same illness sometimes responds differently in two different children. We can't be completely sure what state it is in and how it will react." They again nod in sync, acknowledging they understand.

With that, Nancy withdraws into her own mind, absorbed by the thought of the illness. She talks about it as if it was an entity; an entity with a will; an entity that battles back and moves with the strategy of a seasoned army. She visualizes the initial withdrawal as she hits it with a full frontal attack. It backpedals, wounded, confused. Then the building up of a high fortification able to hold back any advance she might try, the core resting, and building up reinforcements. Then a season of fruitless bombing missions as if they enemy has gone underground and is oblivious to the onslaught raging up above. All the while, she and her minions unsure if the enemy is well hidden and secure or if through some stroke of luck the mass bombing has hit and destroyed the headquarters, killing most and scattering the rest in a fearful exodus.

She plows ahead. "Your insurance will likely cover the treatments for just a few months. It is very expensive to provide intensive care, monitoring, and treatment seven days a week, twenty-four hours a day. After a few months, they will ask for additional medical documentation, which we will provide. Past experience tells me they will label the treatments as too experimental in nature and will stop payment." She sees the look of fear and apprehension creep back into their eyes. "At that time, you will need to begin paying us directly if you want your son to continue the treatments. The choice is yours, but we cannot continue to work on him without payment. We are a private entity. We do not receive government funds. We just aren't structured to provide care for free."

The mother nods in understanding and agreement. The father leans forward in his chair and squirms just a bit. Nancy saves him from having to ask. "As I said, it's very expensive. We discount our fee as much as possible to parents that are paying directly. The insurance company will pay about fifty thousand dollars a month. Should you choose to continue treatments with us we will need thirty thousand dollars, each month, in advance, to help offset our costs to keep the program viable."

Even the mother is a bit taken back, as her hand rises involuntarily to her mouth and she softly moans, "Oh my Lord!"

Nancy jumps in, trying to soften the blow, "It isn't something you have to worry about immediately. The insurance will cover three, four, maybe five months before they withdraw support."

She is surprised to hear the firm, resolute voice of the father. "Whatever it is, we'll take care of it."

The mother now turns her look of shock and disbelief toward her husband and starts to say, "But, how?" and he cuts her off.

"I said we'll take care of it," this said just as firm and just as resolute as the former declaration.

"Very good. Then we'll see Christopher tomorrow morning at 10 a.m. If you'll just see Karl outside, he has the contracts ready for you to sign. If you have any questions," and she stands to dismiss them, extending her hand, "please don't hesitate to call me."

Chapter 6

Nancy sits back down as the couple shuffle out the door to where Karl, ever listening, waits with reams of paper for them to sign. Legal documents, disclaimers, no fault guarantees, all with 'i's' dotted and 't's' crossed, scrutinized by the best medical malpractice law firm in the country. The hopeful parents, generally signing aimlessly, where "x" is marked on each page, or initialing their acceptance of arcane terms with obscure meanings in language they don't fully understand. They follow blindly, like lambs being led to the slaughter. Karl was actually very useful with this. His manner, one that lends itself to trust; she has heard him explain away fears and address concerns better than she could have. At just the right time he reassures the frightened parents, words of "Dr. Glacieux's" expertise and care of each patient in a way that borders on, but never crosses, being untruthful. She gets the impression he understands and fully supports what goes on here.

She is glad the Randolphs came in today. Last month was not a good one. Another of their patients succumbed to their disease. She told the Randolph's the truth, they cannot afford to provide free care. Little Christopher would allow them to replace that lost revenue. Ultimately, her goal is to increase the grants from philanthropic foundations so that they can meet their monthly overhead costs and she would not have to worry about how many children they were treating month to month. Nor would she have to concern herself with shaking down regular, hard-working folks, like the Randolphs, who only want a chance for their boy. She thinks about the luncheon in the city scheduled for today for just such a purpose. That is where the real money is: foundations. The problem is they can be much more intrusive than desperate parents. They require documentation of where and how the funds are used; they look at the results, in short; they ask questions. But that's where the money is. If she could get her hands on a few million, that would solve a lot of problems. It might also ease her conscience some; might allow her to treat a child like Christopher Randolph for free for a few months after the insurance runs out.

Who is she kidding? In this kind of work you can always use more funds, there is never enough. Being honest with herself for just a minute she admits her goal would be to expand the research facility. That's where the answer is, it's in the research. But, young Christopher might serve her well today when she speaks before the representatives of the various trust foundations and other assorted big-wigs JW has rounded up. That's the pitch, she realizes, not only research, but charity. Providing medical care for free is the hot button. Maybe she can get them to fork over some dough. She sneers, and laughs at herself, low but still out loud. She is already thinking about how she can frame her words to get them to believe she would provide 'free' care when she might just as easily justify where the money they donate goes by using it as a 'supplement' to what the Randolphs or some other misfortunate parent can muster up. Christopher lives, the Randolphs come up with $30K, the foundation money supplements it with $20K and "Viola!" she has the $50K she feels she really needs.

Cecilia and Ted Randolph begin the drive home in stupefied silence. The seriousness of Dr. Glacieux's remarks, the pages of disclaimers, cautions, and release from liability indicate that poor Christopher's chances are not good. Each drifts into their own world of contradictory hopes and fears, spinning them in their minds, turning them over, trying to see past the seemingly inevitable outcome. Occasionally, one or the other exposes a piece of what they are thinking about to the other.

"I'm glad she can see him right away."

"Do you want to stop somewhere for lunch?"

They pass twenty minutes of time in this fashion, interacting only three or four times, each on the most simple and inconsequential of topics. Their worn Ford gets a workout as Ted weaves in and out of traffic, gaining a bit on the race to reach their destination sooner than the cars around them. He drives a bit more aggressively than Cecilia would like but she has stopped the useless nagging about his tactics. She now accepts the way he is and has given up trying to change him. Hopefully, he doesn't kill us, she thinks. 'What would happen to Christopher?' flashes through her mind. Ted, more silent than usual hits the right blinker and accelerates into the middle lane, passing what he considers an inconsiderate, moderate moving left-laner that should be moving to the right and letting the better drivers go by.

"Why are you in the left lane?" he mutters in exasperation as he passes the slower moving vehicle. He gives the driver a short, silent snarl as he goes past, darting his eyes to the left so that he can catch a glimpse of what the offender looks like. He quickly signals his intent while simultaneously re-entering the left lane, secretly hoping the slow moving driver can feel his contempt. Within seconds he needs to tap the brakes as his momentum has quickly overtaken the pace of traffic. This old girl will need brakes soon, he thinks to himself, especially with the number of trips we'll be taking back and forth. The tires aren't so good either. With this stream of thought he is brought back to the thing most pressing on his mind since they sat with Dr. Glacieux.

"She says our insurance is good. It will cover the full cost for a few months," he says. That equivocal statement hangs in the air for a few seconds.

"Yes," she mutters, and this time, instead of maintaining a blank forward stare, she turns with a worried expression towards her husband. He does not return the glance, but stares straight ahead as if he is concentrating too deeply on the traffic to notice, yet he feels it, he knows that it's there. After a few moments she goes back to her former posture. Her husband has always been a good provider. They are not lavish spenders. They pay their bills and believe in giving what they can to those less fortunate than themselves. As a result, they always seem to have what they need. The IRS has been good to him, promoting him a few times throughout his career, and it seems always at just the right time. First, when they bought the house, and again when Christopher was born and she stopped working. Humph . . . stopped working, what a joke that is. She gets unspoken scorn from family and friends. They expect that as a stay-at-home mom she is at their beck and call, as if she wasn't busy, and the subtle suggestion from time to time that she could provide more for her family. How did that happen? In her mother's generation it was expected that a woman would stop working and be home to raise a family. Now, a woman is expected to 'bring home the bacon' first and foremost. She is glad Ted doesn't feel that way. They kid amongst themselves how she traded a five-day a week, eight-hour per day job with two breaks, lunch, paid vacation, and a paycheck for one that is twenty-four hours a day, three-hundred and sixty-five days per year, with no breaks and no pay. At least he understands. They agreed she would stay home, especially when Chris was little. Two years later, Aaron was born, and for the past two years Chris has been sick, at first on and off, and now . . . who knows what will be required of her? She looks over at her husband, with that same look, a look of worry mixed with fear. This time he acknowledges her as their eyes meet.

"Don't worry, Baby," he says and releases the firm grip he has on the wheel to pat her left thigh gently a few times. "It's going to be all right."

While just such a reassurance may have indeed helped her put her concern to rest in the past, it didn't this time.

"But what about the money?" she blurts out. "How are we going to come up with that?"

Ted realizes that she never quite allowed herself to believe that Christopher wouldn't make it. Even though his disease has now progressed and the trip to Dr. Glacieux's is a last ditch attempt to stop the advance, she still believes, she still has hope. He stares straight ahead; his eyes water. He, now also, at least momentarily, believes with her.

"Don't worry," he says, careful not to let her see the moistness, fear, and concern that are in his own eyes. "I'll take care of it."

While nearly overwhelmed with emotion his mind still spins. Several outrageous scenarios begin to form but are summarily dismissed. Where can he get that kind of money? The only idea he can justify at the moment is the easiest. When they stop for lunch he is going to buy a lottery ticket, maybe two.

****

Nancy's preparation for the luncheon is disturbed as Karl pops his head into her office.

"Sorry to disturb you, Nancy." he says, "It's Harry and he won't take no for an answer."

She only nods and Karl goes back to his desk to make the transfer. The phone rings on her desk and she makes him wait. After the third ring she figures she has tortured him enough and picks up. With no hint of pleasantness in her voice she says, "What is it, Harry?"

He is silent a second, perhaps two. The irritation he feels about waiting for her is replaced with real anger. While he would have just harangued her about picking up the phone when he calls that becomes less of an issue. "I've asked you not to call me that," he says flatly.

"I know, darling," she responds with faux pleasantness. "But you'll always be Harry to me." It has been over four years since they split up. They maintain a barely civil relationship. They both realize that if not for their situation they would have gone their separate ways completely and irrevocably. He sits on the other end of the phone and struggles to control his rage.

She, bored with his act, this pious self-righteousness, with little time or interest in playing with him says with exasperation in her voice, "What is it Hanif? You called me. Speak!"

Curse her, he thinks. She's nothing but a wench, a Jezebel, a stinking harlot. He swallows the bitter repulsiveness he can taste in his mouth and maintains the same flat monotone speech pattern. "We need more money. You said we would be able to maintain the facility. I can't keep staff and clients around if we don't have the money to pay them."

"I don't understand," she fires back. "We had enough to get us through to the end of next month."

"Sorry, darling. Your American money doesn't go as far as it used to. It's losing its value. It buys less in the rest of the world."

She notices the sneer in his voice, the same disrespectful tone he sometimes uses when talking to her. "Yeah, well, you didn't seem to mind back when you were shacking up with it." They both let the silence do its work.

"Believe whatever you want. We still need the money."

"Fine. I'll take care of it." She hangs up with nothing more.

Chapter 7

If there is anything he has learned it's that individuals can't get away from who they are. Despite changes in locale, or jobs, or marriage, it still comes down to what makes the person unique. Hanif Glacieux was born in France, of a French father and an immigrant Muslim mother. As a boy, he considered himself French; when his parents split up and he moved with his mother away from the opulence and into the slums of France, he lost that nationality and began to identify with his schoolmates. Even though they didn't have the money, his mother thought it important for him to meet family back in Chad, her birthplace, and took him on an extended trip there one summer. Later, it was his father who thought a college education in the States would be best for his future, so he went.

Looking back he is sure each circumstance in his life contributed to who he is now and helped mold his destiny. Having been led to this point, he can look back and see the guiding hand that has taken what he is, uniquely made, and molded him for such a time and in such a place as this. His childhood was not happy. How could it be with a father that dominated the home and took advantage of a submissive wife? A mother, removed from her cultural norm, insisting that he, Hanif, be raised with a firm grasp of her faith. It was the one thing his father conceded, the one thing he felt he could not give the child, some semblance or at least an understanding of religion, it mattered not which.

Throughout all this, including his secular education, his decision to stay in the States, and God forbid, even his relationship with Nancy, he could trace a pattern of strong feeling against injustice. Not fairness, that is something different. Life is not fair. Justice is far different. Justice does not discriminate. Justice is blind. Justice is what he seeks. While he has gone down several roads in life, and those roads sometimes turned into winding paths filled with darkness, dirt, and waste, he nevertheless possessed an inner course that guided him. It is in his genes, he is hard-wired to think and feel and act; it is inescapable, it will always be with him.

He is his father's son. That thought haunts him. For all his zeal and righteous indignation, he keeps coming back to that fact. He knows now that he and Nancy could never have stayed together, 'till death do us part.' He has come to terms with the evidence. He followed in his father's footsteps. Perhaps it is true the saying about the sins of the father following from generation to generation. It often seems so, an alcoholic begets alcoholic children, depression follows depression. How does one break the curse? His father was a womanizer.   His mother stayed at home and became the server of food and played the role of dutiful wife and mother, the role his father expected of her. He, on the other hand, was attracted to Nancy because she was not like his mother.   She was strong, confident, and independent.   He was enamored that someone like her would find him appealing. He lacked the outgoing easiness, the ability to be comfortable in diverse settings, the light skin, the acceptance of important people. Yet for all that, when all was said and done, he too, acted like his father. It is no matter that he blamed her; he succumbed as his father had done before him. He hated himself for that weakness. He hated himself for being like his father.

After he and Nancy broke up he returned to France, to the slums, to his and his mother's home, the home of his youth. All was different somehow.   Seen through the prism of his broken fantasy he was overwhelmed with the knowledge that he did not belong. He did not belong with Nancy. Did not belong in the society she opened up for him. Did not belong in France. As he grappled with these issues he might have easily fallen into an abyss. He sought to fall, and would have, except for a fateful encounter with a childhood friend.

He walked the streets late one night, the dark and sinister streets of what had become a truly dismal place. There was little light and the storefronts were covered with metal gates. Up and down the small square of blocks abandoned cars were left to rust and the place stunk of misery and hopelessness. Walls were plastered with posters displaying the local unrest and graffiti, a Western term, but a uniquely Middle Eastern version, populated the littered walls. As he walked he spied a group of youths shuffling along the narrow sidewalk heading toward him. Leery, and practiced from the time he spent in New York City, he drifted to the far right edge, using only a few inches of walkway for himself. He turned his shoulders to narrow his path even more to avoid the approaching collision. The small swarm did not give and he was not about to be forced off the pavement and into the gutter. Despite his effort he had the misfortunate consequence of brushing against the youth sauntering toward him on the outer edge. The boy uttered a curse in the native tongue and he uttered "pardon me" in clear English. The group chuckled when they heard this and another one lashed out with the single word "Gringo." The meaning clear to all; they knew he was an outsider, one that did not belong, did not understand them, their ways, their pain.   Like vultures, they quickly encircled the prey. Trapped, with his back against an aging, dirty auto, he had no place to run. Then they mocked him, starting with his clothes – they adhered to the mix of tradition and rebellion among the passionate young – he in fashionable sneakers, designer jeans, and a logoed collared shirt, with his head uncovered and the tight, neat, trimmed buzz of a professional, made him an easy target. He embodied what they learned to hate; he represented a world that was made foreign to them by the accident of birth. Cornered, he reacted with the instinct of preservation, eyes darting quickly left and right, he explored any avenue of escape. The motley group consisted of six, all slight in build, any one of which he could have easily overpowered. He bought a few seconds with his frantic claim that he had no desire for trouble with them, but they tossed any reasonableness aside and tightened the circle. They began to taunt and strike him from all directions about the head and shoulders. Pushed against the car he threw his hands up to protect his face and felt the warm flow of blood already streaming from his nose. They pulled and tugged at his shirt with a violence that took both shirt and skin in their grasp. Soon tattered and bloodied, he crouched down making a smaller target and continued to cover his head and face as best he could with his hands and arms. Without thought he called out in his mother's native tongue, saying, "I am a son of Nasrallah." – and again, "I am a son of Nasrallah." The beating ceased, and he, kneeling, bloody and whimpering, said again, unconsciously prayer-like – "I am Hanif, a son of Nasrallah."

The swarm scattered but one remained.

"Come son of Nasrallah," he said. "I know of you." And so, he was picked up from the ground and allowed to get his legs underneath him and was led away to safety. This too was fateful.

He returned to the States no longer Harry Glacieux. He now knew who he was, he was again Hanif. Hanif Nasrallah, a son of Nasrallah. For in this he was true to himself, and knew he belonged and had a purpose greater than himself. He did not know for sure what lay ahead for him but trusted that all that came before had taught him what he needed to know. He would study and wait for the opportunity that he was sure would present itself.

He never could have imagined from where it came.

Chapter 8

Nancy sighs and looks down at her watch, it is 11:34 a.m. She needs to leave in six minutes. Five minutes to get to the car, a short ten-minute drive to the Waldorf, valet park, and five minutes to get to the banquet room. She reviews her notes one last time, alters the order of one of the points she wishes to make, adding a comment of sentiment, even envisioning the pause she will make prior to delivering it. Eleven-forty, time to go.

She arrives precisely at noon for the luncheon. She is greeted at the door by her host, Jonathon Weiss; JW (as the papers sometimes refer to him), playboy, philanthropist, and the only son of the son of one of the original real estate magnates that envisioned and helped build NYC. The gossip pages seek his image and speculate at his wealth and which woman he will have at his elbow this season. Click, click, the cameras catch Nancy with him, and she chastises herself for not dressing more glamorously. Arm in arm, he leads the way to the dais, taking time to introduce her to various personages as they wield their way to the front. They are an attractive couple to look at. He, perhaps a few years younger than she, but a distant observer wouldn't know that. If anything, they would speculate otherwise. The wonders of hair color in a tube.

He is dressed and manicured to perfection. The suit is made of a very fine fabric. It has a shine that emanates from it and almost glistens from time to time as they pass under the light fixtures. Tailored to fit, it seems to enhance his athletic build. The sleeves meet his white dress shirt at just the right length, and even the shirt seems to obey his command, exposing itself and the gold cufflink when he stretches to greet and shake hands with a guest, returning itself to its enclosure, allowing just the slightest bit of white to show beyond the end of the jacket sleeve when his arm returns to his side. His sartorial statement complemented by wrinkleless pants with a stiff, sharp crease, not unlike a military uniform, the extremities extending to just the proper place at the edge of black, shiny Italian leather. Jonathon Weiss is a sight to behold. His face, if it were possible, looks tailored as well. Eyes, nose, mouth, chin in perfect proportion. He is clean-shaven and as they walk he whispers brief comments to her alone. She catches a whiff of faint yet distinct scent that suggests mystery and even with eyes closed would know she is near a man.

She recognizes a number of faces. Prior 'special guests' of past banquets and luncheons; occasionally a face met only at a dinner party, parties in which she accepted the invitation often out of obligation. She does not enjoy those social events. Not that they are distasteful. There is always good food, wine, and conversation. It's more the burden she feels to be 'always on'- on display, on demand; in character as the brainy doctor with a foundation dependent upon her. She dislikes asking people for money. As a result, that is one of the reasons she likes Jonathon so much. He will do the asking.

Jonathon has taken a 'special' interest in Nancy's work. After an initial meeting, one in which she was formally introduced (for everyone knew Jonathon Weiss, he needed no introduction), he surprised her with a gift delivered to her office the next day. It was a small, engraved box, inlaid with various woods, with a small clasp that when opened revealed miniature fine stones and shells. The card that accompanied this treasure included a check, personally written and signed, for her work. A hand-written note on the card said: 'If God were real, your touch alone would heal the sick. I trust you'll put this to good use. Jonathon'. She wasn't sure what to think. Ultimately, she decided it was either a rich man's way of assuaging his soul or a blatant come-on. She passed Karl the check to deposit and tossed the note in the wastebasket.

Jonathon is his usual attentive self. Sitting at her right elbow and keeping her entertained while the luncheon is served they quickly go from course to course. He makes the effort to describe each plate as it arrives, obviously having had much to do with the menu and apparently acquainted with the chef himself. From time to time he describes what the chef is trying to do with both the aesthetics of the bits of food placed on the fragile china and the effect on the palate. In spite of herself she cannot help grinning nearly uncontrollably as she pictures Jonathon with a state of the art satellite dish that obtains culinary shows from the four corners of the earth and he having four on display, picture in picture, over a huge flat-screen in the rumored Fifth Avenue penthouse. Her fantasy is interrupted by his smooth voice whispering near her ear.

"What I wouldn't give to know what is going on in that pretty little head of yours just now." They both laugh as if conspiring in some great scheme.

"Oh, you will never know," she says. "There are some things a girl has to keep to herself."

They often engage in this light banter, banter not unaccompanied with flashes of sexual tension from time to time. Nancy, if honest with herself, being a bit of a tease; and he with the natural desire that comes from imagining the taste of the as yet forbidden fruit.

"Why do you not eat more?" he says, as the staff removes at least half of the small delicacy that had been set before her. "How about some wine?" he presses her. "Do you have any idea what this is costing me?"

"Sorry. I'm saving myself for the dessert," she responds, and it is true. She knows herself well. The butterflies in her stomach will not rest until she has made her presentation.

"Ah, a lover of sweet things then," he responds, misinterpreting her meaning.

As the staff finishes clearing the main course it is time for her to speak. Jonathon stands, moves to the podium and strikes a water glass a few times to get everyone's attention. After his introduction of her, she rises to polite applause. He catches her hand and gives it a reassuring squeeze, whispers a "go-get'em" to her as they pass. He lets his hand linger ever so briefly on the small of her back as they exchange places at the podium.

"Ladies and gentleman, it's good to see you all this afternoon. Thank you for taking the time to have lunch with Jonathon and me today. I do not plan to take too much of your time, nor bore you with obscure medical jargon.

"It was only ten years ago that researchers first discovered a single genome. Today, we have identified nearly six million individual and distinct genomes that hold the clues to disease, and more importantly, the answers we seek to heal all manner of sickness. Think, if you would, of those small puzzles you played with your children when they were toddlers. There might have been six or eight pieces, each shaped to fit a distinct spot on the board, and perhaps even identified by a picture of an animal of some sort, perhaps a dog, or a cat or maybe a horse. As they got older you may have graduated to 100 piece puzzles, then to 1000. The determined among you may have challenged yourselves with 1500 pieces. Each time you moved up to a more significant challenge it took longer to complete. The difficulty increased as the pictures were now less distinct. Say a field filled of flowers, with hues of yellow and varying shades of green leaves. Some of those puzzles would have many pieces shaped similarly just to make it more difficult. In my house, each of our family members would take turns or work together to solve the difficult sections. Today, Jonathon and I ask you to become like that family.

"The task we've taken on many of you are acquainted with. Thank you for your past support and I hope your prayers as well. The puzzle before us is truly beyond the scope of any one person and I am in debt to you all as well as the dozens of dedicated medical professionals that struggle with me, day after day, week after week, and month after month.

"That struggle would not be possible if the work was just part of some mad dream. It is possible only because we are surrounded with the faces of the young boys and girls, the innocent faces that seek only a childhood with some sense of normalcy and some hope to grow and experience life. Just this morning I met with the parents of seven-year old Christopher, a beautiful child with an amazing smile. They would do anything in their power to give that child a chance (right on cue, a picture of Christopher is projected up on the screen behind to Nancy's right – his eyes are bright, his smile showing a missing front tooth, with his head wrapped in white gauze).

"They are a decent, hard-working family, and yet I know only too well that our health care system fails the sickest of the sick. The work we do is hampered by insurance company policy (here she pauses for emphasis) and fine print. By working together we can ensure that sick children like Christopher get the chance they deserve, that their parents will not be held hostage by their insurance company.

"I ask you today to help me continue the fight against brain disease. For surely this child, and many others, deserve care that gives them a chance. Your support helps us continue our goal of finding the key to the mystery of PML. We *will* identify the genome that is weak. We *will* find a way to halt this disease. We *will* find a way to give children like Christopher a chance to grow and live and not die (and here another pause – and with an ever so brief touch of her index finger to the corner of a teary right eye – she ends her appeal) . . . It is because I have Hope, that I can continue this fight without wavering. Thank you all, and God bless you."

As she takes a half step back from the podium, Jonathon quickly rises and joins her. The applause now has much more enthusiasm. It grows to a crescendo as the audience stands, starting from the front tables and moving like a wave to the rear of the room. There are misty eyes amongst the crowd and a number of discreet nudges and confidential whispers between the couples, whispers and nudges that influence the size of the check that will soon be written.

"Great job, my dear," he says into her ear, taking advantage of this moment to give her a quick kiss on the cheek, and with one hand ever so lightly on her hip, guides her gently back toward her seat at the dais.

Jonathon, now in control, centers himself at the vacated podium and closes the meeting with a challenge to match any gift given or pledged today. With a nod of his head the wait staff begins to circulate a donation envelope, making sure each invitee has an opportunity to join the celebrated cause. Coffee, dessert, and cordials follow.

****

At about the same time, Theodore and Cecilia Randolph finish their lunch. He munching the last of the fries they share and she taking a sip of the mutually enjoyed large diet soda. "Would you like more?" she asks.

"Maybe. Let's take it with us," he responds as they rise to leave, gathering up their tray and the paper their food came wrapped in. She picks up the stray unused ketchup packages, and the small containers of dipping sauce – they are only going to get thrown out she muses, and swiftly transposes them from her hand to her coat pocket.

They head out to the suburban parking lot. It's the same cookie-cutter template that has dominated the landscape throughout the country. A fast food restaurant chain building sits separate with an adjacent bank, similarly situated; behind that a strip mall with an upscale coffee shop, a pizza place, a drug store, a dollar outlet, a card store, a weight-loss center, a deli, a nail salon, a pet store, a women's apparel outlet, a shoe store, and all anchored by a supermarket. Cece heads to the right telling Ted she only needs to pick up a few things. He drifts off to the left, to the card store to pick up a newspaper and purchase a lottery ticket. "Make it two," he says to the clerk.

Sitting in the shade with the seat reclined a bit, he is content to wait for his wife to return. He looks at the lottery tickets, focuses on each number and imagines he can see each being selected at random later in the week. It's televised now, you can watch as each number is picked by the machine; balls with numbers, bouncing in the air, followed by a swoosh as one is grabbed from the mix and pulled through a vacuum tube, coming to rest as the camera zooms in so each viewer can see the number on the screen just as the slim, sexy lady with the silky voice calls it out. Ted looks over his two tickets, checks the paper to see the results from the previous drawing. He looks at the six that made up the grand prize and compares them to the ones he just purchased - only one match in four games - that's a good sign. He didn't want to see his numbers come up last week. It's not likely they would come up again so soon. This week the prize will be bigger. Of the millions that purchased the dream last week no one had all six.

He folds the two tickets, covered with random numbers that hold out security for the future, puts them to his lips for a quick kiss, and places them in his shirt pocket.

Chapter 9

Nancy looks to make her escape. She spies Jonathon lingering with a small group still enjoying the last of their mid-day drinks. She can't just slip out, although that is what she would prefer. She approaches stealthy from behind and places a soft hand up on his shoulder to get his attention. He turns and she continues to move past him and walk toward the exit. "Jonathon, I must be going." Emphasis on the "must" and as she moves toward the door, she turns her head to ensure he is not just looking at her ass as she flees.

"Excuse me," he says quickly to the table and motions with one finger up in the air indicating he will be back in a minute. "Not so fast," he calls out as he deftly slides up beside her before she can get away. "I'm planning on taking a little ride around Ellis Island. Watch the sun set against the skyline. Why don't you come with me? It will be fun."

"Fun," she replies. "I'm afraid I don't have time for 'fun' today. Some of us have to work," she throws in his face.

"Now, now, don't be like that.   We've had such a pleasant afternoon," and he looks at her with a boyish look of hurt on his face that she stops and faces him.

"Jonathon, I can't just slip out in the middle of a work day to 'take a boat ride.' I was with a couple this morning, and needed to be here all afternoon. I haven't even checked in on the children yet today," she says as she tries to look genuinely disappointed that she can't join him.

"I understand," he concedes.   "But how about this evening? I could pick you up when you're done. I know this great little bistro uptown..." this time with the boyish tone of one that only seeks one small cookie before dinner.

"I have to be up early tomorrow."

"I'll have you home by ten. I promise," he says with pleading eyes that melt her weakening defenses.

"OK." As she turns to leave, she looks back over her shoulder and says, "Pick me up at 7:30, by the doctor's entrance of the center."

Even now, just a few seconds after agreeing to see him tonight, she second guesses herself and contemplates if this is a mistake - quickly weighing the pros and cons, envisioning the various scenarios that could develop, and questioning her own motives in accepting his offer. She declines the elevator and goes for the stairs, opting to burn the extra calories and wondering what she'll wear.

****

Back at the center she is transformed from the hunted to the hunter. She dons flats, a standard white medical overcoat, hair pulled back out of the way, and glasses alternately perched up close to her eyes or teetering on the tip of her nose as she looks over them. Armed with a clipboard, she stalks the enemy and simultaneously protects, stopping station by station as if tasked with fortifying the perimeter. She is accompanied by a foot soldier, private first class Henderson, similarly in white, but completely so. White cap contains her pinned up hair, white one-piece falls to just above her knee, white stockings, white sneaker/shoes with white laces, also carrying a clipboard. They march from bed to bed, Nancy getting status reports and ascertaining enemy movement. Today is not a bad day. No enemy advances have been detected. No additional casualties. Yet, each victim has wounds, most apparent, some hidden by hair re-grown, sunny dispositions, and the strength of youth. Youth, with its innocence; its spirit; its energy to fight back; to live and not die; to overcome and triumph against all odds - their lives hang in the balance.

"Kathy," Nancy drops the formal 'Nurse Henderson' that she uses in front of the children and which is standard procedure at the center. They are alone, walking past the now empty private room 113, reminded of the previous loss, Nancy tells her about the replacement. "We have a new patient arriving tomorrow, a seven year old boy, Christopher Randolph. I'm sure Karl will pass you his file before the end of the day. Please get him set up in the community room."

"Very good, Nancy. We'll make sure he gets settled."

'The Community Room' is how they refer to the barracks style open area - a rectangular shaped, wide room with beds lined up and down each side of the room, east to west. The room was designed with a southern exposure, lined with windows and additional, angled sky lights in the ceiling to maximize the sun's rays. The beds arranged not as one might expect, toe to toe with a passageway between them allowing the patients to easily see and converse with those in the other row, but both rows facing the same direction, toe to head, facing the sun. It's part of the treatment - increased sun exposure.

A roomful of children, all wearing sun glasses throughout the day. The sight does make for a comical impression. They stock a wide selection of glasses at the center. Each child has at least two or three pairs. Some lightly shaded, more decorative than functional, yet allowing the wearer to bond to the group. Others wear dark shades, the kind that don't allow the visitor to see the expression behind the lens. Many of the children need corrective lenses to see well and new patients get the kind that fit over their current frames, adding a layer of plastic and comedy to the scene. Luckily, the Center has a local donor, the owner of a vision care store. He will replace a child's glasses with tinted shades to their liking. It's all about fitting in. The first time visitor is taken by the room and its occupants. To some it resembles a bizarre frat party with sleepwear a requirement for gaining entrance, only with diminutive students. This is especially true if one arrives while the dessert bar is set up and the little ones all animated and milling about; to others a dream, as the shades with head dress and the assorted caps make for a surreal setting. To the parents generally neither of those, for them it all depends on timing. Timing. To walk into the room when the recent reality of a fallen soldier has struck this small band of brothers is to walk into a scene of sobs and, more subtly, fear. Weeping for the one lost and fear for one's self. During times of fatigue it is no more than a hospital, bed upon bed of listless small bodies, napping at times when other children are running and playing. With any luck, especially with new arrivals, it can be a time of refreshing and wonder. The morning tends to be more active.

Nancy and the staff do the best they can to move those falling into relapse to one of the private rooms. This allows the staff to monitor the child more closely and when required, the patient can be attached to the bags of fluids they need to stay alive. The children notice when one is wheeled off to a solitary room. Even those that are new to the clinic have been around hospitals enough to know that the private room, with the machines and the drips, makes one uncertain how or if they will return; like prisoners of war seeing one of their ragged outfit being dragged off to solitary confinement. What will they be like when they return? Will they return?

They ask how they are doing and beg to visit. A visit allowed is a good sign. They willingly go to cheer up their comrade. To hear the applause and rejoicing that accompanies one of their own returning to the community room is pure joy.

The dessert bar is one of the things Nancy is most pleased with – so much so that she will occasionally take a turn at serving. Not only does it create some excitement each day for the children and the staff, but it is essential in getting these little patients to ingest the mega-doses of vitamins and the minerals that are integral to their treatment. Diet is another key. For all of time man and animals have ingested what grows in the earth. Up until very recently all medicine derived its potency from natural compounds found in nature, and the ones manufactured generally mimic what has already been placed here. What a wonder, a fungus can become penicillin and save lives; a black sponge, found under the sea off the coast of Japan, can have an effect on tumors, blocking cell division. So, one of the primary weapons in her warfare is food; you are what you eat. Will the right diet hold off a disease in remission? Is it possible, that the body can heal itself if given the right ammunition? She thinks back to her youth and recalls their dog munching at green weeds in the backyard to aid its digestion. And the time, before she began her research in zest, when she told her mother about what she had read about a doctor, decades ago, having success when no one else did, treating illness strictly with diet.

Helen Thompson reminded her daughter of the Old Testament story of young Daniel and the fellow captive Israeli children that, when being held in Babylon, they refused to eat from the King's table, instead choosing to eat only beans and vegetables. The story goes on to say that after a period of time that Daniel's and his friend's faces were as plump as and had as healthy complexions as those that feasted on all kinds of food. The Israelites are a peculiar people, their God told them what they could and could not eat, told them how to wash and care for the utensils they used, fed them with manna, brought a million of them out of Egypt, not one of which was sick or lame. Nancy had read some historical accounts about the creation of Israel in 1948 and what led up to it. Against all odds and against an enemy that greatly outnumbered them, it was established. She was old enough to remember the post-labeled 'six-day war' in the 1960's in which Israel decisively defeated a number of armies from surrounding countries in a mere six days. Even as a child she realized these folks, her father's people, perhaps as a testimony, survived the wicked rulers and armies that sought to annihilate them from the face of the earth. Someone is watching over them. If not, they would have already gone the way of other small tribes of people.

These and other stories from her youth swirl in her mind from time to time. Calling out to her and inviting faith. How could a boy take out an unbeatable man of war with a rock and a sling-shot? How could the waters part to let the Jews through the Red Sea? Could a man be raised from the dead? She submerges these thoughts when they come to her. She has seen too much, known too much suffering, experienced too much senseless disease. Yet, they return from time to time, encouraged by something as small as an unforeseen kindness or something as large as nature's majesty beyond what is conceivable by man. Even the human body is a testament of that same majesty. She, a

65

doctor, could more easily believe that God created something so intricate, so beautifully and wondrously made than believe it just happened on its own. Still, even knowing that, her doubts and the reality of what she sees in the world overshadows those feelings and force her to turn away. She goes through the motions, bowing her head respectfully at the proper time, singing the carols at Christmas, and taking part in the solemn events in church and life that intertwine religion and faith.

****

All the children are given a choice.

The base of the 'dessert' is a serving of an ice cream like (sans the cream) soy-based product that is camouflaged with either vanilla, something almost chocolate, or strawberry. The cart contains all the nutrients they need. The requirement is to take one option from each section. The fixings resemble some type of granola, the variation being what the child prefers in it, either nuts or dried fruit amongst the indeterminable mass of rolled, brownish, crunchy things. The nurse carefully monitors the small, measured cups and watches as each child dumps it onto their serving of vanilla, almost chocolate, or strawberry soy. The next step is syrup, best described by the color; blue is surprisingly the most popular. All this is supplemented by the mandatory dollop of camouflaged, whitish, whipped topping that lacks the flavor one might expect. The final selection comes down to either a poor imitation of a sliced, red cherry or a flat, yellowish circular item that is called a banana slice. With the exception of the very first day, when a new arrival is taken back by the excitement of the cart being wheeled in and the children looking over it with interest, no one is fooled.

"What's that?" a new one might ask the nearest child.

"The dessert bar," a veteran might tease with excited eyes and a smile of anticipation.

After the first day they all know it is part of their regime. Yet when there is so little to be excited about from day to day, even the blandest of treats is something that is looked forward to.

So here they come, from all parts of the U.S., all parts of the world really. Sick and likely dying, they come. Parents desperate. Children, most of whom only know that they are dreadfully sick, that something is wrong in their brain. Expecting their guardians to give them something to make them better; expecting some doctor to perform one last surgery and then to be free to run and laugh and sing, to go to school, like other children. The boys want to drive and they talk about it and post pictures and have replicas of different vehicles amongst their possessions; the girls play house with dolls and in their imagination find their true love; not uncommon dreams for children of this age. Nancy is struck by their determined view for the future, their expectation that everything will turn out alright.

Tomorrow they welcome Christopher Randolph to 'The Center for Hope'.

Chapter 10

At 7:00 p.m. Nancy pours herself a last half-cup of stale coffee, brings it to the microwave and zaps it for a minute and twenty seconds, stopping it just prior to the annoying 'ding' at the end of the cycle. She sips as she freshens up a bit in the small but functional personal lavatory – although Karl takes pride in using it when she is not there. She downs the remaining stale swill just before applying the whitening paste to her toothbrush, guaranteeing a fresh, clean smile for J.W. She looks in the mirror, applies just a bit of color to her cheeks and then slips into the all-functional thin black dress from the meager selection kept in her office closet for just such emergencies. Stockings, shoes, a brush through her hair, one final look and she is ready. Not too bad, she mutters to herself as she shuts the light, picks up her watch from where she left it on her desk, checks the contents of the nearly useless small black purse – wallet, keys, phone; then heads for the elevator.

In the lobby, the night security guard at the desk lifts his head from the newspaper and comments, "Good evening, Doctor G. Don't you look especially nice tonight." She winks and flashes a smile at him that makes him wish he were twenty years younger.

"Don't wait up for me, Earl," she playfully throws back at him, as the door swishes open and she feels the cool night air against her exposed skin. This is likely a bit too skimpy, she thinks to herself but then has no time to dwell on that thought as her debutante date is already waiting for her, coolly leaning against a sleek, black, expensive, and shiny import.

"Doctor Glacieux, don't you look especially nice tonight," he says, while sweeping open the passenger door as his chauffer might do for him. The irony of his welcome strikes a chord. She thinks back to Earl and an uncontrollably full mouth grin takes over her features. As she settles into the soft leather, the door closes silently against the frame. She shakes her head and thinks, they're all the same. Jonathon comes around the car and takes the driver's seat.

Playfully she says, "You look especially nice tonight too, Jonathan. I hope we aren't going somewhere that I'd be underdressed."

"Not at all, my dear, I could take you anywhere and I'd challenge any man to a duel if he even suggested you didn't meet the establishment's standard."

"A duel? Would that be pistols at twenty paces or do you prefer a sword?"

"Actually, I've been successful with both," and he flashes his millionaire smile. "Although I prefer the sword. It's so much more fulfilling than a single shot."

Nancy is comfortable with Jonathon; they get along. Their minds are complementary and there is an indescribable 'click' in their conversation. Always on her guard, yet somehow she feels freer to speak her mind with him. It's not that she doesn't care what he thinks, she does. It's just that he can have practically any woman he wants, so what's the sense of trying to be captivating? Besides, she doesn't want to be captured. Meanwhile, the chase is fun. A bit of cat and mouse, maybe even some cheese.

They go to a posh but not overbearing bistro on the Upper West side. Jonathon knows the staff by name, and at one point, the chef comes out of the kitchen to ask him how he liked the soufflé. The owner stops by their booth too, shaking Jonathon's hand in both of his own. Upon being introduced to Nancy, he kisses the back of her hand and urges them to let him know if anything is not to their satisfaction. The menu has no prices listed. The portions are tasty, but small. The white sparkling wine is sweet, but delicately so.

"So, how was the boat ride?" she asks at a lull in the conversation.

"Truth be told, I lost my desire for it when you turned me down. Besides, I was able to linger at the luncheon and pluck a few more feathers for you," he says with a smile.

"Well then, better yet."

"That calls for more wine," he says, eager to keep the conversation going, hoping to get more satisfaction from his as-yet-unnoticed efforts. He fills both glasses himself to the dismay of the waiter, whose inattention does not go unnoticed by the maître de. J.W. handles the bottle well. He has a steady hand. The bottle very near to the rim of the glass but never touching, a slow but steady stream of the intoxicant hits the remaining wine and bubbles erupt to all sides. He stops pouring at the polite level and with a quick, deft twist of his wrist ensures that not a drop hits the table or streams down the bottle. He does the same for his own glass before putting it back in the chiller, again very gently, such so it nearly doesn't make a sound.

"My, you are good at so many things," she says and immediately regrets it. He can only smile back at that comment. She recovers from her faux pas and takes a joking stance. "What? Worked your way through college?" and at that they both laugh out loud.

The evening goes on in a relaxed, comfortable manner. Dessert is brought to the table in dramatic fashion; it has flames shooting from it. They sip cappuccino while the waiter serves the steaming portions. It is getting late, at least for her. Jonathon orders two brandies using only the chateau's name, one she has never heard of.

"Oh...no Jonathon, I have to drive home after this," she protests. He only nods to the waiter who now scurries off to procure them.

"It's just a taste," he retorts. "You must try it. Besides I can't have you drive yourself home. Especially after the wine you've had. I'll take you."

"I suppose I'd be better off with you?"

She points to his now nearly empty glass which he picks up and drains with one grand swallow. "Indubitably!"

"And, how do I get back to the city in the morning?" she questions.

An odd smirk overtakes his lips but he responds quite naturally, "I will send a car. No argument. You'll just have to tell me what time I should tell the driver to pick you up." It is a done deal. The brandy arrives and they wash down the cappuccino with it. This is the perfect ending to the meal, she thinks. Each sip is smooth, silky, and warming to her throat and beyond. It settles her stomach from the too rich food and the too late hour to be dining.

They are brought steaming towels for their hands and luscious chocolate mints for their breath. With that they rise to leave. Nancy notices that they never brought a bill, never asked Jonathon to sign a charge receipt. There is no awkwardness attached to the evening. Literally, it is all taken care of. This is Jonathon Weiss' world.

****

They pass the time pleasantly enough throughout the short ride east to Long Island; the wine and the brandy doing their job. He handles the automobile without wavering. He was right, she is better off with him driving. She directs him through the formal entrance to the community and the few quick turns to her cul de sac. He has never driven her home before. Having avoided the topic all night she cannot contain her curiosity any longer,

"So, Jonathon, how much did you raise today?" she asks. He smiles and gives her a wink.

"You mean, how much did *we* raise today?"

"Yes, that's right. I meant to ask how much did *we* raise today," although she knew that wasn't true.

"Let's just say you shouldn't have to worry about money for at least a year."

With that she spontaneously reaches out and gives his forearm a quick squeeze; his hand still resting on the steering wheel.

"That's wonderful," she gushes. "I can't thank you enough. You don't know what a relief this is."

Jonathon is a man that is accustomed to people showing their gratification to him. If you asked him he wouldn't admit it, and consciously he would deny that it matters to him. At times, the all too obvious toadying directed his way he finds nauseating. He is aware of the fact that he is treated differently than most, the fawning, the false laughter, and insincerity. Yet it was good to hear her thank him. He is a man keenly aware of people's motives and the hidden meanings behind what they think are imperceptible actions. He is a student of body language and facial expression. A man in his position must be or else he would be taken advantage of at every turn. He can't see her eyes, but he senses her response is genuine. The tone of her voice, the brief but slightly firm squeeze on his forearm, the way she turned toward him at just the right moment confirmed what he has thought of her; has always thought of her – she is genuine.

They pull into the already well-lit driveway and the additional security lighting kicks on as well. Nancy is aware of what the proper protocol is, they have been friends for quite some time. He is good to her, has always been respectful. She is not without desire.

"Won't you come in?" she asks since she can't think of anything else to say.

He is calm, unrushed and only says, "That would be nice."

She goes to the door, enters the security code and the lock turns to let them enter. Inside, the motion activates additional lighting and the foyer is now brightly lit. It opens to a living room and she absently suggests he make himself comfortable.

"I've got to get these heels off," she complains, as she continues down the hall, hits the light switch in the kitchen and turns to the right, presumably to relieve the soles of her feet. He looks around the room quickly but returns his glance to the direction she just departed and can't help but imagine seeing her come back. Finding herself a bit nervous, she kicks off the heels in the bedroom and uses the small bathroom attached to the room. She settles herself, brushes away any stray lint, checks her image in the mirror, and heads back out. Stopping at the corner of the kitchen and partially leaning into the living area she calls out, "Can I make you some coffee, decaf?"

"Yes, please," he replies. "That would be great."

He tries the couch, sits restlessly trying to look casual for about thirty seconds then stands again and strolls about the room. There are scattered knick-knacks, a few photos, one of which shows Nancy as a girl with her parents and what must be a younger brother. It is set near a lake. They look like a happy family. The affection is clear from the photo; the way they lean into each other for the shot, a parent, one behind each child, with one arm slung over the child's chest, closer to a hug than the casual resting of a hand on a stiff shoulder found in many poses for the camera. Their heads close to each other, he can see the resemblance. The mother's influence shows in the shape of Nancy's face, the chin, and the cheekbone; the father's not any less subtle, mostly around the eyes. The nose is also similar, and the forehead. She was a pretty child. He could tell she was would grow up to be a beautiful woman. Nancy approaches from behind him, "I still love that picture. It reminds me of a simpler time. Carefree, you know?"

"How old were you, ten?"

"Actually about twelve," she admits, conscience once again of her slow development. "It was one of the last times we went out to the lake. We must have done that four or five times throughout our childhood. There were these rustic cabins, spread out throughout the place, and we would usually meet another family or two there. Each family had their own cabin and the days were filled with exploration and play. There was a large pool. My father taught me to swim there. And a recreation center, with ping pong, a pool table, darts, a great big stack of board games. There was no television, no Internet, no phone except the one in the office. Can you imagine doing that with a family today? The kids wouldn't know how to cope."

"It sounds nice," he replies. "Like the vacations I imagined other kids having. Ours were . . . how can I say it . . . somehow less authentic. We went all over the world, but I don't recall taking a picture like the one I see here. Dad was always connected to the world, even back then." Nancy thinks about the handful of times she heard his PDA vibrate in his pocket while they were having dinner. To his credit he didn't even glance at it. "My mother had friends and social functions to attend, lunch invariably included cocktails, and the dinners went on late into the evening. The children, well . . . we were . . . I think the word is 'cultivated' but perhaps more accurately, 'entertained.' Our days were scheduled out in advance; breakfast at eight, riding at 8:45, archery at 10:00, all while Mum and Dad slept. We'd meet as a family late morning. Mother would gossip about the people she had spent her day with the day before and Father generally read the paper with only an occasional glance and a monosyllabic response directed at Mum or me." Nancy had never quite imagined that Jonathon would have envied anything about her middle-class upbringing. In times of doubt she thought quite the opposite; why would a Weiss be interested in a Thompson at all? It was at those times that she took up the defensive posture of the hunt, he only interested in capturing another trophy to hang on the wall, another notch on the belt.

As if to break the awkwardness of his admission, he strides a few steps to the left to examine the contents of the bookcase. His head is angled a bit to the right to more easily read the vertical titles on the spines. Occasionally he slips one out to see the cover. She watches, not offering any comment to his equally quiet meandering through her assorted collection. She wonders what he is thinking, specifically what seeing her books makes him think about her.

"Have you read all these?" he asks and glances over to where she still stands. God, she is beautiful he thinks and doesn't allow his eyes to linger on her too long, but goes back to studying the bookcase. He continues to move across about half the length of a shelf before he realizes he has stopped actually reading the titles. His mind's eye still has her silhouette in his vision, penetrating his thoughts. Barefoot, feet crossed for balanced, her body turned ever so slightly towards the place where the books lay. He can see the curve of her hips as the black dress clings to her body. It hangs from two thin straps that expose her shoulders and with her body turned just so, the light coming from the other room reveals a softness of breast that stirs him. His heart beats faster and harder.

"Pretty much," she replies. She is cognizant of the fact that she hasn't moved for several minutes and walks closer to where he stands. He angles out a book to see the cover, "Three Cups of Tea" and she grins at her own joke from earlier today and imagines now that he is thinking Chamomile, Green, or Black, while in reality he has a book about an American mountain climber that is saved from certain death by the member of a small native tribe in Pakistan. Jonathon never has the title register in his mind, misinterprets the grin, and slides the book back into its slot to free his hands and turns toward her as she approaches. He puts his mouth to hers and they kiss. She does not resist, returning the affection and draws closer, feeling warm as her breasts compress against his chest as they prolong the exchange. They turn together slightly to his left. He slides his hands down from where they rest about her waist to her hips. She now has her back to the bookcase and she feels the wood press against the sheer material of the dress as in their passion he leans into her.

For a moment her mind is somewhere else, with someone else, against a different bookcase. Sensing the change in her kiss, he withdraws,

"What is it?" he says as he looks directly into her eyes.

"I'm sorry, I was thinking of . . . I was thinking of some other . . . I was thinking about some other time," is all she can think to mutter. Then, realizing how that sounds, attempts to minimize it. "It's nothing really. It was so long ago." Jonathon moves decisively.

"It's late. I should go." She is speechless and in a flash he reaches for his jacket and heads toward the foyer and the door. "I had a nice time, Nancy. Thank you. What time should I send the car?"

"Nine-thirty?" is all she says as he lets himself out and she stands alone, still with her frame leaning back on the bookcase and her hands now wringing through her hair, as she can't believe what she just did.

Chapter 11

She spends the next several minutes fixated, alternately thinking about what just happened with Jonathon and what happened over twenty-five years ago. How could she be so stupid? How strange that her subconscious returned to that prior nightmare? Brilliant doctor that she is supposed to be she belatedly thinks of any one of a number of things that she could have said to Jonathon, but didn't.

She understood the trigger, it was too similar. "Let it go, Nancy," she lectures herself. "It was twenty-five years ago. Let it go! How many times have you reenacted that scene through the years?" The wine and brandy still altering her thoughts she recalls the last time she thought about it - it was in a dream.

She walks barefoot through the house, shuts the coffee and the light in the kitchen. Rests her hand against the hallway wall for support in the dark, and turns toward her bedroom, alone. She knows the night will be filled with restless sleep, restless sleep and dreams. It happens whenever she has a glass or two too much. Dreams.

She slips out of her clothes, goes to relieve herself one more time, brushes her teeth, and goes to bed without bothering to dress. She curls up comfortably and thinks about how she likes the feel of the sheets on her skin and wonders why she doesn't go to bed naked more often. Her mind swirls in a mixture of fantasy and reality - pajamas are overrated, just a social norm - she thinks about what she planned to wear if she and Jonathon . . . then again re-enacts what she did versus what she might have done. Not sure if she is asleep or awake, the old scene grabs her mind too.

It was med school, after one of the final tests and a small group of tired residents went out to celebrate. Celebrations were rare. They had no time and little money. The night consisted of pitchers of beer and not much more besides a few shared hot wings and the free peanuts off the bar. Although it was a college town and not considered dangerous, she accepted an offer to be walked home. It was around mid-night, she didn't like the idea of walking the streets by herself that late at night. She fancied the offer was chivalrous.

Nancy had a small apartment, the kind you see in college towns. Typically, a home divided into as many apartments as the layout and the law would allow. Oftentimes, just a carve-out of the homeowner's domain; an effort to help make ends meet. In her case, it was the latter. The rent was cheap, which was why she took it. It included a barter arrangement with the old widow that owned the house. Once a month she drove the old lady out past the town border to visit the spot where her husband and the rest of the area's veterans were laid to rest.

This was her second year there and it felt like home to her. The two rooms were littered with her stuff. It felt like her own place. She had never had a man to her rooms this late at night, and hoped Mrs. Morrison, her landlord, was soundly asleep. There were to be no parties, and no 'entertaining,' which was Mrs. Morrison's way of saying that no men were to stay over. She liked Bobby, the young man that walked home with her that evening. He was studious, often had the answer that their mentors sought, and possessed an air of confidence that would serve him well in their profession, that is when he finally conforms and gets a haircut. She had to admit, his thick head of long locks (fashionably appropriate on campuses around the country at that time) were such that most woman envied.

As they approached her property, Nancy said, "I'd invite you in, but my landlady, she doesn't allow men in the rooms."

"Well, that is a shame," he replied. "Think she would mind if a friend just used the head? My bladder is gonna bust soon."

"Sure," Nancy said, not wishing to be rude. "Just be quiet," she admonished as they headed up the walkway. At the top of the porch they turned to the left and walked to the semi-secluded side door leading to the apartment. Once inside she hit the light that illuminated the entire living area. It consisted of a small sofa, a coffee table with a few scattered books and a used paper dish as adornment; a work desk; a bookcase with a combination of now dead Mr. Morrison's old books and Nancy's (there was even room for some of her knickknacks on it), a small table with two chairs just off the sink where a mini frig with a hot plate on top of it rounded out the room.

"Give me a second," she said to Bobby and darted to the door to the right of the frig. A girl living alone can't just have some guy use her bathroom unannounced. She quickly tidied up the commode, secured a few items left out on the sink top, picked up the clothing on the floor, tossed them into the hamper, covered it and put the whole thing in the tub. Then she pulled down the clothes, now dry, off the rod, and finally, hid everything behind the shower curtain that she pulled shut. She looked around one final time, grabbed a bra from off the doorknob where it hung from its strap, sanitary pads put away under the sink, tossed a fresh clean tissue over the wastebasket contents, and with that, felt better about having someone else in her personal space.

"Bathroom is through here, Bobby," she whispered as she reentered the living area. He was sitting and sprang up quickly after she made the announcement and literally jogged by her to the now spruced up bathroom. Gee, his bladder was indeed bursting, she thought to herself as she heard the lid slam up and the near instantaneous sound of a steady stream disrupting the still water. She found herself a little embarrassed, not fully realizing how apparent the activities behind the closed door would be to someone in the adjacent living area. After what seemed like a long time, the sound of the bubbling water stopped and a flush wiped away any other sound. Suddenly self-conscious, Nancy quickly moved to the bookcase and feigned interest in the selections.

Bobby came out and announced, "Now that's better! What are you looking for there? Did you forget, classes are over." She glanced over her shoulder and spied him smiling at her and approaching.

"Oh, just keeping my edge. A girl always has to be prepared."

"Stop," he says. "Classes are over. It's time for a little fun," and with that he spun her around to face him and gave her a soft, tender kiss.

"Well, that was unexpected," she said, but didn't pull away.

"Unexpected things are sometimes the most pleasant," he replied, and this time kissed her deeply.

When they stopped she couldn't prevent herself from smiling up at him. "Not entirely unpleasant," and gave him a playful wink. They kissed again and held each other as a couple might do when standing and kissing. Soon his hands were under her shirt, rubbing her back and as he moved a bit closer and leaned against her, she sensed his excitement. Sandwiched between him and the bookcase there was no place to go and she broke her mouth away from his and said, "We can't. You have to go. Mrs. Morrison has very strict rules."

"We'll be quiet. The old bat is surely sleeping. She'll never know I was here," he answered, only hearing the part that made sense to him. His hands slid deftly down her back, lingered a bit at her waist, as he kissed her again, not wanting to talk, they talked enough. This kiss was more forceful and he pressed against her harder. His hands dropped and he grabbed her low and lifted her, forcing her against him and causing her legs to part just enough to set their imaginations and their youthful hormones into gear. He thought he heard her approvingly moan her arousal. Her feet no longer on the ground, she squirmed, but he forced her against the bookcase, the knickknacks rattled and a few fell to the floor as the bookcase swayed with the motion of the couple. He pressed his mouth against hers to stifle any discussion.

"We can't," and she pushed against his chest. It had no effect. He kept her close and dropped her to the ground, firmly planted between her legs. "Stop, I said no," she said, still quietly as to not wake Mrs. Morrison. To him, her protest was weak. It's obvious they both wanted this; hadn't she invited him in; didn't she kiss him back, didn't she get him to this state? He pulled her shirt up and his mouth was on her breast. "Bobby stop, we can't do this," she whispered and he moved back up to her mouth to silence her and continued to drive against her. She hoped he would be satisfied momentarily and stayed prone but he stopped and began to fumble frantically with the button on her jeans which popped open and he reached for the zipper. Nancy felt fear and panic as she knew he was too strong for her. She remembered Ruth. "I said STOP!" and with an instantaneous, lithe, athletic move reached for the nearest item on the floor – it was the gift from her brother that had fallen from its place on the bookcase – she grabbed the barrel of the miniaturized bat with her right hand, wrapped her fingers completely around it with about two inches exposed outside her thumb, and slammed it as hard as she could against the left side of his head. The top of the barrel struck him flush, just at the base of the ear, and he howled like a wolf, toppling over and covering his ear with his left hand with his head angled into the rug. He was completely off her and continued to whelp and thrash his feet as it appeared to her he was driving his head into the ground, trying unsuccessfully to stop the unbelievable pain shooting through his head. Nancy gathered herself quickly, stood up, and while still holding the diminutive bat, stepped over him, grabbed a handful of hair in her left hand and pulled him toward the door. He had no choice but to crawl and move along the floor with her as the pain magnified in his brain with the tug. As they reached the door she put the bat between her legs, turned the knob, swung open the door with her one free hand and finished dragging him through the doorway. "Get out of here. I'm calling the cops."

She slammed and locked the door, clutched the bat and pressed her back against the door, listened to him squirm and cry. The noise became fainter as he stumbled off the porch and into the night.

After a minute, when all seemed quiet outside, she peeled herself off the door, and while still holding the weapon in her hand, ran to the bathroom, made a desperate lunge toward the bowl and vomited.

Mrs. Morrison apparently slept through it all.

****

80

The night is replete with bits and pieces of disjointed thoughts. She wakes up at brief intervals, conscious of the unpleasant, dry feeling in her mouth, and the clock. She is awake only long enough to re-think the most recent thoughts that her dreams create. She struggles to remember parts of the dream in the hope of making some sense of it or perhaps as a sign to guide her.

She recalled a day in high school, specifically one day in chemistry class when the student teacher was left in charge. Mischievous as teenagers tend to be, the students planned and executed a prank that was designed to push the buttons of the young, aspiring teacher that had the unfortunate pleasure of learning his craft amongst those most interested not in learning, but in having fun. The supervising teacher left the room, giving full reign to the young prodigy and as this was the advanced group, it appeared to be the best case scenario for the novice to practice his craft. There had been instances of the class testing the outer limits of the student teacher's patience, but that day they had a plan. At the giving of a sign, when his back was turned, they coordinated an attack that they had difficulty containing their laughter in anticipation. The sign came and each and every student, valedictorian and salutatorian among them, moved with precision, unfolded the frame and donned a pair of sunglasses. The young aspirant completed his writing at the board, finished his sentence as he continued to explain the mysteries of chemistry these young, bright students needed to learn and turned to check their comprehension. His startled face caused a few to express muffled giggles and the rest maintained faces of serious contemplation, as was the plan.

Nancy wakes, turns to check the time and continues to think about how the young, hopeful, student teacher lost control. He screamed and ranted, "So, you want it dark?" and in anger shut the lights, pulled the shades, and placed them in near complete darkness. She doesn't remember what happened next, but feels the still uncomfortable remorse as she settles back into her pillow and wonders what ever happened to the abused student teacher.

She dreams next about a ride in the car when she was a little girl. Her dad is driving, her brother and cousins spread out in the old Rambler station wagon with her uncle riding up front, smoking a stogie. He is loud and full of laughter - they get lost going to the lake. Nancy is the first to realize it and tells them they are going the wrong way. Her uncle is dead now. So are two of her cousins.

This morphing into a bizarre scene at the supermarket, her brother and her arguing over what they will buy, alternating putting in and taking out of the cart items that the other wishes to purchase. She wakes again. It's been a few hours and she laments her broken sleep. With time still before morning, hopeful of some peaceful sleep, she turns again, feels her own nakedness, throws a t-shirt over her bare shoulders, and settles back in.

There is one last scene this night, it is a much more recent event, one that she is sure actually happened. After flying over non-descript dessert, she gets off a helicopter in a swirl of dust and sand. Now she is walking through their research facility outside of Chad. It is air conditioned. The barracks style living quarters are sparsely decorated, each boy has an open air locker, a small desk, and an attached bunk; there are no pictures of parents, or brothers and sisters amongst them. Occasionally, just something cut from a newspaper, a speaker at a podium, apparently some leader from their culture as she recognizes the same face in a few of the photos, a face seemingly angry, head covered in the traditional kufi, bearded, and often gesticulating to an agitated crowd. She stops at one such station and there is a boy that appears to be no more than fourteen or fifteen years old. The same stark living area, a similar newspaper clipping of the zealot leader, there is a heading, written in what she assumes is Arabic, across the top. He sits and works at a small hand-held electronic game with a second device, this one with an ear plug, shutting out the outside noise and isolating him from external stimuli much like you might see a teenager in the States use while sitting on a bus or in the waiting room of a doctor's office. A can of cola rests within reach. The boy glances up and catches her eye. He does not immediately look away as the others had. She is surprised at the blueness of his eyes. His face is round and full. He does not have the ill look of the boys at home. He is evidently one of their 'test cases.' Beyond this uniqueness he has a distinctive hairline, at the temples it recedes a bit on each side then gathers itself toward the center of his forehead and extends down, narrowing until the hair itself creates a point, in the center. Nancy wakes with the vision of his face in her mind and remembers this boy. Partially conscious, she recalls the question she posed, translated to the boy, and his response.

"Why do you have no pictures of your family, your mother or father, your brothers or sisters?"

"It is better I have no memory of them," is all he said and dismissed her by removing his gaze even before his answer is translated to her, and is transfixed again by the game on his lap. Nancy motioned to her host to take a picture. She sat next to him on the edge of the bed. He didn't look up but fidgeted just a bit, creating an inch or two of space between them as if uncomfortable. She looked up and smiled anyway. Click went the camera. They walked away and she said to the host, "Make sure the boy gets a copy of that picture."

It is now getting light and Nancy tries to settle back in to capture a bit more sleep before she starts her day. Her mind, activated by this memory, will not allow her to rest as she runs through the dream again and again, trying to remember details of the visit and make more sense of things there. Nearly an hour goes by and she is about to give up on getting more rest this night but she turns and puts herself into the position she is most comfortable, clears her mind of everything except the sweet imagined place of repose. At last, she slips into a deep slumber. Finally, entering into the restful place her mind and body really need, she doesn't dream, doesn't wake until her eyes pop open at 9:10 a.m. Shit, no alarm. She springs into motion. The car will be here soon.

Chapter 12

Ted Randolph is back at work early the next day. Between missing a bunch of work due to Christopher's illness and his own distracted mindset, he has much to do. His bosses are particularly gracious toward his situation. They really don't hassle him about the time out, don't ask for paperwork or documentation. From time to time they ask him how Chris is doing and he has always felt it genuine and is appreciative of their concerns. For Ted, no matter what he tried over the past few months, he finds himself regularly staring off into space, his thoughts elsewhere. He might be doing the most routine audit and in the midst of it realizes he has gone through a whole section or two of the audit and doesn't really remember what he read. It's usually about Christopher and the family, or some aspect of the illness that will interject itself into his consciousness, but other times not. Wistful reminisces. Imaginative romances. Lost dreams. They take a stand in his mind as well. There are whole blocks of time he feels completely out of sorts. Not depressed per se, but melancholy, as if his life is sweeping past him and he is in the water and struggling just to hold on to a floating piece of driftwood to keep his head above water. He presents a good face to the world. He says the right things; does the right things. He has to be strong. Strong for Ceci, Aaron, and Christopher. He has to be the man.

Today, he can't help but dwell on the meeting with Glacieux. Although attractive, he doesn't really like her. She seemed distant and calculating. While one part of him appreciated her directness, he was not left with a warm and fuzzy feeling toward her. Ted is good at reading people, in his profession he has to be. He attributes it to some innate skill that he is blessed with. A skill that makes him good at his job – perhaps. Or perhaps he is simply observant. Observant and schooled in analyzing what people say and how they say it. His goal is to get at the truth regardless of what the client portrays is the situation. He knows the truth. Christopher doesn't have much of a chance to make it. Poor kid. Poor sick kid. He quickly attempts to change this stream of thought. He can't let himself go down that path again today. The poor sick kid. It isn't fair. No kid should have to suffer so. What did he do to deserve such a fate? Why Christopher and not one of the hundreds of other kids he sees lined across the school bus stops that he drives by in the morning? Why not some deadbeat drug addict like the one he saw, unwashed and pushing a shopping cart along the roadside this morning? Humph. That deadbeat will probably live to be sixty.

Back to work, no time for self-pity today. He finishes up the paperwork on the case he is working and picks up the next from the pile he has arranged neatly in a stack to the right. Harvey Weinberg, self-employed, owns a delicatessen on the North Shore. Let's see what we can find out about ol'Harvey, he muses. Ted pulls him up in the agency's database and scans through a few pages of data, does some preliminary comparisons and smirks at what he sees. Harvey doesn't claim very much income from his mostly cash business. Wife is on the books, minimal income but likely has benefits. He maintains a home in an upper middle income neighborhood. Ted reviews the deductions. Real estate taxes are hefty, mortgage interest also high (both standard with living in New York). Some money to charity, a capital gains loss, a goodly amount of interest on savings, son in college. Ted has enough info to place his income needs within a certain range. It appears Mr. Weinberg is likely not claiming the income he should be. Bastard. Guys like me pay every dime, guys like Weinberg skim the system. His kid probably gets federal dollars for school too. He places Weinberg's file in a separate folder. I'll be visiting him soon, Ted thinks to himself. He'll shit his pants when I hand him my card.

Boy, he'll owe a bundle. We can go back a number of years, make some assumptions, add some penalty and some interest; yep a pretty penny will be coming into the coffers of the U.S. government. Ted knows other agents that wouldn't even make the effort to chase down the cash. They sit back, collect what is coming to them every two weeks, do the minimum, and count the days to retirement. It's probably why his bosses don't give him a hard time, even with his troubles he is worth two of those old slugs, even if he works only half the time. He discovers the fraud, collects the money and his bosses get the credit that comes from his sharp mind.

He notices it's after nine and his stomach reminds him he hasn't had breakfast. I'll go down to the cafeteria, pick up a bagel, check the paper for the lottery numbers – he realizes he talks to himself more now too. He reaches into his shirt pocket, pulls out the ticket and memorizes the first three numbers in each of the games. I won't even have to buy the paper, (as if the fifty cents would make any difference in my situation). I'll just check the inside cover and scan the winners. Then again, maybe I should drive over to Weinberg's deli, shake him down for free bagels, coffee, and newspapers, for life. Scammer! Although what I really need is cash - cold, hard, untraceable cash. I'm suspicious of that Glacieux woman. I'll take a glance at her records too. A pang of conscience strikes him as he types in her information then hits submit anyway. A father has a right to know about someone that he is placing his trust in – no? The initial screen pops up and fear creeps in. I could lose my job over this. The Internal Revenue Service doesn't fool around. Agents are sent packing when they access records that they are not authorized to see. His stomach growls at the further delay and Ted minimizes the screen, picks up his picture ID badge from where it lays on the desk, clips it to his shirt pocket, properly displayed as per protocol, and heads out to the cafeteria.

He strolls through the halls, nodding greetings to those he passes, in most cases not knowing their names or what they have going on in their lives. Do they have trouble like me? Who am I kidding? I don't have the chutzpah to shake a guy down for a bagel, never mind cash.

Never have. Not worth it, potentially forfeit everything I worked for, lose my pension, maybe go to jail? What would happen to Ceci and the boys then? Too risky for my blood. He walks past the elevator and takes the stairs thinking it will help burn off the calories from the bagel, the butter, and the half n half he'll put in his coffee. He thinks about the thousands of times he must have taken these steps; eighteen steps on each level, two levels up, two levels down, at least two times a day, forty-eight weeks a year, minus twelve holidays, for twenty years. There was a time he could have done the math in his head, but not today. Today the thirty-six steps feel like thirty six hundred. He plods along and feels he would fall headlong to the bottom without the assistance of his hand on the rail. He feels older - much older than he is - like an old man. His shoulders stooped, he walks with head down, looking at his shoes, in need of a shine. Worn soles. The laces frayed. He makes a mental note; I've got to get new laces. Silly to wait until one of them breaks when I'm tying them and rushing to get out of the house in the morning. Yes, that's what I'll do. I'll pick up new laces and give them a good shine too.

He gets to the bottom, pushes open the door, turns toward the cafeteria as the elevator door swooshes open. He catches the eye of the young lady from across the hall as she exits and gives her his best smile, which she returns. He slows to allow her to go ahead of him. She accepts his polite gesture and walks quickly past. He lingers behind but his eyes are drawn as if pulled by gravity down to the material of her skirt swishing left then right as she walks. He quickens his pace to stay within range, not allowing anyone to get between them. He follows her path, in mock interest of the wares available in the cafeteria, the same goods that he has seen morning after morning for so long. He knows what he wants. She hesitates and looks at the hot food, the eggs, the bacon, and leans toward and over the glass so that she can see them clearly beyond the steamed glass, one foot rising off the floor as she leans over and her mouth is slightly open as a child might do when scanning a candy rack. Ted unconsciously licks his dry lips and feels his heart beating in his chest. He catches a whiff of her perfume but veers too close and her foot brushes against the side of his pants leg.

"Oh, I'm sorry," they both utter in the simultaneous awkwardness when one brushes against a stranger and neither knows who is at fault. She decides against the eggs, more window shopping than serious, and moves along the counter to where the dry cereal, fruit, and yogurt wait. She takes a yogurt and a banana, walks past the bagels, rolls, and assorted pastry and she is gone; the temptation now out of sight. Ted focuses his attention briefly on the bagels and the server greets him with a "sesame with butter?" question that she already knows the answer to, deftly cuts and butters it to his liking, puts it on a paper plate and leaves it for him to pick up. He smiles at her and says, "Thank you," picks it up and glances over to the cashier area where he can just catch the youthful profile and portions of the sculptured legs on heels as they whisk her to the plastic utensil station. Ted mechanically goes to the coffee area, makes a cup in his usual way, places a plastic lid on top of the Styrofoam cup and swallows hard. Dang – if she isn't put together. I bet she's not a day over twenty-five. Not married either, can you imagine that?

He wonders what others would think of him if they knew what goes on in his head. "It's just a little fantasy. No harm done," he justifies within himself. "Look but don't touch, that's my motto," he continues. He has been faithful all these years. Still a guy has needs. When was the last time he and Ceci . . .? He heads back to his office, paper plate and cup in hand, catches the elevator door just before it closes. He half hopes she is in the elevator, but it's empty. I wonder how I can find out her name? I didn't see her wearing a badge, another rule breaker among us. If she'll break one rule . . .

He fantasizes away the short ride, exits the elevator and heads for his office. He looks down the hall hoping to catch a glimpse of her but finds only the dull print on the wall opposite his gaze. No sign of her above or about the cubes. As he settles back in behind his desk, he turns his attention to making a rip in the lid so he can sip his coffee and he realizes he forgot to check the newspaper. Dang – maddening distractions! I'll have to remember when I go down again this afternoon for coffee. He consumes the bagel, punctuated with sips of hot coffee, and tries to imagine how a conversation with her might go. How might she be interested in a guy like him? Before long he has visualized a way, like a scene in a play, both of them interested in only one thing. Passion, like in the movies; desperate lovers; but it is all a script, not like real life. Cripes – I don't even know the girl's name! He wonders what he would do if the opportunity he has created in his mind's eye actually presented itself. Would he go with her if the invitation came? How could he? What would he say to Ceci? How could he look her in the eye afterwards? She would be too hurt. She doesn't deserve to be treated so. She deserves a faithful husband. I do love her. I would never want to hurt her. It wouldn't be fair. He wets his dry lips, swallows hard, feels his blood pumping and imagines pressing against her and her wanting him.

****

At home, Ceci helps Christopher into the car and tries to encourage him about the new doctor, and the new place they are going to. "They have experience dealing with kids that have your condition. They know the best way to help you," she tells him.

It was a rough night. Her sleep was broken more than once. A lighter sleeper than Ted, she heard him first, just like when he was a baby. She tries not to wake Ted when Christopher is up in the night, rationalizing that he has to go to work.

She lives with the thought that Christopher needs her.

The first time he woke was around two in the morning. He threw up in his bed. She heard him gag with the effort not to wretch and was by his side before he had even finished. She comforted him and took care of the practical things too. They removed his soiled pajamas, cleaned up in the bathroom, and put on fresh things. He sat in the small rocker as she took care of the bedding and when done, she tucked him back in. Ceci placed the sheets and clothes, damp and distinctly scented with a mixture of stomach acid and bits of that evening's dinner, into the washing machine. She prayed for Christopher, prayed for strength, and by the time she returned to check on him, he was asleep.

The second time it was just before 4 a.m. He cried out for her, "Mommy, Mommy!" and she went to him. He was sweating and dizzy. "Mommy, mommy, my bed is moving. Mommy, Mommy, I don't feel good." She cradled him close and hoped he wouldn't throw up again. She reached for the pail they keep near the bed at all times and tells him it will be OK.

"Mommy is here with you." She held him against her with her left arm and clutched the pail in her right hand. "Mommy is here. You're going to be OK. There, there, go back to sleep now. Mommy is here. Go back to sleep. Mommy is here. Everything is going to be OK." She prayed silently and moved the lock of hair from off his damp, warm forehead. Lately, he has been running a slight fever. "Mommy is here. It's going to be OK." Ten minutes later she woke up, gently placed him back on his pillow, fixed the covers about him and quietly slipped out of the room.

Back in their room, Ted stirred in his sleep, she was careful not to wake him. Bad enough one of us isn't getting a solid sleep, she thought. She drifted off for what felt like only a minute, waking to the sound of Ted moving about the room, trying to get dressed in the dark. "Ted, why are you up so early?" she said with an unintended complaint in her voice.

"I'm sorry, honey. I was trying not to wake you. I couldn't sleep. I'm gonna go into the office early, get some work done. You go back to sleep now. I'll see you tonight," he said and gave her a peck on the cheek and slipped out of the room.

The post-rush hour traffic is not too bad, and as a result, they are a bit early arriving at the clinic. Ceci maneuvers the family mini-van into a parking spot not too far from the door and cheerfully tells Christopher that they are here. She is clearly excited but Chris looks out rather stoically at the brick façade and glances up at the overcast clouds that cover the sky. "Mommy, it looks like rain. Be sure to take your umbrella with you," he reminds her.

"Yes, Christopher, it does. Thank you for reminding me," she replies. Even with all he is going through he still thinks about her; worries about her. Just a few days ago, she was checking on him in the middle of the day and he remarked how she looked tired, and suggested she take a nap. Today, he is worried about her getting wet in the rain. What a great kid, she thinks. He has a thoughtful spirit.

Inside they are greeted at the reception desk by a nurse in the typical white attire, small white cap keeping her hair in place. Ceci is handed a clipboard and is asked to complete paperwork. There are a few pages for the patient's medical history; allergies, current medications; a card with emergency contact information, home, cell, e-mail – she leaves blank what she feels is irrelevant – are they going to e-mail me she thinks to herself - and then goes back and puts it in, thinking there is a chance they will forward pertinent articles or instructions to her that might help her take care of Chris when he comes home. She wonders how long he will be in this time. In three months it will be Christmas. It would be nice to have him home for Christmas. Dr. Glacieux said she would be willing to treat him for as long as she thought the treatments could help him. If he is well at Christmas, he could come home for a few days, then she would bring him back. His birthday is in the spring. They should do something special for that too.

Deep in her own thoughts, she hasn't noticed that Christopher wandered off. The nurse, busy, is not at her station when Ceci goes to return the clipboard. "Where is that boy?" she says aloud to no one in particular. She looks down the corridor in each direction. No Chris. There are three sets of double-doors: one straight ahead, one set back to the left, another set back to the right. Each has a rectangular piece of glass so you can see if someone is coming as you approach. It's quiet. There's only the sound of her footsteps as she goes from door to door, agitated at having to look for Chris but increasingly hectic as she glances through the glass and into the hallway behind the center set of doors, then to the doors on the right. They are marked 'Doctors and nurses only – No admittance'. She scurries across the open venue to the last set on the left, 'Restricted Access, No Admittance,' statement on each swinging door, and worriedly looks again. There he is, down the hall a bit, peering into one of the rooms through the glass. Ceci checks behind her, no nurse, and briskly walks in and heads for her son. He doesn't appear to hear her coming. "Christopher," she scolds. "What are you doing in here? You aren't supposed to be here. This is a hospital. You can't just walk around wherever you feel like." The glass is a bit high for him and he is leaning into the door and is on his toes so that his eyes rise just above the wood and allow him to see in. "Get away from that door. Don't be so nosy." He doesn't turn his head or move. She approaches and looks over his head and into the room that has mesmerized him. She sees a child on a bed, its head wrapped, a ventilator taped in place and pushed down its throat, the ugly apparatus covering its face. Hoses, perhaps a half dozen, heading into and out of the still body; bags hang from a hook above; machines line the room, with lights blinking and numbers flashing, one has a graph moving left to right. It's as if you can feel the heart beat with each peak and valley on the screen. If you listen closely you can hear the incessant 'beep' 'beep' noise marking the beats. A clear cylinder unit, its internal gear moving up and down, regular and consistent, keeps necessary air in the lungs. The child's chest rises and falls in unison with the machine.

"Come," she says and rests a hand on his shoulder. "We shouldn't be snooping on people we don't know."

Chapter 13

At precisely 9:30 am the doorbell rings at the Glacieux residence. Nancy, not nearly dressed, trots toward the door, looks through the peep hole and upon seeing what appears to be a driver, goes to shut down the alarm before realizing she went to bed last night without setting it. I should be more careful, she thinks. She opens the door just enough to expose her still wet head and tells the driver, "I'll be a few more minutes."

"Take your time, ma'am," with a formal tip of the cap comes the reply and he turns to wait in the black limo parked in her driveway. JW is a class act. If only she had reacted differently last night when they kissed . . .

Fifteen minutes later, she heads down the driveway to the waiting car and reaches down to pick up the plastic bagged papers left on the driveway sometime earlier that morning. She hates when people leave these unwanted items sitting on the ground, littering the neighborhood and their property. What are people thinking? How lazy can they be?

The driver springs into action as she approaches and stands with the rear passenger door open for her. She settles into the seat, comfortable on this chilly, early fall morning. The leather was heated in advance and her wish for a cup of coffee is soon fulfilled as the compartment is equipped with that novelty. The car moves quietly over the road, the turns nearly unfelt by the passenger. Ahhh, a chauffeured ride to work is a great way to start the day. She sits back and lets her shoulders sink into the leather, inclines her head back and shuts her eyes for a few seconds. She rethinks what little she can remember from her night's dreams. Now, with her mind occupied in the present and her subconscious pushed down beneath her awaken persona, she recalls even less. My brother was in one, what were we doing she questions herself? And then there was the boy she can still picture in her mind that she met on her trip to Chad. What did he say to her? Something about not remembering? The rest is completely gone; she could not conjure up the images that were so real just a few hours ago.

Like in our dreams, only a few moments of time had transpired as Nancy can tell from the fact that they had not entered the highway yet. She lifts her arm to better focus on the hands of her watch. The driver, who evidently is more aware of her than he leads on, offers the opinion that they should arrive at her destination in fifteen minutes, adding that traffic is light this morning. She gives him a smile, directed into the rear view mirror where his eyes pick it up and then quickly dart back to the road.

With nothing to do she occupies herself by pulling off the plastic and spreading out the local paper that she picked up. Nancy glances at the headlines and advertisements, not really reading any one in particular. She looks at each picture and reads the caption underneath explaining who or what the picture is in reference to. Sometimes, when skimming through it in the past, she would see an acquaintance that was the chairperson of a particular charity or promoted into some job and had even had her own picture appear. Jonathon probably arranged some coverage for their luncheon yesterday but it might not be in this local community paper, and surely not until next week, if at all. He is much better at marketing her and the Center than she is. She nearly loses interest when a photo of a ribbon cutting catches her eye. It's a picture of a young African-American woman holding an overly large scissor and standing in front of a store. On either side of her is an elderly white person, a man and a woman, each holding an end of the ribbon that the young lady is about to cut. The caption above reads, 'Grand Opening – Second Chance Window Treatments.' The writing underneath explains, "Lakeisha Williams, celebrates the opening of her new store with sponsors Andrew and Melissa Cartwright." To the right of the picture there is another heading and a short summary.

Water Meter Hero Realizes Dream

Lakeisha Williams, a former water authority worker, celebrates the opening of her new store in Cannonsville. Ms. Williams, is the young woman that came to the rescue of Andrew and Melissa Cartwright who had been trapped and left for dead in their basement after a horrific home invasion last April. Ms. Williams told the Sentinel, "I can't believe this is actually happening. I am so grateful to Mr. and Mrs. Cartwright. Without their help, this wouldn't have been possible."

Andrew Cartwright, still conscious after beatings, tied and bound in his basement for three days, was overheard by Ms. Williams as she did her rounds. Mr. Cartwright said, "Lakeisha came to our rescue. It was her concern for us that allowed us to live. We would have died in that basement if she hadn't come by that day and stopped what she was doing to check on us. She rang the doorbell and I came to and tried to make some noise but my mouth was taped over. After a minute, I realized Melissa was silent and still and I figured she must have died already. We have been married fifty-two years."

Lakeisha told us that she had about given up when no one came to the door but went back over to the basement window one more time and this time heard Mr. Cartwright as he cried over the loss of his wife.

"It was a miracle," added Mrs. Cartwright. "Lakeisha is like our angel. Her timing was perfect. Now Andrew and I get a second chance and Lakeisha does too. We are so excited about her new store. You tell everyone to come by and say 'Hi.' She is really talented. Customers won't be disappointed."

Readers, when you stop by, be sure to say 'Hi' to Melissa Cartwright too. She'll be helping Lakeisha most mornings in the store – Second Chance Window Treatments is located in the Prestige Shopping Center on Shore Road. Their hours of operation are Monday to Saturday, from 9:00 a.m. – 4:30 p.m.

Nancy sat in wonder and admiration. Fifty-two years. She remembers now reading about the story when it first appeared in the news. The old guy loved his wife so much that upon the thought of having lost her, although nearly dead himself from three days without food or water, and with his mouth taped shut, his groan was heard outside the walls by the woman that came to read the water meter. That is great love, she thinks to herself. She wonders if anyone will ever love her that much. Harry was a disaster but when they got married she thought it would be her one and only time. Who gets married thinking they will break up?

With her and Harry it was probably inevitable. They came from different walks of life and even if they had worked things out better, now, with him taking up a renewed interest in religion, it would likely have broken apart anyway. Better sooner than later she muses. When they met she was taken by his dark looks. Handsome, and with a serious but somehow innocent appearance, she liked him right away. He was working a civil servant job in the town planning office and she went in just before closing with the blueprints her contractor had given her to file for a permit on the work she was having done. He listened to her story and took the time to make sure she had all the paperwork she needed and waited patiently, past closing time, while she filled it all out. Then he double-checked each part to make sure that when it was turned in there would be no problem. She thought he was so nice, so unassuming, and different than the men she knew. She learned he had a degree in engineering and he seemed bright. He read the blueprints, which she could neither make heads or tails of, and pointed out to her a section that did not match what her contractor had put down on his part of the forms. He called her Mrs. Thompson, even after she suggested he use Nancy, and finally corrected that by saying emphatically, "It's Ms. Thompson," and waved an unadorned ring finger in his direction. "I'm not married."

He had the look of a little boy who had been corrected by his teacher. He mumbled an embarrassed apology and put his head down into the work. That look won her over. She teased and bantered with him the rest of the time she spent there. Upon her getting ready to leave, he rose, put out his hand and said, "Ms. Thompson, it's been my pleasure to serve you." That solemn, quaint, formal statement made her laugh and although she hadn't intended to, she asked him out.

"Harry, you've been so helpful, and I've made you stay late. Why don't we get something to drink and maybe a bite to eat?" When he hesitated, thinking he might be worrying about the cash he would need, she said, "It's on me. It's the least I can do."

"Oh, no Ma'am," he said, "it's not that. It's just that the Town Planning Department has rules. I can't take a gift from someone that is seeking approval for a permit. It might not look right." She laughed.

"I'm not bribing you Harry. If you don't want to go with me, just say so."

"No, no, it's not that at all, Ms. Thompson. I do want to go with you" and he stopped short realizing he may have appeared too anxious.

"Well then," she broke the silence, "if you do want to go with me and you don't want me to pay for you, we'll go Dutch." That solution made him smile.

"Very well," he nodded his head in agreement. "Give me a minute to shut down my computer. I'd like that very much."

When they sat down at the Momentum Sports Bar it was apparent he was nervous being with her. She figured he was in his mid-to-late twenties. She was already thirty-five, but could pass for younger. He drank down his first beer in several thirsty gulps and was well into his second before she had even sipped through the foam on her first one. The nervousness gone, Harry became a perfectly cordial source of entertainment. He was articulate, passionate, good looking and extremely attentive. The rest is history.

She picks up the cell phone and dials his number. "Hanif, it's me. I just thought I'd let you know that I can wire you some money, hopefully by the end of the day."

"Praise be to Allah," is his reply.

Not knowing how to respond to that she simply says, "Yeah, OK. I'll let you know when it's done," and hangs up.

****

Hanif Nasrallah had already been up for several hours, he had washed and prayed but had not eaten. He would fast this day. Fast and pray. Her call had disturbed his contemplation. When he first heard the phone he intended to not answer but he could not resist looking at the ID and when he saw it was her, he picked it up. He always catered to her. It's as if he has an iron rod through his being and she, fully magnetized, pulls him in. When they first met, he was totally helpless. Now, he resists but cannot overcome. He recalls the day they met as if it was yesterday. He can still see what she was wearing, how she walked when she entered the town office, and with her first words something stirred within him. She leaned onto the counter, not knowing who to address. He was sitting to the left and not able to take his eyes off her. He could do nothing but listen. As she spoke, her one hand moved animatedly and the other clutched a set of blueprints as she explained her predicament. He did not hear every word, just jumbled batches strung together. "My contractor says," "He didn't realize," "Now it's an emergency." All the while her lips moved and her eyes danced and her hair, her hair shined and swayed with her as she told her story. The counter was purposely high and as she leaned into it her breasts rested on top. The top two buttons of her shirt were open and he could see the white skin, and the material stretching to where it met the third button revealing yet more white skin. He thought it would burst open under the pressure and had trouble keeping his eyes from it. He was close enough to see how the flesh pushed against the opening, yet the small, cream-colored button held the two pieces of stretched cloth together. He was embarrassed to move from his seat behind the desk. Finally, she stopped talking, and when he said nothing, she looked hard at him and said, "Well, can you help me or not?"

At that point he might have agreed to just about anything she said. His desire was to help her.

Thinking of her now, rekindled the feeling he had that day and it made him uncomfortable. How can she still have this pull on me? How can she make me react in such a way? He tortured himself over these questions. His spirit sought to soar and yet his flesh could not be contained. What is she – a witch, a devil? How can she have this power over me? I can understand before, but not now. It is me? Do I have some innate flaw? Is it my sin? Is it my father's sin that has flowed down and come against me? Perhaps I should beat my flesh into submission. What is the answer? To whom do I turn to understand this? With these scattered thoughts in his mind he throws his head on the ground and covers his face with his hands and weeps for his condition.

When he stops, he feels better. He rises, washes his face, and takes food – today is not a day to fast.

From the first day, he sought to please her. She was not at all like his mother. She had her own mind, made her own decisions. She was strong mentally, physically, and emotionally. She was successful and he convinced himself that did not matter.

When they married he would rise early, have the coffee ready and would often make breakfast for her or run to the store before she got out of bed to buy her something fresh that she might like to eat.

The time with her went by quickly. She opened up the realm of possibilities that the world held. She exposed him to new and different people and experiences. Yet, he knew that they were drifting apart. He had hoped a child would bring them closer together but that was not the way it worked out. He is brought back to the question of whose fault it was and who controlled the levers?

She began to resent him. She accused him of having an easy life and mocked him because he stayed with his soft, safe position in the Town Planning Department. She said he had no ambition and threw herself more headlong into her career, the doctor, the soon to be brain disease specialist. She became a martyr to her dream of finding a cure.

At first he supported her, how could he not? But as the realization sunk in, as he saw the sick child move from ill to invalid to bare existence, he lost hope. Nancy did not. She was away most of each day and had no interest beyond her work. They related less and less in every way. He suspected she had interests beyond him outside the home, how could she not as their marriage became inactive like her patients. He began to leave the house before she woke up and would be asleep (or feign so), when she arrived home late, as always. They sometimes went days without hardly speaking. Just a note on the kitchen counter or a message left on the answering machine.

She drove him away. He found sustenance at another well.

Gloria began working in the town offices as a summer intern. She was the daughter of the County Supervisor and said she was only there so, "Daddy could keep an eye on me." Gloria could be described as feisty. She had dropped out of her freshman year of college and her father made sure she didn't have the chance to just sit around the house all summer, and so, put her to work. Gloria pushed the limits of 'casual office attire.' She flirted openly with all the men, each eyeing her carefully and yet keeping distant due to her connection, her youth, and the fear of being caught. She was not overly bright but did not have to be, her assets were elsewhere. Hanif knew that she did not love him. She simply used him because he was willing and because he was not fearful of being caught with her. She wanted to make Daddy pay for forcing this job on her. Hanif didn't care. Gloria apparently learned things in her short time at college that helped satisfy him. He used her too.

Nancy would have never known. She did not suspect he would wander off after another. He had all he needed or so she thought. Gloria and her father argued at the end of the summer when she informed him that she was not going back to college in September. In her desire to hurt him, she hurled her promiscuity in his face and it was not too long after that she and Hanif were discovered in a compromising position during work hours. Losing the job allowed Nancy to find out the truth.

She controlled him from the first day that they met but now the tables are turned. Now he controls her, she can do nothing but follow his suggestions. He was the one that first mentioned the facility in Chad. He was the one that kept her on a short lease and demanded she provide the funds to run it. Weak woman that she has become, her desire has become her weakness and he exploits it.

Chapter 14

Ceci and Christopher returned to the reception area and sat down again. He munched on a granola bar she brought and washed it down with a drink box as they waited. Within a few minutes the nurse returned, and seeing the empty wrapper and the drink box still in Christopher's hand, looked disapprovingly at Mrs. Randolph. "Mrs. Randolph, you did read the facility instruction pamphlet that was provided to you?" Ceci nods yes in in response. "Well then, you must commit to following it to the letter. The treatment your son is entering requires strict diet. You are not to bring anything in for him to eat. Both of these items contain contaminants. Food dyes, preservatives, sweeteners, to name just a few. Do you understand?"

"Yes, yes, of course. I'm sorry, I didn't realize . . . he was hungry," Ceci says apologetically.

"What else did he eat today?" the nurse inquires, pencil and clipboard in hand, ready to take down the full extent of her faults.

"Uh, nothing really. Cereal with milk - Cheerios, and a small glass of apple juice," she says defensively.

The nurse inquires further, "Regular Cheerios or fancied up, like Honey Nut or . . .?"

Ceci cut her off. "Regular, plain, store brand Cheerios. Low in sugar, I think."

The nurse purses her lips and continues writing. Thinking better of it, and realizing she has inadvertently made her upset, the nurse smiles at her and says kindly, "It's fine Mrs. Randolph. Don't be overly concerned. We just have to keep track of everything the child eats from this moment forward. It's fine, really." She rests her hand on

Ceci's shoulder and passes her a tissue for her eyes, which had watered nearly to the point of tears. Ceci accepts the tissue and the gesture, blinks away the water and pats the corner of each eye.

"Now, let's get young Christopher settled. The children are excited that we have a new friend coming in this morning. Come with me," and she holds her hand out as if she is leading them into an amusement park adventure. They head toward the center set of double doors. It does seem kind of magical. Arching over the top of the doors are the words, emblazoned in the colors of the rainbow, 'THE CENTER FOR HOPE' and the rainbow continues down the left and the right until it hits the floor on either side of the doors. They open into a narrow hallway, which leads to another set of double doors, this time completely made of glass. Entering, Ceci and Christopher see a huge, rectangular shaped room with beds running parallel on each side. The group continues down the wide, open, center aisle. On the floor, which is polished to a smooth sheen, they come to a hop scotch game pattern that had been painted onto the floor. Several children are in the midst of playing. At the end of each row of beds there is an open square, and each corner has its own set of activities. On the immediate right, a number of children sit playing games at what looks like stone tables, each with a game board built into the face of the table. Ceci recognizes the black and white squares that can be used for checkers or chess, and another that looks like a backgammon board, and even at a distance, she recognizes a third, which is being used for Chinese checkers. The corner contains a large bookcase, with six shelves, filled end-to-end with books. One child looks up from what she is reading. Another, with her back to them, turns her head fully to take a good look at the newcomers.

On the immediate left, there is an area with plants of various shapes and sizes. A few children walk among them. One child, with scissors in hand, works at the shape of a small bonsai. As the Randolph's walk through, each child becomes aware of their presence, and looks toward them. Ceci feels their eyes upon her, relating, knowing she is the boy's mother. But mostly they peer at Chris. Some smile. Others give a wave, either shy or boisterous. A few glance toward them, but make no visible reaction.

The room itself is flooded in light. Two long banks of skylights, angled North to South, take up the bulk of the ceiling. It is a bright day, yet the room is not as warm as expected. Ceci has to squint to see, but Christopher is wide-eyed. Nearly all of the children have sunglasses on, and depending upon the style and shading, you can't really tell what is behind each lens.

Even though the room is filled with activity and the buzz of children, they pass a child that lays on his bed, glasses left on the bed-side table, eyes closed, blanket pulled up to his chin and seemingly asleep. Ceci notices Christopher looking hard in the direction of this child and his lips move. She recognizes the habit of her son to mouth a quick prayer, he is a sensitive and intuitive child.

About a third of the way in, they stop in front of a bed on the left. It's a single bed, metal frame, with sheet, blanket, and two pillows. A small chest sits at the foot, and an end table to the left, a light with an adjustable arm is attached to the top of the modest metal headboard.

"This will be your bed Christopher," says the nurse.

A child approaches. "Hi, I'm Sammy. We're going to be neighbors. This is my bed here," and she points to the next bed before thrusting a small white hand out to shake Christopher's. Mrs. Randolph would have guessed Sammy to be a boy if she only looked at the child's face, but she is adorned all in pink: pink sweat shirt, pink softie pants, pink socks with individual toes. Her head wrapped neatly, it completely hides her hair. She smiles big and is missing one tooth on the bottom. "You're Christopher. Nurse Clement told us you were coming. Would you like to see my bird? Her name is Precious. You are going to love it here," she continues until Nurse Clement intervenes.

"Samantha, slow down. Let Christopher get settled. He hasn't even seen the rest of the center."

"Oh, can I help show him?" She beams at the nurse as she takes his hand and begins to lead him off even before Ms. Clement nods her head in approval. Ceci and Ms. Clement follow and watch as Sammy leads Christopher to the end of the two rows of beds and into the glass enclosed room in the left corner. It is labeled 'Sanctuary' and Ceci can see she brings Chris directly over to a cage that contains a blue and white bird. They stand together trying to get the little thing to play with one of the toys that hang from the wire strands of the cage. The room has a wide number of cages and an assortment of birds, reptiles, and small furry creatures. Another child sits on the floor and hand-feeds a floppy eared rabbit that is loose on the floor. Sammy and Chris join her and the three of them entertain themselves by caressing and feeding the pet.

Nurse Clement chats with Mrs. Randolph while they watch the children play. "The Sanctuary is enclosed because we strive to keep the living area as sterile as possible. As you read in the pamphlet, we believe in a holistic approach to helping the children. They are sick, but keeping them secluded, in a typical hospital bed setting, surrounded by artificial light, hasn't done them a bit of good, and won't help them fight their disease. We encourage every child to adopt a pet. We work with a number of veterinarians and animal shelters. They provide us the animals, all of which need care. They are either sick or injured when they arrive here. In the Sanctuary, the children take care of them and help nurse them back to health. We believe it is important for the children to have a pet that needs them, that they know is ill, and that they can take care of and help recover."

"Yes," is all Ceci can think to say.

Nurse Clement glances at her watch and uses the speaker system on the wall to call out to Sammy, reminding her that they have more to show Christopher. The children scamper out of the Sanctuary, hand in hand, stopping at the hand sanitizing station on the wall, then trotting across to the right corner activity. It consists of a gate with a short, clear, glass wall all around. It is filled with sand, like a gigantic sandbox. Sammy carelessly removes her pink socks and makes Christopher remove his sneakers and socks as they enter the area. The sand is warm and jettisons from under each foot as the two children run across the area to the water's edge. On one end, the water cascades down a stack of slate rocks, making a short waterfall which creates a splashing sound and small waves. The water flows in a semi-circle, past the edge of the encased miniature river. Fish swim gracefully along the bottom, one occasionally passing close to the edge, the light bouncing off its scales, magnified by the sun and the angle of the glass, making it shine through the curved glass in a glorious display of its colors and subtle shading. The children squat in the sand and put their faces close to the glass and peer, eye to eye, to the swimming partner until it pushes past them with a firm swish of its tail. The beach has assorted pails and shovels in various colors and sizes. In one section, the remnant of a sandcastle still stands, one wall broken down by a giant foot. "The sand is completely sterilized every three days. The children love the beach. Many of them spend at least a little time here each day."

"Yes," Ceci responds. "When he was well, Christopher always did like it. We took him when my husband was on vacation."

"He will be well cared for here, Mrs. Randolph," offers Nurse Clement.

"Yes, it appears so." Ceci nods in agreement.

"It's nearly visiting time, Mrs. Randolph. I think we can leave Christopher with Sammy for a bit. Would you like to put his things away at his station?" the nurse suggests. "I have a few items to take care of before any visitors arrive." With that the two women turn and head back to where Christopher will sleep for the next few months.

Ceci refolds her son's clothes and places the larger items into the chest at the foot of the bed. She slips the smaller items into the two drawers in the end table. She places his bible on the end table. Although she had gone over the list they gave her three times, and had meticulously packed the correct number of each item requested, she goes through it again as she unpacks his things. It's not the first time she has settled him into a hospital room, but this time she feels a calm assurance that she hasn't felt before. This time it will be different, she thinks to herself. Her thoughts are interrupted by the voice of a woman approaching.

"Hello." Ceci turns to see a well-dressed woman with her gloved hand extended toward her. "I'm Melinda Robinson, Samantha's mother."

"Hello," Ceci responds and extends her hand. The two women engage limp fingers in greeting. "I'm Cecilia Randolph. Christopher's mom. My friends call me Ceci." A brief silence follows as they each gaze at the other, not sure what to say next.

There is a lot you can tell from a glance. A lot is revealed in a face. On the surface, it's apparent the Robinson's have money. Ceci can easily pick out the designer look of her suit, the matching shoes and handbag, discreet but good jewelry, hair neat, with a salon look. Ceci self-consciously presses out an imaginary wrinkle in her plain polyester dress with both hands. She then reaches up with her right hand to replace a loose strand of hair back behind her ear. Below the surface, seemingly etched into her face, is the tired look of a mother with a sick child. Even beyond the prettiness and the carefully applied make-up, Ceci can see Melinda Robinson's trouble. It's apparent around the eyes and the corners of her mouth; a look of fear, a tired, achy look in the depths of the hazel iris of her eyes.

Melinda Robinson is taken by Ceci's smile, notices she is plainly dressed, with little make-up, and appears to be embarrassed - Melinda is unsure why. "The first day is always a bit awkward," she offers. "So, where is your son?"

"He is at the . . . at the beach - with your daughter. She has perfectly taken him under her wing, like her little bird." Ceci responds. And they both smile at that thought.

"Yes, I suppose she would," and she stands on her tip-toes and looks over to the sandy area to try to catch a glimpse of the two children. As she removes each glove, Ceci can see the manicured, soft hands. The gloves are deftly stuffed into her clutch and she removes a pair of sunglasses and slips them on. "Forgive me, they keep this place so God-awful bright. Do you have a pair to put on? I'm sure we can find something for you." She walks over to Sammy's end table, opens the top drawer, finds a pair with pink frames and passes them to Ceci. "Try these, they are not too ostentatious." Ceci thanks her and slips them over her eyes.

"How long has Samantha been here?" she asks.

"Nearly seven months. She loves it here, and it seems to help her. She has had one relapse, needed more surgery. And, as you can probably tell, is still healing. She has gorgeous red hair, the kind any woman would die for," Melinda responds naturally. The irony of what she said immediately striking them both.

"She is a beautiful girl. She is going to be a beautiful woman someday," Ceci says, trying to be encouraging.

"Yes, I hope so," Melinda responds, and whispers again, "I hope so."

Ceci attempts to fill the silence. "Seven months is a long time. We're hoping we can take Christopher home, that he will be well enough that is, to come home for Christmas." Still silent, Ceci tries to distract her from her thoughts, "Where do you live? How often do you get to visit?" she asks.

"Connecticut," Melinda absently makes the one word reply. She is still caught in the web of thinking about her only child's chance of becoming a woman. Then remembering that a more complete answer is required, she follows up with, "I come pretty much every day, except if I absolutely can't. We had a terrible snow storm in February, and there was a fire on the Throgs Neck Bridge in the summer. You may have read about it," as a way to justify her answer.

Ceci approaches her, places her hand on her new friend's forearm, and pulls her back from the dark thoughts. "You can't think like that," she says and peers through the sun dampening lenses into Melinda's eyes. "Samantha is a beautiful girl and she is going to be a beautiful woman when she grows up. She is going to have a full head of red hair that all her friends will be envious of."

"Yes," Melinda smiles back into Ceci's eyes. "Thank you," and she hugs Ceci, pressing her wool suit into Ceci's dress and holds her, as if gathering strength. Both their eyes tear behind the glasses. Ceci reaches for the tissues on the nearby end table and pulls one and then another quickly and hands one to Melinda as they separate. The women sit on the edge of the bed, side by side, hand in hand, and any awkwardness that existed, any perceived difference in their stations, any of the usual conditions applied to friendships in this world, simply melted away.

They sit and talk, share some of what they have gone through, what hospitals they had been in, what the various doctors had told them, the rejoicing of the remissions and the fear that grips when the relapse comes.

"I, we," referring to her husband, "don't ever want her to think that she won't make it. We've never talked with her about the possibility that she might die and she has never spoken to us about it either. It's always, 'when you get better' or 'when you are fully recovered' and yet, even here, in the seven months, we have witnessed five children that didn't make it. Five in seven months! Each bed represents a child and stares us in the face each day, and reminds us of what can happen. Reminds us of what the doctors tell us will likely happen. This bed here, Christopher's bed, was Allison's. I don't even think Samantha cried, at least she didn't in front of me. They were great friends. They spent whole days, weeks, even months together. Samantha told me, when I pressed her about what she was feeling about Allison, 'Allison was happy, Mom' she told me 'She was not afraid to die.' Can you imagine that? Just a child, and yet, seemingly more together than most of the adults around her.

"So, we persevere. I don't have to tell you what it's like. We do whatever we can to give Samantha a chance to live. My husband, Don, had been totally consumed by his work. He is an investment banker on Wall Street. Samantha's illness changed him, changed him for the better. He was only concerned with making money and he would justify all the time and hours at work by saying he was 'doing it for us.' But now, he would give it all up, would drive a school bus if it would mean his little Sammy would be all right. He leaves work to get here to see her during the day when she seems to have the most energy. He never did that, not in ten years. I know what he's doing; he's trying to show her how much he loves her and is trying to make up for missing most of her childhood. It's sad, really. But, he is a better man. Humph, he even treats me better. I mean, he was never mean, and he gave me whatever I wanted, but now he is more attentive. Kinder. More caring. He gets it. Life is short and there are no guarantees. Nothing can be taken for granted."

Ceci sits with her on the edge of the bed. Knee to knee, hands clasped, she sits and listens. She looks into her friend's shaded eyes and nods her head from time to time. Saying nothing, she is still a great comfort. A comfort drawn from knowing that someone else knows what you mean, knows the truth of what you are saying, knows how you feel; someone who has walked in your shoes and understands the pain.

"Don actually took an unpaid leave of absence when it became apparent that the doctors didn't think Samantha would recover," she continued. "He, we, couldn't accept that. His firm has been very good to us. They encouraged him to take the time off and when they found out how much the treatments cost, the partners, all ten of them, each gave twenty thousand dollars of their own money to help pay for Samantha's care here. Our insurance wouldn't pay for it; experimental, unproven, was how they labeled it – what were we supposed to do? Just let our child die without trying? Don spent three months researching possible treatments. First, he learned what he could about the disease itself. He read medical journals and what studies he could find. The firm has some contacts in the pharmaceutical industry so he got a chance to speak directly to some of the top researchers. He called all over the world to speak to various doctors looking for a solution. He spoke to dozens of parents trying to learn how the disease manifests itself and to catalogue what was tried. Initially, he hoped surgery would be the answer, but that only prolongs the illness, at best, and each one is more dangerous to the patient than the one before. Samantha has had three now," she paused to reflect.

Ceci continued to hold her hand and nodded, knowingly. "We considered more radiation, of course. But that hadn't worked before, you know." Her shoulders move slightly forward and up. The corners of her mouth move a bit up as well as she purses her lips and shrugs in defeat. "Then there were various drug cocktails to consider. Bombardment. One does one thing, one does another, a third produces an effect that a fourth could piggy-back on. Each with its own set of side-effects and dangers. One affects the liver, another the kidneys. All make you nauseous and drowsy . . ." her voice trails off.

"There was a trial starting up in Boston a while back. Did you hear about it?" she asks, and Ceci shakes her head. "We were too late to get Samantha in it. Thank God for that. It was disbanded only a third of the way through. They lost two of the ten subjects in only eight weeks.

"Don ended up knowing more than some of the doctors we spoke to. He knew the questions to ask and wouldn't tolerate their evasive non-answers. Finally, we decided on here, 'The Center for Hope'." She makes the same movement of her shoulders and Ceci can see beyond the shadowy lens that her eyes open a bit wider as she says it and the corners of her mouth turn down, not in sadness, but in a combination of wistfulness and resignation.

"Dr. Glacieux believes in treating the body and the person, not only the disease. We like that," she says as she takes a tube out of the drawer in Samantha's end table, squeezes a small amount on the fingertips of her right hand and rubs them over her exposed neck, chin, both cheeks, and around the sunglasses. "SPF 60," she explains to Ceci. "Here, you should use it every time you come." She passes the tube to Ceci, who does as she is told. "The sun is good for the children. The body produces its own Vitamin D. Did you know that? That is, of course, if it doesn't give you skin cancer first," referring back to the sun. "Plus, this place is fun. Look around, have you ever seen anything like this?" Ceci follows her friend's gaze as they take in the game area, the books, the sanctuary, and the beach. "Dr. Glacieux is treating the whole person here, not just the illness. We all have physical and emotional needs, these kids perhaps more than the rest of us. She gives them something to live for, even something that needs them, like Samantha's little bird. It all seems to work together. So different from what we've come to expect from hospitals. It's peaceful here. The beach. The sound of the water. It . . ." and here she hesitates for the right word " . . . it ministers to me," and she gathers up her forgotten tissue, lifts the sunglasses, and pats the corner of each eye.

"Even with the awareness that we come to this place with, and even with the empty beds that make the danger that lies in the Recovery Hall all too real, we still think our child will make it. By some miracle, their body will respond and begin to combat their disease in a way that will put it at bay. Samantha believes it, and maybe that's a part of the battle plan here." She hesitates again. "It just has to work."

Ceci ventures, "What exactly goes on in the Recovery Hall?" It's Melinda's turn to look back into her new friend's eyes and she tries to provide some comfort. "Well, it's exactly that. That's where the children go to recover . . . if they've had a set back or if they become too sick to stay here in the group." Deep silence envelopes the two mothers. Melinda is the first to speak. Whispering and leaning toward Ceci's ear as if they are being overheard by hidden microphones, she says, "One of the mothers told me that when their daughter was moved to Recovery Hall, they saw a child that they seem to be just keeping alive. Literally . . . keeping . . . alive!"

Chapter 15

Sammy and Christopher sit in the sand, their toes making pathways through the warm fine grains of sand. He is relatively still, listening to the water and her babbling. Sammy is in constant motion, her arms moving front to back and side to side. Her hands cupped or with fingers spread, moving sand in patterns that only she can see. Christopher closes his eyes and tilts his head back, allowing the sun to warm his whole being. The rattle of the water echoes in his ears and he feels himself drifting off. Images of him with his brother come in and out of his vision. They are running, each holding a string being pulled by a kite and the wind he cannot see. Alternately, he hears her talking and bringing him back to the present, which he resists. He is at a picnic table, food spread over it. His brother sits across, his parents, one on each side, with his dad nearest him. They are all smiling as if one of them has said something funny. The smiles fixed on their faces, he does not know what is being said, yet still they go on laughing and smiling. He is startled by a touch on his forehead. His eyes spring open. Samantha's face is over him. She continues to move her fingers from his forehead to each cheek.

"Silly," she says. "It's only sunscreen. You must use this every day. Too much sun isn't good for you."

"Thank you, I guess," he replies. "Although I'm really not worrying about getting sick." And the two of them giggle at his small joke. "I think I'm going to like this place. I mean I wish I didn't have to be here, that I could be at home, sleep in my own room, go to school, you know, normal stuff."

"Yes, I know," she says back. "But, yes, I think you will like it here too. There's always something to do and you'll get to know all the kids. The food is not so great, even after you get used to it, but it's . . . it's still nice."

"So, what do we do next?" Christopher inquires hopefully.

"Well, how about we find you a pair of sunglasses?"

"OK, I was beginning to feel a little left out."

With that, she takes his hand, leads him out of the gate that constrains the sand. They get their socks and his shoes and she takes his hand again, causing him to hop and skip across the floor with her to a small cabinet set in a nearby corner. "These are kinda like extras," she says. "You can have your mom order you a pair or two from the catalogue at the nurse's station. But one of these will do for now." She hands him one pair she thinks will fit. He glances at himself in the small mirror attached to the back of the cabinet door, barely gets a second to evaluate, she takes that one back, hands him another, and then a third, in quick succession.

"I thought the first pair was good," he says.

Sammy only shakes her head. "This last pair is soooo much better," she corrects. He shrugs and nods in agreement. "Still, this is just until you get your own. You have to pick out something that you really like. Everybody does. You have to find a pair that say 'Christopher' and nobody else."

"I didn't realize sunglasses could talk," he replies.

"Well, they do. Look at mine. Don't they just scream 'Sammy'?"

He laughs and nods. "Yes, yes, I see what you mean. Let's go find a 'Christopher' pair."

She takes his hand again but this time walks. They head back the way they came, past their moms sitting on Sammy's bed, also hand in hand. "We'll be right back," Sammy calls out as they go by. "I wonder what those two are up to?" she whispers to Chris.

"Looks like your mom is looking out for my mom. Did you see those glasses?" and they both laugh out loud. "Your mom is so pretty," Christopher says. "You look like her."

"Do not," Sammy retorts.

"Do too."

"Do Not," she replies emphatically and reaches up and straightens the kerchief on her head.

"Are you going to tell me when you walk through the mall with your mom people don't think you are mother and daughter?"

"I don't know what they think," she replies. "They probably think, 'there goes a pretty lady with long brown hair, and she has a sick girl with her.'"

Chris doesn't know what to say so he says nothing for a few steps, then he says "Don't worry Sammy. Your hair will grow back. I know it will. Then they will say 'look at that woman with her pretty young daughter, my, doesn't she have the nicest brown hair.'"

"Red."

"Red?"

"Yes. Pretty young daughter with the nicest red hair," and they both laugh again. Sammy is cheered up. She begins to swing their hands as they walk and they push through the double doors and go up to empty nurse's station. "The book is right here," and Sammy goes around the corner of the desk and scoops it up from its normal place.

They sit in the lounge alone together with the catalogue of sunglasses and their thoughts. Christopher feigns interest in them and Sammy tries to make it seem that he is picking out his own glasses. Ones that scream 'Christopher,' but they both know she is picking them out for him.

"So, how are things when you're home?" she asks as she turns the page of the catalogue and points to a hideous pair where the lenses are shaped like oversized stars and the frames come covered in red or purple glitter. It's a question that two healthy children would never really ask. But Christopher knows what she is asking by it. The real question is, 'You're a sick kid. I'm a sick kid. How do your parents react to you differently because you are sick?' He thinks a little before responding. His initial reaction is to answer like he would if he was talking to his grandmother or his aunt, something like, 'OK, I'm feeling pretty good most days,' but realizes Sammy would know it is at least a partial lie.

"OK," he starts. "My mom seems tired all the time. Tired and worried. She doesn't spend the time she needs to with my brother. He knows it and I know it. Sometimes I think he doesn't like me. I mean he likes me all right, it's just that he doesn't like that I get all her attention. That she is always worrying about how I feel or if I've eaten enough or trying to somehow make up for the fact that I'm sick most of the time. I don't know what he does when I'm in the hospital. I know it can't feel good, bounced around from neighbor to aunt to grandma, while mom and dad, spend time with me each day. It's messed up."

"I'm sure he likes you," Sammy replies. "It's not your fault you're sick."

"Yeah, I know it's not my fault, but I hate having the world revolve around me. I wish I was invisible. I wish they could just be normal. I wish we could just be a normal family. Everything is about me, about my brain, about some test or doctor appointment. We can't plan to do anything. It's always. 'if Chris is well enough . . .' I hate it," and tears start to well up in his eyes. Sammy darts back over to the nurse's station, pulls a tissue for him, grabs an extra and darts back, handing him one. "Other times, I get the feeling they are only doing things because I'm well enough. Two weeks ago, Mom dragged us all out on a Saturday afternoon. We went to this cheesy lake we've been to a dozen times, just like when we were little. Dad was working on the lawn. Aaron had just gotten home from soccer practice. He wanted to go to the store and get new cleats because he was still using the old pair from last year. Mom, she makes everyone get in the car, act like they're happy, and off we go to stroll around the lake."

"I think that's nice," Sammy says. "I've been stuck here. I wish I had gotten to go. I bet there were ducks at the cheesy lake?" Chris nods. "How about swings or a slide, did you do that?" Chris nods again. "Camera?" Another nod. "And what did you do after that – ice cream?" Chris shakes his head.

"Italian ices," he corrects.

"So, you spent a few hours with your family, got some fresh air, exercise, took some pictures of the fun, and had Italian ices. That sounds *horrible*," she says in mock jest. "Think Chris, why do you suppose they did that, even after they've been there a dozen times?"

"I told you, because Mom made them. Because I was well enough."

"Yeah, but maybe she didn't 'make them' as you suppose or even if she did, maybe she needed to go out, get some fresh air, see you smile, just spend some time as a family, just like a normal family," she says with some exasperation in her voice. She is winded. Christopher can hear it in her voice. "Geez, they even took pictures. Think. They wanted to have pictures to remember the time the family went to the lake. Your mom, she . . . she wants to . . . she wants to make sure you know you are loved." She draws out the second tissue and dries the stream of tears rolling down each perfect cheek before they drop to the ground. She heaves one large sob, takes a deep breath and continues. "Someday, maybe someday soon, all she's going to have is that, some pictures. Some pictures to help remember you by. That and the knowledge that you knew you were loved. That's why they do what they do. You're sick and they will do all they can to help you. Help you anyway they can. But mostly, mostly they want you to know you are loved. That's it. That's what everyone wants, to know they are loved. With us the time is just shorter, that's all."

Christopher is overwhelmed. Tears stream down his face as well but he doesn't move. He lets them flow around his mouth and splash onto his shirt and does nothing. Says nothing. Sammy notices his lips moving but no words come out.

Finally, as if awaken from a trance, he says, "Sammy, what's down that hall?" He points toward the restricted access, double doors that he had wandered down earlier that morning. "I . . . I saw something. In the room at the end. I looked in the window."

"That's the Recovery Hall. I've been there. If you get too sick to stay in the center with the other kids, or if you've had surgery and need some time to recover. They put you in a room there. It's private." She pauses a bit, then goes on. "Sometimes . . . sometimes kids don't come back. You know?"

"Yeah, I know," he says, and they are quiet a minute. "I saw something . . . someone, in the room at the end. I don't know who it is but she, I think it is a girl, she is all hooked up to hoses, machines, bags of fluid hang around her and she's still breathing. I . . . I don't want that to happen to me. I don't want to be all hooked up like that. They don't make you, do they?" he asks. "They can't make you, right? I mean if you don't want that, they shouldn't make you, right?"

"I don't know," she says slowly. "It's not up to you. I think your parents make that decision. I hope I just go in my sleep, peaceful like. I don't think my parents could let me go; not if they had a choice. They would keep me alive. I don't think they could live with themselves if they didn't do everything possible to help me. Even if I have my way I'm not sure how they will live after I'm gone. They don't seem to accept the possibility that I won't be with them for long. They still talk about the future, things like me going to college, getting married someday, as if all this goes away somehow. I know they are just trying to keep my spirit up. They don't want me to give up, and I'm not. I'm not giving up. It's just that I can't change how I feel. I know I'm sick. I have good days, but I'm still sick. I'm usually OK in the morning but I get tired all the time, usually not long after lunch, and then I just want to rest. I need to rest. That's not normal. That's not getting better," she says with a firmness that reveals her acceptance of her fate.

"Oh, don't be so sure," Christopher chides. "You're not God. You don't know His plan for your life. The Bible is full of stories where God healed those who were sick. Jesus even healed some that were already dead. You have to have faith. I'm going to pray for you and I'll get my mom to pray for you too."

"Thank you, Chris. That's really nice. Yes, I'd like that. Please pray for me, maybe that will help," and she smiles, patting her eyes with the tissue. Then she takes hold of his hand and walks him slowly back to the center.

Chapter 16

Ted stops in the cafeteria on his way out, leaves the newspaper in its stack and fingers through the pages until he locates the lottery numbers. One. Two. Three. Not one hit in three. He drops the pages, not interested in the rest, turns and leaves. Rationalizing, he knows the odds are astronomical, and yet, occasionally someone does win it all. People do get all six numbers and do win millions; you see their pictures from time to time, big grin, holding a large check, looked on enviously by the lottery officials and reporters, a spouse or family member nearby with a gleam of lust or unbelief in their eye. It can't happen to me, he thinks. Nothing in my life is that easy. He settles into the worn seat of his tired automobile. This car reminds me of my life, he thinks. Worn and tired. Tired of making the same trips, running the same errands, being passed by younger and faster models with bright paint, not dull and graying, the dash smooth and sleek, not faded and cracked. The odometer reads 122,000 miles, time to change the oil. I've got to get a filter and some oil, maybe I can get to it on Saturday, if it's not raining, he recites to himself so he won't forget.

Glancing at the folder he placed on the seat next to him, on his way to Weinberg's deli, he should be more excited. He used to be, when he had someone to skewer. He pretty much already knows he is right or he would not make the visit, but the confirmation is in the look. The look they give when he identifies himself, or if not then, when he begins to speak to the suspicious facts. He would speak and pat the folder as if to tell them 'it is all in here.' All the evidence needed, right here in this folder. Their eyes go to it, and he gauges their reaction. That is, when he becomes sure he has them, and when he begins to talk

119

about exactly what the law allows in such cases, and the threat, the underlying threat of what might come next. He follows that bit up with what he labels 'the nice guy.' I'm here to help. This is all just preliminary right now. You have a chance to make things right. The department will work with you if you cooperate fully, etcetera, etcetera, effectively manipulating the situation to achieve his goal.

Today is the day. His estimate is substantial. If he sees fear, he sees himself saying, 'if you cooperate fully,' and giving a knowing look.

He has had offers before. He never encourages it but he still enjoys seeing them squirm. They hesitate and stumble, not knowing what he truly means. Is this an offer? Can they trust him to take cash under the table and not make this worse than it already is? They might say, "I'd like to work something out too." Or perhaps, "Is there something you have in mind?" They turn it around, leaving the door open for him. And they dance a bit until one or the other has the guts to come out more plainly with what both of them are thinking. Ted is under no allusion. A cheat will always cheat again if given the right circumstances. It's in their blood. They cannot get away from it, this self-preserving, self-indulgent way of life. This is too perfect. They've kept from the government their earnings, now he only needs to get them to suggest they would do it again. In their self-interest, costly, yes, but it still saves them money. That's the name of this game. He tries to encourage himself. He envisions saying, "I'm sure we can work something out. Do you have time now? Is there someplace we can talk privately? We will need your full cooperation."

Ted finds the deli, parks, and enters with a plan in mind. He's timed the visit - he knows the lunch crowd is over and all the owner would be doing is cleaning up for the day. Tough, that can wait. He emerges two hours later, folder under his arm. It's a bit fatter now with hard evidence. Ted is smug in knowing he is right. He pegged this guy, from the fraud, to the dance, and most importantly, about his character. Human nature is fairly predictable. Humans have the same flaws. They are tempted with the same things and there are very few saints and martyrs left in the world. He thinks about his role, not in the big scheme of things, but in the portion he can get his head around; this one scene, in this one act of a multi-act play.

Weinberg is a cheat, plain and simple. Probably has always been a cheat. He's owned the deli for fifteen years but IRS only concerns itself with the past three. "Why shouldn't the Randolph's get what they need?" He throws the question out to the silent interior of the car so that he can hear it out loud with his own ears. He mulls the thought and searches for a way to rationalize his actions. He suppresses his conscience and denies the fact that he dwelt on taking Weinberg's money. Well, not Weinberg's really. It's the government's, or should have been, if Weinberg paid the tax he owed. And what of that? How would the government have used it? Baked into the enormous federal pie of dollars to be doled out, be abused, or be paid to other federal workers; workers like those around him at the Internal Revenue Service. Not one of them would have done the work to catch this guy. Not one would have made the extra effort to visit, confront, and collect what was due. So, it would not be stealing from his employer. How can it be taking from his employer if his employer never would have known the deceit existed? And what about Weinberg? What would a public accusation do? Wouldn't the penalty and interest exceed what is fair and proper? His accounts would be frozen. What about his workers, the landlord, or the vendors that innocently delivered product to his store, all expecting to be paid? What if Weinberg doesn't have the money? What then? Jail? All this helps no one.

Ted suppresses his argument, jogs his memory and concentrates on what he needs to do. Something practical, something real - stop at the auto parts store, pick up five quarts of oil and a filter. Next, swing by the Center. It's Chris' first day. See how he is settled in. Maybe run into that doctor lady.

Glacieux. What to do about her? He knows he shouldn't have looked at her file. The Internal Revenue Service has rules against that kind of thing. Snooping. Illegal access. Unauthorized viewing. It goes by a number of names, all meaning the same thing. Still, doesn't he have some sort of right to know? She is drawing big bucks from the insurance company and Ted is pressed, pressed to the wall with the expectation that he will have to come up with those bucks soon enough.

Who wouldn't look if they were in my shoes, he thinks. This could provide some leverage, a guarantee of sorts. It's not for me, it's for Chris. Ceci would eventually ask, suspect that he was up to something. It's like the woman has radar. She can sense when something is amiss. He can't do anything wrong around her. It's as if her conscience has become his. Wouldn't Ceci be upset if she knew what her dear doctor was up to? That Glacieux is a slick one. He immediately didn't like her the day they met. She must have read their application listing his occupation; she made no mention of it. Most folks usually kid him about it, "IRS, I bet you have some stories to tell." She said nothing, didn't flinch. Smooth, that one is.

Ted takes care of the oil purchase and heads over the bridge to Manhattan. Driving unconsciously, stopping at red lights, signaling, changing lanes, while going through each document he studied once again, only this time in his mind. He knows the order, the numbers of each form and can visualize the sequence in which he pored over each section, comparing the main to the detail. Hers was done by a professional accounting firm with a good reputation; they know the law and the loopholes. Still, he can't help but be suspicious. She would know if things were being hidden. Professionals like her claim innocence, but they know. She wouldn't know the fine lines, maybe not know how the documents were doctored. Doctored, that's funny, and grunts at his own inadvertent joke. But she would know. The research facility is a separate legal entity. How convenient; an arm's length away from her personal file. Smart.

Turning into the visitor parking lot he scans the doctor's area. Each of the three cars he finds in a short row closest to the entrance possess a symbol of success, either as a hood ornament or logo embossed in the grill. He glances down at his bag of motor oil and wonders what they pay to have their oil changed. He should have been a dentist like his mother suggested. He wouldn't be spending time this weekend with greasy hands, that's for sure. He parks and walks up to the entrance, the sliding glass doors open, anticipating his arrival. He paces up to the nurse's station and identifies himself. The nurse is efficient, asking for his driver's license, comparing its picture closely to the man standing before her.

"Thank you, Mr. Randolph. If you will please sign in on the visitor log," and she directs his glance to a clipboard nearby to the left on the desk. "I'll be right with you. I just need to make a copy of your license for our files," and with that she turns away and walks the few steps to the rear of her area where the copier sits. He dutifully fills out the log, glancing up and at the back of the prim nurse, notices no paper coming out as she picks his license off the glass and turns to find him watching her. With a smile that suggests she doesn't mind being admired, and with another quick glance at the document, she stretches forth her hand to pass it back to him.

"You're keeping digital files?" he inquires.

"Yes. We maintain a very secure facility. You have to these days. We can't have just anyone walking in to see the children. Your license is called up the next time you come, in case the nurse on duty doesn't know you Mr. Randolph."

"Please, call me Ted," and he allows his fingertips to linger ever so briefly on hers as they rest on the countertop with the passing document. He glances at her name badge, a rectangular, gold-toned strip, pinned just below her left shoulder, and from this distance has to strain some to make out the neat bold letters, 'Nurse Ashley' and with that can't help but have his eyes drawn to her full and erect form, the top two buttons of her white uniform open at the neck and the brown skin set against it, inviting. She shows no surprise and before it becomes awkward he speaks, purposely using her name, as if to suggest his gaze was only to find it out. "So, Nurse Ashley," he fumbles. "How long have you worked here?" That allows them both to resume their proper position for the remaining minute together as she guides him to where he can find Christopher.

"Hey buddy. How you doin?" he calls out in exaggerated, mobster style, Brooklynese.

Christopher, startled, turns his head around, calls out "Dad!" and leaps up from where he is sitting on the edge of the bed with a book. He runs to him energetically and throws both arms about him nearly causing Ted to lose his balance.

"Easy there slugger, you'll knock your dear old dad over." Returns the hug and adds a kiss on the top of Chris' head as they embrace.

"I'm surprised to see you. Didn't you have to work today?"

"Ah, nothing is more important than my boy." They walk the few steps, his arm over Chris' shoulder, to where he had been sitting on the edge of the bed.

"Dad, this is Sammy."

"Hello, there Sammy," he booms and reaches out his hand to shake hers in greeting. She is laying still, her head propped up on a few pillows, blankets covering her small frame. Her hands are folded neatly on her stomach. She extends a limp hand and he gathers her fingers in his huge hand and notices that they are cold. "Sammy, what kind of name is that for a young lady?" he asks with a wink and a grin.

"It's Samantha, Mr. Randolph. It's nice to meet you," she replies politely.

"Samantha. That's a beautiful name," he says. "Are you showing Chris here the ropes?"

"Yes sir. Don't worry about him. He's in good hands," she replies, her voice and her face reinvigorated by his friendly banter.

"Well . . . Samantha, thank you. Thank you very much," and he turns his attention to Christopher, who is still standing and listening to the exchange. "Whatcha reading there, kiddo?" Ted points to the book Chris had laid face down on the bed when he had jumped up.

"It's 'Pinocchio,' Dad. We have the movie at home, but this is the real book. I was reading it to Sammy. She picked it out. We were just to the part where Geppetto talks about wanting a real boy."

"My favorite part is when Pinocchio's nose grows when he is telling a lie." Ted laughs, thinking how convenient that would be when working with his clienteles.

"We can read more tomorrow, Chris," Sammy pipes up. "Show your Dad around. I'm tired now anyway. I'm going to rest," and she settles back into the pillows, straightens the covers, closes her eyes, and refolds her hands. She looks peaceful.

Christopher leads Ted away so they won't disturb her and begins to tell him all about his first day there. Ted is pleased to see Christopher so energetic and animated. He mentions Sammy several times as he relays their activities together.

"That Sammy is a real looker, Chris. Now don't get too smitten on the first day. Girls don't like that." Chris blushes at Ted's comment.

"She's worried about her hair growing back. She has red hair," is all he can think of to say.

"Well, she's pretty as a picture right now. It's good you made a friend here on your first day," Ted replies and places his arm across Chris' shoulder as they walk throughout the Center.

"Mom made a friend too. Sammy's mom, Mrs. Robinson, was here this morning just after we checked in."

"That's nice son. How is mom today? Did she like it here?"

"She's good. Yeah, I think she liked it a lot. Tell her she doesn't have to come here every day. I'll be fine. There's a lot to do here and she can call me or I can call her. Really. She should take it easy."

"I'll tell her son, but you know your mother, I'm not sure she'll listen. Besides, she likes to see you every day. She's got to look out for her boy. That's what mothers do." Ted gives his son a wink and pulls him closer with the one arm on his shoulder.

They finish their walk, a slow loop around the Center, Christopher explaining all the amusements, and are back at his bedside. Sammy is sleeping. Ted bends down toward his son's face and whispers, "I love you, Chris. I'm gonna go."

"OK, dad. I love you, too." Ted holds Chris' head in his hands, tilts it slightly forward and plants a gentle kiss on his forehead.

As he turns to leave, he notices it is just five o'clock and wonders if Nurse Ashley is getting off now.

Chapter 17

Late afternoon and she hasn't even shown her face downstairs. As a matter of fact, she hasn't even left the office. Not for lunch. Not for anything. She arrived a little after ten and Karl had already signed for the package and laid it on her desk so she would be sure to see it when she arrived. He knew she had been expecting it.

Every month it's the same routine. It comes, overnight delivery, from the facility in Chad. The package contains the results from last month's testing. Nancy turns her office into a war room. The conference table becomes covered with paper. The uncovered whiteboard has a combination of new scribbles and past conflux of notes for further review. The old compared to what has newly arrived. She barricades herself in her office and throughout the day she calls out to Karl to bring her fresh coffee.

In the afternoon, he offers to pick something up for her to eat and that is the only time that he even receives a glimpse or some brief eye contact. She acknowledges the kindness offered, looks up at him with a smile, and says, "Thanks, but not now. Just coffee." Her desk is littered with phone messages. Karl lets her know when he brings in one from Jonathon Weiss. She stops to read that one, but it only indicates that he had made a deposit into the trust account. She adds her own note to it – call Harry - in her unprofessionally neat, legible script, compliments of the private grade school - her parents had sacrificed in order to be able to send her and her brother.

While scattered looking to the casual observer, Nancy is methodical in her approach. The results are set in three formats: individual, group, and comparable trends. She examines the individual ones first, looking initially for any slight upward tick in white blood cell count. Each subject has a blood test taken every seventy-two hours, an uptick would be cause for further scrutiny. She has come to know the advancement in the disease is preceded by a slow and steady weakening of the blood. She knows the trend, knows the point in which the fear of a recurrence is real and not just the normal reaction of a healthy body, fighting off an ordinary illness or infection. The blood doesn't lie. She trained the others, when a certain point has been reached, they begin to test the blood every day. It's only when the trend line breaks that they go back to the standard. The results are displayed in graph form, visually alarming. Trend up, up, steady, steady, up, steady, up, steady, up, up, up . . . Should they hit a certain point without a period of steadiness they would need to move quickly and radically. This month's showed no such severe anomaly. Nancy senses a disappointment and as a result has to fight back the feeling of reprehension that troubles her conscience. Her rationalization is carefully structured. It's not that she wants any particular subject to have the illness advance, but seeing that and combating it successfully, shows progress. It gives a unique opportunity to study the enemy and potentially create a defense that cannot be breeched. It's not as if she gave them the disease or wished it upon them; you either have it or you don't. If you get it, you will get sick. You will die. She reminds herself that is not her fault. Life and death are not in her hands. Yet, she strives to prolong existence and dares to try to beat the grave.

Next she examines those that show any periodic increase of white blood cells whatsoever. These are potentially just as significant but increase the scope of what may be connected. They also complicate things as what may not be connected is thrown into the mix. It increases the size of the haystack to a field. One might be able to find something in a haystack if one looks long and hard enough because it is limited. Finding that same item in a field is much more unlikely. Of course, if you're not in the correct field, then it's impossible. These subjects are mostly healthy, yet they carry the same genetic traits, have the same genome scheme and the pattern that tends to succumb to the disease. Somehow their bodies have discovered a way to ward it off, to rout it before it corrupts them.

Nancy sits at the table, puts her elbows on the laid out papers, closes her eyes and rubs her temples with her thumbs. Of course, this is just one avenue she is considering. What comes first; the chicken or the egg? Does the enhanced white blood cell count indicate the disease is moving forward or does the disease sit dormant and simply wait for the count to the rise? Does it cause it or merely react to it?

She goes to the imaging, the brain scans, and wonders for the thousandth time, what the brain does. Does it defend itself? Can it produce its own toxin, a toxin that kills the cells of the disease while they are forming or in their nascent stage and leave the rest intact?

Do we weaken our God given defenses with what we put into our bodies? Do we cause the walls to crumble by what we think or what we do? Is it just heredity that is to blame?

These and other thoughts go through her mind as she sits with the evidence around her. She takes a deep, cleansing breath and continues to gently massage her temples as that seems to temporarily relieve the feeling that her head is going to explode. She goes to her desk, coffee cup in hand, locates the bottle of extra strength pain reliever and takes two, washing them down with the now tepid coffee.

Karl's head pops around the corner of the entranceway. He sees her at her desk and calls out, "Nancy, Harry's on the phone. Do you want to take it?" Not looking up, not saying anything, she nods her head in the affirmative, and Karl goes off to transfer the call. This time she picks it up before the first ring is completed.

"Hi, Hanif. I'm reviewing this month's report. I've been going over it since this morning. There doesn't seem to be anything that moves us forward."

"Well, we can't expect too much too soon. These things take time."

"Yeah," Nancy replies. "By the way, I'll arrange for another wire tomorrow, enough for the rest of this month and next."

"Good, we can't move forward without funds."

"I've been thinking though. Wouldn't it be good if we could enlist more girls?" And as he says nothing, she continues. "I mean, having more females could be beneficial in the long run. Don't you agree?"

"I hear you, but it's not that simple. There are strong customs and traditions that encourage families to consider the males more worthy, more able." And now it is his turn to pause. "Women don't hold the same place in our society."

Nancy considers this for a moment, then says, "Yeah, but still. There has to be some families that are progressive thinkers. Some that want their daughters to attain the same goals as their sons? Maybe we can increase the stipend? You know, provide some good old capitalist incentive program?"

Hanif chuckles at this thought, but admits, "You might be on to something there, Nancy. I'll have my people work on that."

"OK, anything else?" There is a short lull and as he says nothing, they have nothing else to discuss. "I gotta go," and she hangs up the phone without waiting for a response.

Nancy's mental process always considers the counter argument to everything she thinks. She begins to wonder how the parents of those they enroll in their research actually give up their child. Boy or girl, tradition and custom aside, how does a parent make that choice? In Western culture, most children are cherished by their parents. They give all and do all to see them cared for. Nancy sees this first hand, with every child she treats at the Center. Yet in Hanif's part of the world, they willingly give them up. Not so different than the ancient days she reasons, child sacrifices were part of tradition in many places of the world. Today we would label such things heathen practices. Today it would not be politically correct to label it so, but isn't the end result the same? Isn't it just the same old belief that God wants or will reward their faith or their sacrifice? Nancy continues in this stream of thought, her left hand still on the phone from when she placed it down, the right holding a pen and blankly staring across the room, seeing but not processing the framed print on the opposite wall, a print of children dancing around a maypole. She picks up the thread of thought again in her mind. Today they do more than that, not only do they sacrifice themselves but they take with them innocents that just happen to be in their path. That's a significant difference. It might be one thing to allow your young to kill themselves, but to teach them to kill others in the process? That is truly heathen.

She comes to herself, breaks the gaze, looks around the room, and removes her hand from the phone. She ponders her role, providing money to families that are willing to allow their child to be part of her research. The guilt rises within her and permeates her consciousness - she is taking advantage of their poverty. She wants more females in her study and so told Hanif to offer more. Their culture and their tradition be damned, offer them more money. Nancy knows it will work. The temptation of money will be too great. It will break down someone who is weak, or desperate, or greedy, or selfish. Money is the root of all evil. She corrects that thought; it's the love of money that is the root of all evil.

She speaks to donors and omits the part of the story that would be distasteful, only telling them of the possible good their donation can achieve. She deceives them, deceives JW as well.

Now her head is back in her hands and her thumbs again massage her temples in a vain attempt to get some relief.

"Nancy, are you OK?" It's Karl. "I'm getting a snack downstairs, can I get you something?" She looks up.

"I'll be OK, Karl. Thanks. Yes, get me some chocolate, with almonds if they have it."

"Sure thing."

As he goes off she calls out, "And a fresh cup of java too."

She hears his, "Got it," as he retreats toward the elevator.

Sitting in the quiet she acknowledges, that no, she is not OK. She wrestles with what is right and feels powerless to steer her boat out of the dangerous waters. Waves rock and batter the hull. Water seeps in and its weight limits her options. She is in too deep. The tide is against her and the rudder useless. Not able, nor willing, to chart a new course, Nancy feels an overbearing sense that her fate is out of her control. There was a time that she could have altered it, but that moment is past. Now there is no option. She must sail through and dreads the cost.

Wishing to forget her pain Nancy goes to the bathroom, opens the medicine chest and picks through the vials, reading each label. She pops one open, shakes out two small yellow pills, and throws them back into her mouth quickly before changing her mind, turns on the water, cups her hand underneath to catch some to use for a cleansing swallow. A few drops dribble through her fingers, down her chin, and onto her dress. She stands and looks into her eyes in the mirror, the shadows reveal dark circles underneath. She examines her face, takes a stray hair and plants it behind her ear, takes one more hard look into her face, not recognizing who she has become, turns, and marches back to the paper strewn table to search some more.

****

Later, tired of the work but refreshed from the chocolate and the coffee, her head no longer pounding, and better yet, feeling less overwhelmed, Nancy goes downstairs to check on the kids. She enters the lobby area from the staff door to the right of the nurse's station and heads directly to the clipboards that contain the day's data points. Every child's temperature is taken every four hours when they are awake and a third of them have their blood checked daily. Notes indicate that Samantha Robinson is fatigued in the afternoon. That is fairly common, but ominously her temperature rises a bit in conjunction. The acetaminophen still works to lower and maintain it until she goes to sleep. She is only out of the recovery ward two weeks and Nancy inserts instructions to check her blood daily. If she heads off the charts, Nancy wants to know before it gets out of control. Her back is to the reception area, her head down as she goes through each page on the clipboard. She is wearing the standard issue white physician's coat, her hair hanging loose, soft brown curls fall across her back.

"Excuse me, Nurse. Do you know if Nurse Ashley is still around?" She turns and is surprised to see Mr. Randolph. He, in turn, is surprised to see her. "Oh, I'm sorry, Dr. Glacieux. I thought you were one of the nurses. I'm very sorry."

"That's all right Mr. Randolph. It's perfectly understandable." After a short pause, she says, "Do you need something? Is there something I can help you with?"

"No, No. Nothing. She was kind enough to bring me to see Christopher and I thought I would ask her how he seems to be settling in."

"I see. Today is his first day. How does he seem to you, Mr. Randolph?"

"Fine, yeah. He seems fine," Ted responds.

"Oh that's good. I'm not surprised. The staff does a great job and the kids . . . the kids all seem to get along. They have a bond, an almost instantaneous bond . . . due to their illness. They tend not to be as petty as children can sometimes be toward each other. More mature. More forgiving of faults." She turns the page of the chart, finds his son. "Christopher is running a mild temperature. Is that normal for him?" she asks.

"I'm not really sure, Doc. My wife would know better." Ted is slightly embarrassed at not knowing this and thinks about it harder. "Yeah, now that you mention it. Ceci has said something about that. Yeah. She did say he runs a little warm. Is that something we should be worried about?"

Nancy gives a short smile, not surprised that the father would not know for sure something so basic about their child. "We monitor it here, Mr. Randolph. Every four hours. Nothing to worry about right now. Are you headed home?" She wishes to end the chat and get back to work, turning the page again on the clipboard and focusing again at her work hoping he takes the cue that he is dismissed.

He doesn't move or say anything, so after five or ten seconds, she pulls her glasses down on her nose, peers over them and inquires, "Is there something else, Mr. Randolph?"

"No, No, Dr. Glacieux," he stutters uncomfortably. "It's nothing. I . . . I can see you some other time. It's Christopher's first day . . . and you're busy. It's nothing." Nancy takes her glasses off and gives him her full attention.

"It's OK, Mr. Randolph. What is it? Do you have a question?"

He exhales, actually blowing his cheeks out, forcing the air out his mouth so that it makes a noise. "It's kinda awkward, Doc. I work for the Internal Revenue Service, you know?"

"Yes, go on," she now warily encourages him.

"It's just that you run this whole place and I understand, doctors have overhead and insurance. To run a place like this, wow, it's really something." He looks at the ceiling and raises his arm pointing toward where the children stay. "The accountants they don't always do things by the book. They say they are looking out for their client. They might suggest or do things that a doctor, like yourself, wouldn't really know about, that might be viewed differently from the Service's point of view. You, uh, know what I'm getting at?"

She hesitates, tilts her head, winces a bit, as if she is talking to someone simple. "Not really, Mr. Randolph. Are you saying my accountants made an error or that they misled me? They really do have a good reputation. You can call them if you have questions. That's why I pay them." She struggles a bit with her patience. She thinks he might have some question about the disease or the treatment; that she was prepared to answer. But taxes! Really!

Boy, is she cool, he thinks. She's going to try to turn this around? Stand behind the fact that she doesn't know or maybe she thinks he's too stupid to figure things out? "Listen Doc. I've been doing this for a long time. I've seen all kinds of things. You're obviously a smart lady. But it ain't that simple. You send money out of the country." There, he laid down the gauntlet. "And while that, in and of itself, isn't illegal, it does raise some red flags." Too late to stop. "You can't just do what you want with that money." He looks directly at her and thinks, did she just flinch?

Nancy has had about as much of this as she can take. Still, he is the parent of a patient and besides that, she doesn't want to get any publicity whatsoever. This wouldn't be good if it got in the papers.

What does this idiot know? What does he suspect? Caution is the word, caution. "Well, I don't know what it is you think you know, Mr. Randolph. But I am sure, whatever it is, you're mistaken. So please call my accountants and get the answers to your questions. I've got to get back to work."

"OK, doc, if that's the way you want to play it. I'm not going to submit anything official on this. I'm just going to keep it close to the vest," and he pats his inside jacket pocket as if he has something stored there. "You're treating my son. I respected that. I appreciate that. Let's just keep this between us," and with that, gives her a wink and strolls out of the lobby.

Nancy frowns, takes out her cell phone, finds the accounting firm in her contacts and dials.

Chapter 18

Outside, the wind whips the dying leaves onto the driveway and into circular patterns, gathering them up near the garage door. Ted hates this time of year. Not the fact that winter will soon be here in her full fury, but that he has the annual leaf raking chore to do. Ceci smiles to herself as she replays his latest tirade in her mind. "I rake and bag the leaves that gather on the side of the house and what happens? Within a week there's another pile sitting there, killing my grass, and they aren't even my leaves. Sheesh, that lazy neighbor of ours lets the leaves sit and sit until every last one has dropped. They blow around and guess where they end up? On my lawn! So, what can I do? And they're from his tree! Can you believe that crap?" Still smiling, she knows he is only venting what he feels. It's probably good for him, no sense keeping things bottled up inside. It doesn't hurt anyone. He would never say anything to the neighbor. He spouts and rants a bit to her. It's just his way. He does the work. He is a good man. He is a good husband, a good father, and a good provider. Ted is a good model for the boys too. He treats her with respect. They eat dinner together as a family each night. They go to church together on most Sundays. That is, when Christopher is well enough to go. When he is not, Ted offers to stay at home with him so she and Aaron can still go. He knows the weekly service means a lot to her. It is her refuge. It's where she gets encouraged and where her faith is increased, and she sees her friends. It helps her face another uncertain week. Of course, she prefers it when they can all go together. Ted needs to get to church too. She senses his struggle. He can't seem to just accept like a child. He questions and attempts to make sense of things. "If I make it to the Pearly Gates, I've got some questions to ask," he has said at various times. Still, he is a good man with a kind heart (when you get to know him). Ceci doesn't doubt God's mercy and she's sure he'll get his chance to ask his questions. Although, she thinks, when one sees Him face to face, will we be able to speak at all? She thinks not; it will be too wondrous. She smiles again, picturing Ted at the Gates and speechless as he looks toward the throne and catches a glimpse of his Creator.

Ceci looks at the clock and is pulled back from her revelry into the reality of life. It's 9:15. She needs to get ready to go to the Center to visit Christopher and she still needs to do a load of laundry. Ceci heads up the stairs and can't help but think about how their lives have changed. She and Ted are not old. They have a good marriage. They still love each other. But things have changed. They don't seem to make the effort to work on their relationship much anymore. She feels a little unwanted, a little undesired. She stands in front of the mirror, analyzing the flaws in her not-so-youthful figure. How does a woman with two children, approaching middle age, compete with what is out there in the world today? She imagines that's why Ted has lost interest. She too, always dutiful, and yet now when she gets to rest her head on the pillow, that is all she really wants to do, get some rest. There are times she is glad when he's watching TV in another room and she settles into bed, pulls the covers around her, warm and alone. One might defend her, thinking about all the nights she had to rise early or was awakened during the night when the boys were babies. More so since Christopher has been sick. A decent night's sleep makes a world of difference.

Gee, it's not like there is any romance going on around here, she muses. It's not as if that lug Ted makes any effort. It's no wonder women flee to soap operas and cheap romance novels. It might not be your own romance but at least it fans the flame. Romance, that's what's missing.

She strips off the flannel pajama pants, unbuttons and discards the top with her eye catching her naked image in the mirror. She quickly pulls out one of a stack of white cotton underwear. Her grandmother would call them 'bloomers,' drops it onto the floor and steps into it, pulling them up and over her belly and covering her stretch marks. Next a non-descript, white, support bra, hooked and strapped, to hold everything in place. Now covered sufficiently, hidden like Eve in the garden, she is willing to look again but still can't help but see where life had taken its toll. She is envious of the women on TV that prance about nearly naked, with their near perfect bodies, and entice their men unashamed. I don't have time for this, she thinks. I've got to get dressed and get going. Grabbing a pair of jeans, she hurries to dress and meet her day's obligations.

****

Outside the cold fresh air feels good on Nancy's face. A scarf is wrapped around her neck with the loose end tossed over her shoulder flutters in the wind. It feels like it may snow. The sky is full of thick clouds and their shadows cast a gray dullness over the landscape. Not much sun for the kids today, she thinks, as she arrives at the Center. Humph, they might not even need the sunglasses today. It will be a good day to see their eyes.

The past few months have been good. Uneventful, but in her business, that is good. Jonathon is convinced the donor base they have built up will come through. The bonuses on Wall Street will be decent this year and the holidays always seem to bring out the urge to give. Plus there is year-end tax planning going on. There have been no serious reoccurrences among the children, the enemy is at bay. The Christmas holiday will be here soon enough and it is always a special time for the children. A number of them will be allowed to spend a few days at home. The reduced number to care for will relieve her staff a bit too, and she'll be able to allow more of them to be off. She saw Mrs. Randolph yesterday and she's anxious to know if Christopher can go home for the holiday. Nancy is glad she will have good news for her. She reviewed his blood work before she left and there continues to be the steady improvement in his condition that she has seen throughout his short time with them. He doesn't even run the slight fever that seemed to be the norm when he arrived. Still, Nancy suppresses any feeling of glee. She's reminded of an old saying, 'it is always calmest before a storm,' and has learned to not take whatever progress she feels they are making too much to heart. Now she moves in caution. It doesn't take much to dash any hope that is built up. The enemy sleeps but is swift when it arouses from its slumber. Still, it would make for a nice holiday for the families and for her staff if nothing were to disturb the calm that they are currently enjoying.

****

At the Thompson home, Nancy's mother is in the kitchen amidst a whirl of activity. A morning like this, cold outside, but warm inside from the oven running, scented with cinnamon and sugar always makes her feel good. In the background traditional holiday hymns play, and at times, she sings along, "Oh come all ye faithful, joyful and triumphant, oh come ye . . ." Her work becomes easy. She is joyful in it. She knows her family and friends will enjoy the homemade medley of cookies that she'll give as gifts or arrange on a platter for dessert after a holiday meal, and that they will be appreciated. Folks don't bake so much anymore. Homemade goods add a special touch to the holidays.

Helen removes two cookie sheets from the oven and sets them on the side to cool. She has completed two batches already this morning. She started with the easy ones but now looks over the striped rainbow cookie recipe. She goes through the list of ingredients, finds and arranges the various items she will need and places them within easy reach on the counter. She'll need a break before she starts these, they take more time, are more tedious to produce. Still, they seem to be everyone's favorite. She gets a lot of compliments on them. Her family and friends rave about the chocolate, the stripes and filling, the height of the stacked layers, and more than that, it is traditional Helen Thompson fare. They look forward to it. They expect it. It's a lot of work, but after all, it's only one time a year, and a special time at that. As she clears the table of the remnants of the prior batch, she reaches to grab hold of the handle of the rolling pin and feels a sharp pain in her side. It causes her to fall into the chair and clutch her side. "Oh Lord," she instinctively prays, "Please heal whatever caused this. Touch my body, 'By your stripes we are healed'," she recites. As she sits and rubs the spot, the pain subsides some and she is a little less uncomfortable. I'm getting old she thinks. Pain just from the effort of making a few batches of cookies. Maybe I'll do these tomorrow instead. She wonders what will happen to the rainbow cookie tradition when she is too old to make the effort. One of the kids will probably just buy some. They will go from homemade to store bought, just like that. Her cookies will become a memory, a distant memory. They'll buy them for a few years just to not make her feel guilty about not baking and they will compliment her, "Oh Mom, these are nowhere near as good as the ones you used to make," and, "Can you believe what they charge per pound for these?" But at some point they will just stop or in some mix-up Nancy will think David was going to buy them and David will think Nancy was going to buy them and they will find themselves on Christmas Eve without any rainbows.

When Nancy was a young girl, she and Helen used to work on the Christmas cookie project together. This was before Nancy began to make her own life. Now it's not expected of her. Who will do this when she doesn't have the energy, she wonders? Who will do this when she is gone? There was a brief time when Helen Thompson dreamed about passing on the tradition, passing on something of herself beyond just the photos and the ever fading memories. When Nancy got married and the time for having children had arrived, she fantasized about bringing her grand-daughter to her home, and to pass down more than a recipe on a card. To pass down a virtual piece of herself, some of the essence of who she is, and have that at least live on. Essence in a rainbow cookie? She knows that's not it. It's not about a cookie. It's about love and sacrifice and doing things simply because you know it will bless other people. It's one of the many small ways one life can touch others.

Thinking about her second child, David is another story. He doesn't seem to want to settle down. They've had this argument,

Helen and her son. The traditional husband and wife team, staying married for life, has no appeal to him. What house did he grow up in, she questions? Can't he see how happy she and George have been all these years? The statistics all favor monogamous marriage arrangements. Health, happiness, even sexual satisfaction all increase, yet he still rejects their lifestyle. Truth is, she worries about him. He's not a kid any more. Who will take care of him if he doesn't find a wife? Grand-children, can she ever expect any from him? She fears not. Beyond that she clings to what she believes for him, 'if you raise up a child in the way he should go, he will not depart from it,' she quotes. And yet, they've argued about faith too. Argued so much that they no longer talk about it. Helen has resigned herself to simply pray for him and so they now maintain a civil mother-son relationship. They love each other, that is without question. But someone like her, someone sure of what they believe and convinced that that belief will bring peace within and life everlasting, cannot but wish that others would find what she found. This is especially true of one's children. As pastor likes to say, "The only thing you can bring with you to heaven is your children."

****

Hanif Nasrallah wakes up in a cold sweat. His sleep, what little he was able to get, has been broken into short bursts of restlessness. He got the call he has feared, last night around ten, which would have been three in the morning in London. He doesn't hear from his brothers in the U.K. very often, and when he does, it is normally through an intermediary, but there is no time to waste. They discarded their normal protocol and called him directly. It won't matter now. The possibility being compromised means that they must pull up stakes and move. He purchased his tickets last night. He rises and immediately begins to plan his day. He has much to do in the next twelve hours.

Chapter 19

Christopher brings Sammy her breakfast – she sits in bed. He carefully balances the tray with one hand and lowers the legs on either side so it will sit straight over her prone body and allow her to eat. "Chris, you are too good to me. Have you had your own breakfast yet?" she inquires of him.

"Not yet, I'm not hungry. I'll eat in a little while. But look what I've got for you, all your favorite things. The nurses say you have to eat. Keep up your strength," he responds with enthusiasm as he places the tray over her blanket covered torso. Sammy offers a weak smile and reaches for her sunglasses. Christopher wears a puzzled expression and continues to look at the tray of food as if he could will her to eat what he has brought.

"The light, it hurts my eyes," she says as way of explanation to his look.

Chris looks at the skylights above their heads and sees only the gray December clouds. He looks about the room and of the children still milling around, he doesn't see anyone else with their glasses on. "I brought you some of that orange marmalade you like. Do you want me to put some on the English muffin for you?"

She sighs dramatically. "I'm not an invalid, you know," and picks up one side of the muffin, and using a knife, begins to spread some of the jam onto it. They sit quietly as she finishes the task and begins to eat. Christopher notices that she puts it down after a few small bites.

"What do you want to do today?" he asks.

"Oh, I don't know. I do want to see Precious. I have to change her water and make sure she has enough seed." She pauses as there is really no other desire she has. "We can talk about that later. Right now you need to go get your own breakfast." When he protests, she stops him and orders, "Go get your breakfast, Christopher Randolph. I'm not taking 'no' for an answer. Go!" and she extends her arm and points in the direction of the cafeteria.

With that, Christopher slides away, looking back at his friend as he goes. Sammy closes her eyes underneath the glasses and that makes her head feel better. She opens them, takes another look at the tray and grabs the small, white, paper cup which contains her morning allotment of vitamins and minerals, notices the addition of an elongated white pill and throws the whole mixture into her mouth. She lifts the orange juice and in two good swallows washes the pills down.

She wakes to the sound of Mrs. Randolph and her mother sitting on Christopher's bed, trying to be quiet, but still giggling like a pair of school girls. Keeping perfectly still, she takes a quick peek with one eye, doesn't see Christopher, then closes it and continues to lay still. The sound of their voices, especially her mom's, is soothing. Mrs. Randolph continues, "So, what you're trying to tell me is that Sammy's illness has somehow become a blessing. It has helped your marriage and your family?"

"Well, I really won't put it that way. But yes, Samantha's illness forced Don and me to reevaluate our priorities. What was important before became less important. The uncertainty, the fear, the struggle helped us realize how precious and fragile the time we have is. And Don, to his credit, applied those feelings not only to Samantha, but to me as well. As I told you, he is so much more attentive now. Even though we have stress and fearful days, through all this, it has bound us together. It's *our* struggle. We're in it together, the three of us. In the evening, when we are home by ourselves, he comforts me, and that sometimes even leads to . . . sex." Melinda whispers the word to her friend. Sammy can barely keep a grin from appearing on her supposedly sleeping face. She has always been a mature child for her age and she is smart. She had asked Melinda 'where babies came from' years ago and Melinda had been honest with her. Melinda

143

continues, "It's not that, it's not that at all." And here she pauses for the right words. "It's that I know he loves me, no matter what we're going through or what we will go through in the future. I know that he loves me."

Ceci's eyes water. "Wow, that's fantastic. I am so happy for you Melinda. I know Ted loves me, but I don't feel that. I hate myself for placing blame, but Christopher's illness has become our burden. It's like the four of us each carry the burden by ourselves, independent of each other. I let it consume me. I can't do enough. I hope and I pray. I take care of the house, and Ted and I make sure Aaron has what he needs and that he's looked after, but things are not the same. I'm not the same. We, as a couple, are not the same. I'm so embarrassed. I can't talk to anyone else but you about this. I'm Christian. I'm supposed to have unwavering faith and peace in a crisis. Our families are going through the same experience and you, you are not even religious, and yet your family has overcome this trouble and mine has not." She sobs openly. Sammy knows she has to keep perfectly still now.

Melinda moves closer to her friend and puts her arm around her, pulling her close and letting Ceci sob into her shoulder. "Ceci, you are the best woman I know. You and your family are going to pull through this. I know you will. Maybe that God you talk about put us together, at just the right time, in just the right place. Ted loves you, you know that, and I've seen the way he looks at Christopher and how Christopher lights up when he sees his dad or his brother. The Randolph's are going to make it. Don't cry dear. This is just a dark time, but there are better things to come." Mrs. Randolph stops sobbing and is drying her tears when Sammy hears another voice coming toward them.

"So, how are my girls today?" It's Don. "Hello, Ceci." She turns and he sees her red and puffy eyes "Oh . . . I'm sorry. I'll . . . go. I'll come back in a little bit."

But Ceci has already grabbed his extended hand. "Don't be silly. You stay right here. It's just silly girl talk. It's nothing."

144

"Donald, what are you doing here? Why aren't you at work?" Melinda asks as he leans over and gives her a kiss on the cheek.

"Nothing is more important than my girls. How is the little one today?" He steps toward his daughter and gently plants a kiss on Sammy's cheek. She plays the perfect actress, gives a huge faux yawn, raises one arm and stretches to demonstrate that she is just waking.

"Daddy!" she cries. "Give me a hug." He reaches down, envelopes her small body in his two strong arms and hugs her to himself, lifting her nearly out of the bed.

"Don, be careful," Melinda cautions behind him.

"Oh, she's not going to break," he says, but still softly places her back down. "How is my angel today?" He removes the sunglasses still perched on her nose and looks into the prettiest pair of hazel eyes he has ever seen.

"I'm better, now that you're here, Daddy," Sammy replies and gives him her best 'I feel good' smile.

"Hmm . . ." he says warily, as he glances over to the barely touched breakfast tray that Melinda had moved from off the sleeping child and left on the end of the bed. "It doesn't look like you ate very much breakfast."

"Oh, that old stuff." Samantha dismisses it with a wave of her hand.

"Well then, I've got something for you." He reaches back to the white paper bag he had tossed on the bed.

"Don, what did you do? You know Dr. Glacieux doesn't allow food to be brought in from the outside," Melinda cautions.

"It's quite all right dear," he says and turns to give her a smile. "I have one for you too, and Ceci, if she would like."

"Very thoughtful, but that doesn't make it right," she chides.

"It is all right, dear. I cleared it – in advance – with Nurse Cratchit. They're from the organic bakery I told you about on Third Avenue. I went by there yesterday, got the ingredients and faxed them over yesterday. They're approved." Then quickly, "Let's try one of these bad boys." He passes out the square cakes filled with grain, nuts, and seed he is so proud of.

"Is there a nurse Cratchit here?" Ceci wonders out loud, not realizing Don was just trying to poke fun at the stringent rules they have regarding food. Even Sammy laughs for the first time today.

"Where is Chris?" Don says, and stands up to look around the room, hoping to see him, "I've got one for him too." Sammy enjoys the cake. While it's better than the normal fare, that isn't what makes it special. Don makes a face as he eats his. "Well, they are a little dry, but they're supposed to be good for you. Probably help keep you regular, honey." He jostles and pokes Melinda playfully in the ribs. If one had come across the three of them sitting in any other setting than the one they were in, one would think they were just a picture perfect family with no problems.

Ceci, conscious of the rare chance for some private family time, rises and says, "Excuse me, I'm going to find Christopher."

Still anxious over her condition, but fortified by her friend's words and the example she just witnessed, is filled with a new determination. This thing is not going to beat us, she says to herself. She wanders about the place, not merely looking for Christopher but looking at each child and imagining what they had gone through. There are a few parents around – mothers. Don is the only father. She listens hard to each conversation as she walks past, using the out of context pieces to fashion a life scenario unique to each. One child is encircled by his mother and what is likely his grand-parents. The old couple, wrinkled, small, and tired, looking on their grand-child and wishing they could take away the pain. The grand-father sits on the edge of the bed and holds the child's hand in both of his, gently patting it in a way that would suggest he believes that will make the child feel better. It probably did.

Who can dismiss the effect of a concerned human touch at times like these? Even in those war movies that Ted likes to watch, with the horrible scenes of men dying, you see their buddy, holding their hand and telling them it is going to be OK, even while they know it's only a

146

matter of minutes before their life slips away. Sometimes the wounded ask someone to stay with them. To hold them while they depart. Ceci looks back toward the Robinson family and sees the three of them together on Samantha's bed and prays. She is reminded about Jesus' admonition to visit the sick and those in prison. Somehow, in her current frame of mind, she has a glimpse of understanding. It's the reassurance, at a dark time in life, brought in the form of a human touch - that someone cares. In an odd turn of events she comes to think that Samantha and Christopher, surrounded by their family, and the grand-child that is having his hand patted comfortingly by their grand-father, are better off than many. Surely better off than those that die by themselves or even those that go through life, sick or not, uncertain whether anyone really cares for them.

****

Ted spends the day in his usual manner. It is four o'clock before he knows it and he thinks about going home. He wonders what Ceci is planning to make for dinner. They have a meal that they affectionately call 'slop.' It's actually pretty good. They haven't had it for a while. I could go for a nice plate of slop, he thinks. It's macaroni covered in a sauce with ground beef, onions, and condensed tomato soup - it's better than it sounds. The cooks don't seem to mind when it is referred to so disrespectfully. Ceci's mom used to make it when she was a girl and one of her siblings coined the phrase; she and her sister have kept the family tradition alive. She'd make it for me if I call and asked her to, he thinks, but decides against it, not wanting to trouble her with his yearning.

Regardless, he hopes she has dinner ready. He has a commitment he has to get to tonight. She'll probably remember. He's supposed to get up to the church by 7 p.m. He and a handful of other men have agreed to take turns caring for the building; general maintenance, minor repairs, that sort of thing. He always has a bit of internal agitation when it's his turn. It's not the work itself, he rather enjoys it, and enjoys the company of the guys he works with. Being around them encourages him, helps his faith. Ted would rather work than just sit around and talk or listen to a redundant, hopeful message. He enjoys it more than the pious prayer meeting, and the pious prayer meeting types. His agitation stems from two sources; first, from past experience, to see if the other guys that committed actually show up. It is annoying when he expects the work to be shared by three and only two show, or worse yet, if it's only him. Second, and this bothers him more than if he has to do the work by himself, is the nagging fear that he is only paying tribute. Not actually paying money, although he is sure many do that instead, but that he is relying on what he does for the church - the painting, the distribution of turkey baskets, the grounds keeping, even the prayer meeting. Are they all just works? Is he trying to earn his way to heaven? Is that what He makes of them?

Still, it's pleasing to Ceci to see him act so, and while that is not his primary motive in doing these small things, it is surely part of it. He wishes to make her happy and knows that she believes beyond what he has allowed himself to. As busy as she is, she does many things to help the church meet the needs of the people. He imagines her motives are pure and that perhaps there is still hope for him.

Ted understands his struggle. He is uncertain which camp he is in. Is he like the man in the Bible praying, that beats his chest and cries out to God, 'Have mercy on me. I am a sinner.' Or is he lukewarm and at any moment to be spewed out?

It's odd. Christopher's illness doesn't trouble him in the spiritual sense. While he naturally questions the why, and even though his wife and others pray and believe it will be, he doesn't have faith enough to expect a miracle. He knows Christopher believes; that's enough no matter what happens. Ted wishes his pain would be less. Would take the illness upon himself to allow his son to live a full and healthy life. With this thought Ted closes his eyes and makes one of his own infrequent prayers. 'Lord, take me. Heal the boy and take me instead.'

Chapter 20

It's evening and Nancy arrives home happy. She had the opportunity to pass good news to a number of the parents; the news that their child was well enough to go home for the holidays. As she pulls into her driveway, lined with lights to mark the gentle curve up to the doors, she is especially glad for the automatic garage door opener. The day had turned bitter, the wind had picked up its intensity and the temperature dropped. As the door slides steadily up in concert with her wish, she thinks to herself, I'll throw on some comfortable clothes, have some soup and sit by the fire. She waits until the garage door closes firmly against the ground to block out the pending winter tempest, steps out of the car, and reaches into the back seat for her briefcase. As she turns toward the door leading into the house, she is surprised to see the door ajar and the light from the hallway behind it shining through and around the small opening. Odd that it wasn't pulled shut, but in her pleasant reverie she thinks little of it. It must be the wind, she thinks as she reaches for the door knob, turns to hit the garage light shut, and enters the warm confines of her home. She turns to the left and drops her bag on the floor, but out of the corner of her eye she notices another light, this one coming from the bedroom. Nancy looks harder and sees items strewn about on the floor. Her heart leaps within her. She bends down to pick up her bag and determines to go back to the garage, all the while keeping her eyes fixed on the open bedroom door, looking for any movement and listening to hear if the intruder is still somewhere in the house. She tries to be silent as she opens and closes the door behind her.

Back in the garage she looks for something that she can defend herself with. Hanging from a nail in the wall she sees a crowbar and snatches it up, gauging its weight in her hand. She grasps it firmly near the curve, holding it up in the air and testing her ability to use it by cocking her wrist a few times. Satisfied, she moves further away from the entryway, down the side of the car and to the rear of the garage, closer to the exterior door, in case she needs to get out quickly.

Secure in this defensive posture, she is able to take a few deep breaths and begins to think more clearly. She reaches into her bag for her cell phone and dials 911. The operator grasps her whispered meaning, and after determining that she appears safe, takes the information needed to find the house, and cautions her to remain where she is until help arrives. Nancy, her eyes never leaving the door that leads into the house, crouches with crowbar in hand. Her heart races, she still holds the cell phone and looks at the time display, 7:34 p.m.. Worried about how long it will take them to reach her, she thinks about running out but quickly nixes that idea due to the wintry weather that she can hear from her spot near the door. Perhaps she should go to the car, start it, raise the door and escape that way? What if the intruder hears the car starting or the garage door opening – what then? What if he appears at the door? I could throw it into reverse, nail it, and crash through the as yet unopened garage door, she muses. What if he has a gun? What if he shoots through the windshield like they do on the cop shows? Maybe I should just put it in drive, surprise the bastard and pin him like a piece a meat against the wall. She pictures herself triumphant, sitting on the trunk of the car and calmly smoking, when the cops finally show up, the car plowed into the wall with the bastard pinned and bleeding on the hood of the car. She looks down at the cell phone – still 7:34, shit.

Think Nancy, think, she encourages herself. She takes a few deep breaths, checks the cell phone again, 7:35, whew, time is still moving. Figure ten minutes to get here, nine more, shit. After another minute she is able to dismiss fear and remove fantasy from her thoughts. There can't be anybody still in the house. She opened the garage door when she got home, duh, if anyone was still in the house they would have heard the noise. On top of that, if they were in the house and meant to do her harm, then they would have attacked her as she entered. Reassured, now thinking logically, she needs to see what they took from her, what they did to her home. She warily approaches the doorway with the crowbar raised. She swings the door fully open and shouts, "If anyone is in here I'm giving you sixty seconds to get the hell out," and she listens for any sound of movement. She waits about half that time and enters with the crowbar in both hands and lifted over her shoulder, ready to strike. First to the bedroom, she pushes the door the rest of the way open and takes a half step back to survey the room. Not too bad, she thinks. The contents of a few boxes had been dumped. There are scattered papers on the floor. Her armoire left with its doors open and she can tell it had been rifled through. Jewelry box intact, she lifts the lid and looks in. She doesn't keep anything too precious sitting out, but there is some gold in there; a ring and a set of earrings from her grandmother are still sitting in the bottom tray, another set of earrings, diamond studs, sit undisturbed. Odd, why would someone bother to break in and not take the stuff that could score them some quick cash? Still clutching the crowbar, she goes from room to room. Throughout the house there is general disorder but she can't put her finger on anything that is missing. Flat screen is still on the wall. Stereo unmoved. Her mind goes through any item of value that a thief might be interested in – nothing missing.

The doorbell rings and she trots toward the door, crowbar still in hand, but relaxed and at her side. She reaches up for the alarm and notices it is unarmed – son of a bitch – did I forget to set it on the exact day some bastard breaks into my home? She opens the door and lets the policemen in with a, "Hello, officers. I'm Nancy Glacieux. I called about the break-in. Come on in, I've just been surveying the damage." The two policemen enter, a middle-aged white guy leading the way followed by his younger, African-American partner. Both have their hand on their holster but seem to relax as they sense there is no danger. "I walked through the house. Whoever did this is probably long gone. I haven't been home all day."

"That's fine, Miss," says the more senior officer. "You're probably right, but would you stay right here and let me and my partner double-check? Thank you." They leave her by the door and begin to do their walk through.

Nancy goes into the living room and plops herself down on the couch and shakes her head, annoyed. How did I forget to set the alarm, she thinks? She makes a mental picture of her actions as she left this morning. I was unrushed, following my fairly rigid routine. I dressed in the bedroom, unplugged my cell from the charger on the nightstand, went to the kitchen, picked up a banana, found my keys in my pocketbook, and exited through the garage. I could swear I set the alarm from the console by that door. It's right in my face as I am leaving. How could I have overlooked it? Did I forget something, turn and get distracted as I approached the door?

"It's all clear, Miss," says the officer, as he and his partner return to the living room. "Have you looked around? Can you give us a list of everything that was taken?"

"I have, but I don't see what, if anything was taken. Odd, right?" Nancy responds.

"Yeah, I'd say. I see you have an alarm. Was that set when you left this morning?" the lead officer continues.

"I would've been pretty sure, but now," and she hesitates. "I'm still pretty sure."

"Well, we'll need a list of anyone that might have access to the house, housekeeper, maintenance person, uh, relative, babysitter, anyone you can think of. Do you know of someone that would have wanted to do this?" Nancy shakes her head. "Do you have any idea what someone could have wanted?" and she shakes her head again. With that, there is a knock at the door.

Nancy and the officers each look at the other. The lead officer nods his head indicating that she should answer it. The front door is still open and through the clear glass storm door she can see, standing directly under the porch light, two men, both neatly dressed, overcoats buttoned up against the weather. The man closer to the door holds up a badge and without waiting says, "Nancy Glacieux?" Upon receiving her nod, he continues, "I'm agent Walker, with Homeland Security." He moves the badge to indicate to her he has proof. "This is agent Williams." He turns slightly to give her a view of his partner, who stands stoically behind him. "May we come in?"

Nancy pushes open the storm door and says, "Sure, join the party. Homeland Security? It was just a break-in. I already have the Village police here." As they enter they come face to face with the uniformed officers. The officers quickly identify themselves by title and last name, the Homeland Security guy flashing his badge again. The Village officer's names are Ross and Roberts and Nancy can't help but grin at the thought of how the partners are paired up, guess alphabetical works, she internally jokes.

Agent Williams moves toward the officers and indicates they should walk with him, says, "Officers, can I have a word with you?" He leads them down the hall and into the other room out of earshot.

Nancy addresses the remaining agent, "What is this about, Agent Walker?" As he hesitates to gather his thoughts to respond, she continues, "Is this about that idiot Randolph?" Agent Walker looks puzzled at this comment so she continues, "The guy from the IRS, Ted Randolph. Did he put you up to this?"

"I'm sorry Ma'am, I don't know the idiot Randolph you mention," but he takes a notepad out and is jotting down the name as he speaks. "We aren't here about a tax issue. This is more serious than that," and he hesitates again. "You do know why we are here?" emphasizing the 'do' and looking directly at her, nodding his head as if he can influence her decision.

Nancy contracts her mouth left, closes one eye making a comical face, tilts her head, and mimics, "Nooo, I don't." Emphasis on the 'don't.' "Whhhyyy don't you tell me?"

Agent Walker doesn't seem to appreciate the humor. "Ma'am, Ms. Glacieux, this is a serious matter. This is a national security concern.

We have reason to believe you are involved in plots against the government."

"Plots against the government!" she spits back and laughs out loud. "That's absurd. Who put you up to this? Is someone filming this?" and she looks around as if she would spy the hidden camera.

"Ma'am, I can assure you, no one 'put me up to this.' There are no cameras. You need to come with us for questioning." Abruptly, he adds, "Get your things, Ma'am. The officers will stay here and secure your home until our forensic team arrives."

"What? You've got to be kidding!" she shouts in disbelief as the three other officers return to the room.

"No, Ma'am. I'm afraid not. Agent Williams will escort you. Please get your coat and whatever personal belongings you wish to bring. We need to go. Now!"

Chapter 21

Nancy is led into an interrogation room. The square table, overhead light, and two-way mirror gives the situation an ominous and surreal feeling. Sitting across the table are two agents of Homeland Security, Agents Morris and Fitzsimmons. Both have a blank legal pad, posed for note taking. Fitzsimmons has a manila folder stacked neatly under his. A digital recorder sits in the middle of the table. Nancy wonders if they're going to play good cop, bad cop with her.

"So, gentlemen, would either one of you like to explain to me what this is all about?" She has the confidence of one who knows she has done nothing wrong and isn't about to be bullied.

"We ask the questions here, Ms. Glacieux," says the agent who identified himself as Morris.

"OK, then ask," she snarls back. "I'm the one that had my house ransacked. The other agent said a forensic team is heading there, God knows what for. You better know what you're doing because if my rights are being violated my lawyers will have a field day. Am I under arrest?"

This is followed with, "You don't understand. We ask the questions," this time thrown out with an unmistakable glare. Bad cop, she thinks, and decides it might go quicker if she just responds to their questions rather than antagonizing them.

Agent Morris begins. "As you are probably aware, the agency is continuously investigating individuals in this country that might pose a threat. We look at a number of activities. We monitor phone calls to try to determine the movement of money across borders." Here he hesitates for effect before continuing. "Dr. Glacieux, we have taped conversations of you discussing the transfer of money to overseas accounts."

"You guys are listening to my phone calls?" she calls out in anger and disbelief. "This is America, not Nazi Germany. Is it illegal to talk on the phone now? Illegal to send money overseas? This is total bullshit."

After an appropriate pause, Morris nods to his partner. Fitzsimmons reaches into the folder and slips a photo out, turns it so it faces her and slides it under the light, towards her as Morris says, "Have you ever seen this man before?"

Nancy recognizes the face instantly. It's more accurately described as a boy. He has dark skin, a round face, and an unmistakable hairline. It's the boy she saw in her dream a month or two ago; the boy whose hairline receded on the sides and met in a distinct point in the middle of his forehead. Several thoughts go through her mind, each coupled with fear of the unknown. She is cognizant that an answer is expected of her and feels their eyes upon her as she continues to look down at the photo. Determined to give nothing away, she looks up, her eyes going from one agent to the other. "I can't say for sure. It looks more like a boy, not a man. " Then looks back down as if studying it further for clues.

"Well, he seems to know you," agent Morris strikes back, causing her to involuntarily meet his eyes.

"I'm sorry, Agent Morris, I can't place him. I'm a doctor. I've seen thousands of children. I wish I could help," Nancy responds and gives a shrug as if she has nothing more to add.

Agent Morris gives the same look and nod to his partner as if it is a predetermined sequence of events. Fitzsimmons pulls a second sheet from the folder in front of him, turns it to face her and slides it across the table as he had done with the photo. With his other hand he slides the photo off to the right so that the second sheet is centered in front of Nancy. "This is a manifest of air travel you made in April of last year." Morris continues, "Do you recall making this trip?" He gives Nancy time to nod her head in agreement as she looks down and sees her name listed on a flight manifest for a flight from JFK to Brussels and the connecting flight on to Chad later the same day. "Can you explain this?"

"Sure," Nancy responds hesitantly as she fashions her statement with care. "I did take these flights. My husband, my ex-husband that is, grew up there and I went for a visit."

Morris presses her. "This young fellow in the photo, he is from near there as well. Does that help jog your memory?"

Nancy takes her time, careful not to let her tongue slip. She is not about to give them information they don't have and continues to maintain a calm appearance. She reaches for the photo as if to reevaluate her original perception, studies it a bit and begins to shake her head without looking up at the agents. "No, I'm sorry. I don't recall seeing this particular boy," she lies. "The whole place is filled with boys that look like this. I'm sorry, I can't help you."

Fitzsimmons interjects, "Dr. Glacieux, we can help you. Look again, try to remember. Information you provide can help our investigation and we, in turn, can help you." Good cop, she thinks, and takes another long look at the photo.

"I'm sorry, Agent Fitzsimmons. I wish I could tell you more. But, I can't."

Morris utters a deep, exasperated sigh, scribbles something on the pad, looks back up at Nancy and says, "Dr. Glacieux, this boy was picked up in London the day before yesterday. He was caught in the midst of executing a terrorist act. Luckily, and I do mean luckily, the authorities there stumbled upon him during a routine check of their transportation system. Hundreds, if not thousands of lives, were potentially saved," and here he stops for effect. "The boy implicated you. He had a picture of you and him, sitting together on a bunk."

Nancy's eyes dart left and right several times in rapid succession. The shock to her system renders her inarticulate. Her only movement is an involuntary, minute shaking back and forth of her head in denial. "No," she mutters more to herself than to the agents. "No, that can't be." She continues to shake her head in disbelief.

Agent Morris, recognizing her weakness, continues. "The boy says he saw you at a training camp about 20 kilometers outside the capital of N'Djamena and that you supplied the funds to run the camp. He says you visited and the timing of your travel plans indicate that he's telling the truth. So, what's it going to be, Doctor? Are you going to cooperate with us?"

Nancy doesn't really hear Agent Morris after that. She doesn't know where she is or what time of day it is. She simply sits and rocks her head in denial, her lips moving but only muttering to herself in whispers over and over, "No, that can't be." Finally, Nancy stops speaking, stops shaking her head and looks up but through the agents, her gaze resting on the far wall as if in a trance. Fitzsimmons can't wait any longer, "Dr. Glacieux, Nancy, tell us what you know!"

Nancy is trying to process the information she has been told and evaluate the situation. The boy caught in London; a terrorist camp; Harry a fanatic; money she accepted 'for research' sent overseas. Fear grips her. What will happen to her work now? Nearly a full minute goes by before she is able to say, "I don't know anything. I obviously don't know anything at all. Call my Father. I want a lawyer. I'm not saying another word." Her gaze doesn't leave the blank wall.

Chapter 22

Within an hour of receiving the call, George Thompson arrives at the offices of Homeland Security. He has no information other than Nancy is being held for questioning. He dressed and rushed over. George is not the kind of man that gets flustered in a crisis. However, initially convinced that this must be some kind of error, he finds himself more anxious the closer he gets to the office. He approaches the front desk with apprehension. After identifying himself and providing documentation, he is scanned for metal and weapons before being brought into the inner offices. Chaperoned until met by Agents Morris and Fitzsimmons, he is ushered into a small conference room and offered coffee, which he declines. Anxious to avoid unnecessary pleasantries he seeks to move the conversation forward so he can speak to his daughter. "Gentlemen, can you tell me what is going on? There must be some mistake."

Morris takes the lead. "Mr. Thompson, this is a serious national security matter. We have reason to believe that your daughter has information that could help us in our investigation."

"OK, I'm assuming you have asked her?" and upon receiving nods continues. "My daughter would have told you if she knows something. She is an upstanding member of the community. Her reputation is impeccable. She wouldn't be involved in anything unsavory or illegal. Of that, I can assure you."

"We would like to believe that, Mr. Thompson, but the facts put that view in jeopardy. If she is as innocent as you say, then you can help her by getting her to tell you what she does know. Her cooperation would be favorably viewed. If she is not involved, the information she provides could remove any doubt of her innocence."

"What are these facts, gentlemen?" George Thompson queries in such a manner as to display his disbelief that they actually exist.

"I understand your concern for your daughter, Mr. Thompson," Morris replies. "And while I'm not at liberty to reveal everything about the investigation to date, I can let you know that a terrorist that has been captured in London has positively identified your daughter as a participant in the group's activities. We have evidence, and she has admitted to us, that she visited the region the terrorist is from last spring. In addition, we have been monitoring phone calls of suspicious persons, and on more than one occasion, she has been caught on tape speaking with one such person specifically about transferring funds to overseas accounts."

"Hmm… I'm not exactly sure what all that means, but let me speak to her. I'm sure there is a reasonable explanation."

"Good," Morris exclaims, but before he can continue, George interrupts.

"I'm no lawyer but I need some assurance that the conversation between my daughter and me will be private. No tape recording. No listening in. Do I have your word on that, gentlemen?" There is a pause and an exchanged look between the two agents. Morris answers.

"If she gives you information can we be certain that you will tell us?"

Thompson snorts a short laugh. "Well, my wife would say that liars shall not enter the kingdom."

"And you sir?" Morris enjoins.

Thompson shrugs. "What would you like me to say? If I say 'yes, I'll tell the whole truth' without knowing what Nancy will tell me then I run the risk of harming my daughter. If I say 'no,' then you won't believe anything I say anyway." The three of them remain silent seemingly not knowing who should speak next. Thompson continues, "So I guess the question is would I lie for my daughter?" He hesitates again as he ponders that question. "The only thing I can say is 'that depends.' If she murdered someone and I knew, I would tell you. But if you sought to punish her for something that she was not responsible for… would I help you make a case against her? While I don't know for sure, I don't believe I would outright lie. No, I don't think I would," he states emphatically. "Now, do I have *your* word, and can I see my daughter?"

Realizing they received an evasive answer the agents still think it best to allow Mr. Thompson to speak to his daughter under the rule he established. In cases like these, time is of the essence, people disappear, cells scatter literally overnight. They give their word that they will not 'listen in' on their conversation.

"Daddy," Nancy cries out, and runs to him from where she had been pacing back and forth in an attempt to figure out exactly what she should do. Pushed to her limit, unsure of what the agents know or don't know, frozen with fear, uncertain what lays ahead for her and her work, she had even silently prayed. While not elaborate, not even consciously, she had found herself pacing and praying. Every few turns, when unsure of what to think or what to do, her mind would form the words, 'Lord, help me. I don't know what to do.' Seeing her father near allowed her to release some of that fear. She throws her arms around his shoulders and weeps against his chest.

George Thompson hasn't seen his daughter vulnerable like this in many, many years. It takes his already soft heart and melts it further. After a minute the sobbing and weeping begin to subside. He passes her a tissue, which she uses to dry her face and with one last heaving sigh, she is still. He leads her back to one of the chairs, pulls a second one up close to her and sits, face to face. He holds her two hands in his own and tries to reassure her that everything will be all right, that they will figure something out. Agents Morris and Fitzsimmons watch from the other side of the two-way mirror.

"Daddy, I don't know what to do. They are trying to link me to some terrorist plot. My house was completely ransacked earlier today and Homeland Security is sending a forensic team there. I'm afraid.

I'm afraid I'm being set up. I didn't do anything. Nothing like this . . . I would never . . ."

Her father interrupts her, "I know you wouldn't honey. Don't be afraid. We'll figure something out," and he pulls her closer and wraps his arms around her once more. They part and she touches the tissue again to the corner of each eye but she is done crying. "They told me you went on a trip last spring and that they have tape recordings of you speaking to someone about transferring money overseas. Is that true?"

Nancy's eyes dart left and right and some of the fear rises back up inside her. She moves closer to her father as if to hug his neck and whispers into his ear. "We can't talk here. They are listening."

He understands her concern but pulls away and looks into her eyes but still whispers. "It's OK. I have their word that they won't listen or tape our conversation," but he can see the doubt in her eyes. "Trust me. I have their word," he repeats.

Nancy is silent for a few seconds and considers what her father said. He is such a good man, she thinks to herself. This is just like him, honest and trusting. Her father is the most honest man she has ever known. Perhaps that is why she asked for him at a time like this. There is an underlying belief, somewhere deep down within, that her father can fix anything, that his counsel will be wise, and that if she listens to him, things will turn out all right.

She thinks about an incident from her childhood. Their family had gone to one of the infrequent Sunday dinners out at a restaurant. She doesn't recall if it was for a specific event. It was a Chinese restaurant, the kind where you sit down at a table or a booth, not the take-out version with the counter, the pencils, and the ordering process of circling numbers on a long sheet - a pint of this and a quart of that. No, this was a nice dinner, where they take your order and pour you tea into a fragile cup with a delicate pattern that sits in a matching saucer. She was ten, maybe eleven, and old enough to decide between right and wrong.

In the midst of her memory, there is a knock at the door and Agent Morris opens it.

"I'm sorry to disturb you. Mr. Thompson, your son is here. It seems your wife has taken ill. She was rushed to the hospital and he insists that we interrupt you."

Nancy let out a soft, "Oh, my God."

George Thompson receives the news as if he had been told what time of day it was. "Thank you, Agent Morris. I'll be just another minute." Morris nods and leaves the room. George Thompson turns to his child. "Don't worry. Don't be afraid. Your mother is in good hands. You don't need to worry about her," he says reassuringly.

Nancy understands and says, "You go. They aren't going to let me go anywhere. I'll be here when you get back. Go check on mom."

"Is what they say true?"

Nancy doesn't answer him directly. "Make a call, Dad," she says. "Call Jonathon Weiss, tell him I need a lawyer. A good one. Go now, and don't tell these guys anything."

George Thompson leaves the room and in the hallway seeks Agent Morris who meets him.

"I'm sorry I had to disturb you," he starts, but George holds up his hand to stop him.

"It's OK. She didn't really tell me anything except that she didn't do what you suspect and I believe her." As they walk to the front George continues, "Between me and you, I'd check out her ex. He is a bit of weird bird. I don't know the whole story but sometime after they broke up he got all religious. Muslim. If you are dealing with terrorism, I'd start there. His name is Harry. No. No, he changed it. Now it's Hanif. He goes by Hanif Nasrallah. I think he lives somewhere in the city. That's all I'm saying and you didn't hear it from me – got it?" Morris nods thoughtfully but doesn't tip his hand that Hanif Nasrallah is the suspicious person he referred to earlier, so this admission adds nothing to the investigation.

By this time they approach the front desk, David is sitting off to side, both legs tapping in a fight or flight motif. As they near his senses react to the movement. "Dad," he calls out when he looks up.

"Son. Thanks for coming," and gives him a hug. Then he turns and says, "Agent Morris, can David here go see his sister?" Morris shrugs indicating he has no objection but is thinking this is another chance to hear some of what Nancy knows. "Same deal as me. No listening. Do I have your word?" Morris agrees and realizes just how sharp Thompson is.

****

David enters the room without knocking. Nancy is still in the chair she was sitting in when her father left. Bent over, her head is bowed with her eyes closed. Her hands clenched together on her lap. She evidently hadn't heard the door slide open so David just stands there awkwardly, not knowing whether to make a noise or back out of the room. As if she senses a presence Nancy opens her eyes and spies him standing at the door.

"David," she cries and rushes to him and throws her arms around her brother.

"Hey. Are you OK?"

She takes a step back to look into his face and nods yes. "I'm worried about mom. What happened? Is she all right?"

"Yeah, I think she will be. She's had a pain in her side since this morning and after Dad left it got worse. So she called me and I took her to the hospital. She asked for Dad. I mean, I don't really know if she's OK. They're checking her out. I could tell she was in some pain but don't you worry, it's probably something minor," he says trying to put her mind at ease. "What the hell is going on here?"

"I'm in trouble," she says. "We can't really talk here. The walls have ears." With her eyes she points toward the mirror on the wall.

"Nope, Dad made them promise they wouldn't listen in."

"Sure," she replies with a smirk that makes them both laugh. "Isn't that just like Dad, thinking that other folks have as much character as he does."

"Yeah, Dad always thinks the best of people. I wish the world was like that."

"Just a few minutes ago, while he was here, I thought about one time we went to that nice Chinese restaurant in town. You remember the one, just off Main Street down in the Village?" David nods. "And one time the waiter brought over the bill and Dad looked it over, as he would usually do to make sure it was right." Dave nods again. He remembers this too. Nancy goes on, "So, he gets the waiter's attention and tells him there is a mistake on the bill. The guy starts apologizing and offers to bring us cookies. But Dad finally gets to tell him that the mistake was that he didn't charge us enough. Do you remember that?"

"Sure do," Dave says. "I thought something was wrong with him. I mean, I was like eight. Who tells someone that they weren't charged enough for something?"

"Yeah. I didn't know what to make of it either," Nancy replies. "And you, you start to give him a hard time. 'Dad, what did you do that for?' you said, or something to that effect. I remember Dad's answer as if it was last week. He said, 'David how would you like it if you were a waiter and someone took advantage of a mistake you made? That fellow probably needs this job and what if I didn't tell him about the error and his boss finds out and maybe fires him. That wouldn't be right. Not only that, but we ordered this food. We know what it cost. The prices are right on the menu, so we should expect to pay what we agreed to pay when we ordered it. We aren't looking for something for nothing, David. We're regular folks. We pay our way'."

"Yeah," Dave says, "I remember. I even tried to argue with him after that."

"You were always a little thick, Dave," Nancy shoots back.

"I think I said something like, 'But Dad, he made the mistake. It's not your fault.' Dad said, 'It still wouldn't be right.' I can't tell you how long that bothered me. I mean, jeez."

"Dad always talked about character, and that your actions and words make or break you," Nancy says. "That and what you do when no one is looking. When you think that no one will find out. No one would have ever known if Dad just paid the bill he was handed, but he still had the waiter change it. I think the point might be that while nobody else would have known, Dad would have known."

"Yeah, Dad is the most honorable person I know. I look at my life and I try to do good. I respect Dad, and Mom too. If it was her, she would tell the waiter too, but only because she wouldn't want to sin. I don't mean any disrespect. I love Mom. I don't really know what her reason would be. I'm not judging her, I'm just guessing." And here he pauses to reflect. "I'm so far off from either one of them. I shouldn't say anything."

"Don't be so hard on yourself David," Nancy interjects. "You're kind and good. You go to the mission and serve meals, you support that child from Africa every month, and the work you do at the research center. The kids love you. All that counts."

"Thanks Nancy. I do those things but I get something back by doing them. I'm not sure they count for much. I'm not like Dad. I don't always do what's right, especially if I get an advantage out of it. I'm going to tell you something I've never told anyone else. It's not a big deal, but it gets to what I'm trying to say. I was traveling on business. My boss and I were waiting to catch a flight. We're sitting at a table, laptops open, working, and we decided to get coffee. So I offer to go find some and he stays and watches our stuff. I get to the counter and it is busy, I wait and finally get to order, I go down the counter to where you pay. The clerk comes, I've got my card out to pay, and she tells me they need a minute or two to make some fresh. I say sure and she goes about her business. A few minutes go by and a different clerk sees me waiting, asks what my order is, and goes back to find it. Now I'm a little pissed it's taking so long for a simple order and they seem confused back there. On top of that I'm annoyed it's overpriced airport fare. The second clerk comes back with the two cups in hand. She puts them on the counter near me and doesn't appear to be thinking I might not have paid, so I and slip my credit card back in my pocket, pick up the coffee, and turn away."

David doesn't look at Nancy but is shaking his head at the remembrance of his actions. "I still can't believe it. I don't need the money, and on top of that, I would have just put it on my expense report. It wasn't even going to cost me anything!" He continues shaking his head, re-living the scene in his mind. "I'm walking away partially exhilarated, partially mortified. I'm annoyed that it took so long, that I had to ask for it twice, and that it is overpriced to begin with. Essentially, I justify my action, and all the while I'm heading back to where my boss is sitting and I'm thinking about our father and how disappointed he would be in me if he was watching."

It's silent as David allows his conscience to lash his spirit. Nancy, sitting and knowing what her brother is experiencing, deals with her own tormenting thoughts.

"Nobody's perfect, Dave," she says. "At least you can fix that. Just go back. Fly there if you have to. Pay for the coffee."

He snorts in response, then says, "Naw, it's no big deal. It's nothing to them. They spill coffee and replace orders all the time. That might work for some people – restitution. It's deeper than that. I know what's right and I don't do it. You can't imagine how that makes me feel."

The siblings sit in silent desolation, not concerned about where they are or who might be listening. Nancy speaks first.

"I've done wrong too, Dave. Much worse than you. Maybe I should be in jail. I've used people and I've taken their money for a selfish pursuit. I took an oath to save lives, and in what has become a single, desperate desire, I now use children, sick children, in a vain attempt to restore life. I'm so stupid. How could I have thought for one minute that I could play God? We have no control. Death comes to us all one way or another. Some young, some old, some sick, some by accident, disease, or war but the end result is still the same – death. I . . . I need to come to grips with the fact that I'm losing Hope."

Dave looks tenderly at his big sister and sees the heart of a much younger Nancy, sees the heart of a person born to do great things. "That's not true," he replies. "That's a lie straight from the pit. I never looked at it that way. You were given a talent that you are using to the best of your ability. I've never seen anyone more driven and there is no one else on the planet that would care as much as you. Boy, you are stupid," he mocks in his brotherly way. "Do you think for one minute that it was some coincidence that you became a doctor? Or that in your residency it was chance that you got to work with one of the finest brain surgeons on the East Coast to set you on the path to get to this point? You're wrong, Nancy. Trust me on this. You were given a gift. You were born for this reason. You're going to solve this thing and many, many children will benefit from it. Don't ever doubt it."

"Listen to you," Nancy replies. "I didn't know you wanted to grow up to be a preacher."

"I just might," Dave says. "There's still time. Besides I've always thought that if I really believed, I mean really, really believed, I would have to be a full-time missionary." In spite of herself Nancy cannot refrain from a full, throaty laugh out loud. "What?" Dave says in mock offense. "It's not *that* hard to believe."

"Mom would be happy. Maybe that's what she's been praying for all these years."

"Yeah, likely. I mean I'm not religious in the normal sense of the word, but I've got faith. I believe. I'm like the third guy on the cross who overhears Jesus being hassled and shoots back, 'Hey, leave him alone. He's done nothing wrong.' As a matter of fact, I take solace in the answer he gets too, 'I say to you today, you will be with me in paradise' – a lot of church folks have got it wrong. I've argued with Mom when she tries to get me to walk like she walks, do my weekly pilgrimage to church, pray for everything like she prays for everything, or do whatever the preacher says to do. That's not me. That's not how God made me. He made me as I am. He knows how my mind works, how I struggle to make sense of the world He dropped me in to. That might be fine for her, might be fine for a whole lot of people, but not me." He hesitates to take a breath. "We are alike in this one way. I never wanted to be a hypocrite and I can tell you never wanted to be one either. But that don't mean we've fallen off the course. I'm still finding my way but you are doing what God made you to do. Don't ever doubt that, and when we struggle, which I expect to do until the day I die, we just gotta remember, it's His mercy that saves us. Nothing we can do on our own will get us there. It's all Him."

Chapter 23

David leaves Nancy in the holding cell and heads back down the hall the way they had come. Agent Morris jogs up next to him as he walks quickly toward the entranceway. "David," he says, "can I talk to you a minute?" David says nothing and continues walking. Morris continues, "Did your sister say anything that could help us in the investigation?" This causes David to hesitate his step and Agent Morris slows to step with him. For the first time they face each other.

"Go to hell," Dave says, then continues his brisk pace towards the door.

Meanwhile, reports had been coming in from the field. Nasrallah's apartment had been swept clean. The forensic team working at Nancy's has come up with nothing. The PC's hard drive was taken out before they arrived. There are no papers indicating collusion, no fingerprints of any consequence. Hanif doesn't even appear in a photo. Another team was checking on travel arrangements. It too, came up empty. It's as if Hanif Nasrallah never lived in the city. Dammit, Morris thinks to himself as he sits at his desk and reviews what information they have. Glacieux was involved, of that he is sure, but at what level? She seems sharp, but they have her on tape talking about money transfers. Where did she think the money was going? Something doesn't add up. He knows his boss is not going to be happy that their net is coming up empty.

On that happy thought the intercom on his phone calls out, "Morris. We've got Glacieux's lawyer up here at the desk."

170

"I'll be right there," he responds. He picks himself up, empties the last half-inch of cold coffee from his cup, and heads to meet the lawyer.

Shit, he says to himself as he enters the reception area and sees the civil rights lawyer, Clarence Williams. This guy is a pain in the ass. He is talking to another gentleman, sitting on his right. Wow, look at that, it's friggin Jonathon Weiss. This lady is connected. This is only going to get harder.

"Gentlemen," he calls out with hand extended as he approaches. Both men rise to meet him. "Counselor," he says with a nod to Williams and shakes his hand. "Mr. Weiss," he says as he turns to Jonathon, again extending his hand. "I'm Agent Morris."

"What have we got here, Morris?" Williams quizzes him without further pleasantries.

"We're holding Ms. Glacieux. The boys in London arrested a fellow prior to him blowing himself up and he implicated your girl. Said she was there, at the training camp in Chad. Said she provided the dough. We've confirmed her visit at around the timeframe the fellow gave us. On top of that, we've got her on tape, talking with a second suspect about transferring money overseas. It's pretty clear she was involved at some level."

Jonathon burst in, "That's absurd. Of course she was transferring money overseas. We support a research center over there. The woman is trying to heal sick children for God's sake." Williams places his hand on Jonathon's arm indicating he should stop speaking. Morris listens and watches.

"What are you charging her with?" Williams astutely changes the subject.

"We're still investigating. At the moment - nothing."

"Well it all sounds very circumstantial to me Morris. Are you sure you're not making a big mistake here?"

"I wouldn't be doing my job if we didn't step in and bring her in," Morris says.

"Very well. I'd like to see my client now." Williams picks up his briefcase, indicating their chat is over. He and Jonathon are escorted to a small conference room and they wait for Nancy to be brought to them. Jonathon moves about the room, side to side, like a caged animal.

"What do you think, Clarence? Can they hold her?"

"Yes. Under current law, they can hold her indefinitely, but I don't think that will happen in this case. They'll determine within a day what they'll charge her with, if anything."

"I realize now that I shouldn't have said anything in front of Agent Morris. But it's so stupid. She runs a research center. Of course she's sending money over there."

"True Jonathon, you shouldn't have said anything. But don't worry, old friend, your little outburst may just as well have put some doubt into our dear agent's head. He thought that was significant, sending money over. It's no wonder they brought her in. I get the feeling from how he reacted that he didn't know that. A legitimate reason for sending money changes everything. No harm done, old boy, but please, let me do the talking from now on. That's why you're paying me."

The door opens and Nancy rushes in. She makes a bee-line for Jonathon and hugs him. "Boy, am I glad to see you," she says.

When released, Jonathon, with a sweep of his arm, turns her attention to the well-dressed man standing patiently a few steps away. "Nancy, this is Mr. Clarence Williams," he says. "Clarence is a dear friend and arguably the best civil rights attorney in the country. Clarence, this is Dr. Nancy Glacieux."

"Ah, Dr. Glacieux, I am so glad to finally meet you," Clarence says as he steps forward and extends his hand in greeting. They touch cautiously and briefly. Jonathon can tell by the scrutinizing look that both parties have begun evaluating the other. They don't smile as one might if this had been a social setting.

Nancy recognizes the name, has even seen his picture in the paper, and tries to place what case he had been associated with that made him familiar to her. Clarence for his part, had only his friend's description of Nancy to go on. He does not travel in quite the same circles as Jonathon. Their friendship began a long time ago, before Clarence Williams had become 'the' Clarence Williams, back when he was a struggling civil rights attorney, defending the poor and weak. As a result, he was rather poor himself for most of his career.

Jonathon had sought Clarence out, heard of a case he was working. It pitted Clarence and his client against the city establishment. The client was accused of murder but the whole thing had the appearance of a set-up. Just one more case of a poor, black man going to jail for something he didn't do. Jonathon passed Clarence the funds necessary to hire the support staff he needed to stay in the game. The client was found innocent by a jury of his peers. In the process some bad cops lost their jobs. Clarence Williams may have been poor but he was never weak. He somehow maintained a private practice and represented those that came to him when a public defender was their only option. Clients that knew the public defender wasn't giving these poor souls the representation they needed to prove their innocence.

Clarence didn't take every case that was brought his way though. No, he turned down cases. He even rejected cases in which there was a good prospect that he would be paid. This was quite difficult for him when he was behind on paying the rent and when his own children went to school with holes in their shoes and wore clothes that were handed down from others. His wife, always needing to be frugal, learned to stretch a chicken over more than one meal. There were times she needed to feed an extra mouth, some 'client' who had no family or had been abandoned. She'd serve them a hot plate and later make up the couch with sheets, pillows, and blanket if they had nowhere to sleep. No, Clarence Williams did not usually have the privilege of defending those with money. He shouldered the burden of those he thought were innocent; innocent and not getting the representation they needed to prove it. As a result, he often fought against the establishment. He disliked when those in power used it to intimidate and stifle others, just because they could, because they had the power.

As they stand there, circumspect and uneasy, Nancy recalls the article she read about Clarence Williams. He came from the projects in the Bronx, the oldest of four boys in a single parent household. His mother worked two jobs and instilled her boys with the fear of God, and of her. They went to school. She took them to church. Clarence Williams went to City College, worked in the evenings to pay for books and to help out at home. Against all odds, he went to law school, passed the Bar, and became a lawyer. Clarence Williams worked in the toughest sections of the city, was known for representing those that appeared guilty, and yet, more often than not, were acquitted when he fought for them. His notoriety brought him a handful of high profile cases and he began a scholarship program for the disadvantaged. The article celebrated the graduation of the first winner, a valedictorian who had dedicated her commencement speech in his honor. The picture in paper showed him with tears streaming down his face and clapping as the young prodigy was called to the podium.

Clarence was not unacquainted with Dr. Nancy Glacieux. Jonathon spoke of her and of the work she was doing. While disheveled and with her eyes red and puffy, Clarence could still see why Jonathon was attracted to her. "Thank you for coming," she says. "I'm at a loss of what to do. They are accusing me of things I haven't done."

"We'll get to the bottom of it, Dr. Glacieux," he responds. "Please sit down. Tell me exactly what transpired since the agents picked you up and exactly what was said by whom as best as you can recall."

"Please, call me Nancy." Jonathon continues to walk about the room. Over the next forty-five minutes she relays everything that happened from the time she arrived home to her last interview with Agent Morris. Clarence occasionally stops her mid-sentence and asks a clarifying question, but for the most part he just listens. Jonathon, eventually weary from pacing, takes the seat next to her. His expression conveys his worry.

After hearing her story and asking a few more questions, Clarence feels sure that she had not knowingly supplied funds for terrorism. It seems likely that her ex conned her. While the research center is real, it is apparent from Nancy's acknowledgement of knowing the young man in the photo, the man she had seen when visiting the facility, that Hanif Nasrallah has ulterior motives. Still something troubles him. "Nancy, why didn't you tell Agent Morris about the research center? It would appear to me that this fact would have taken some of the appearance of guilt away. Why did you lie to him about that?"

Nancy takes a deep breath and says, "I didn't want him to know."

Jonathon shifts in his seat and exclaims, "Why in heaven's name not!"

Nancy looks from Jonathon to Clarence and back to Jonathon. Both men remain silent, waiting for an answer. "I was worried about the work. The publicity that this will create could be devastating." Again, both men say nothing and look at her with skepticism waiting for her to explain more fully. Exasperated and desperate, Nancy sits back in the chair and rakes her hands through her hair. She turns to Jonathon, more worried at the moment about what he might think of her than her own situation. "Jonathon, there's something you don't know. I . . . I couldn't tell you. It was a burden for me to carry. Mine and mine alone. The facility in Chad did research . . . does research. But the reason that it's done there is not for public knowledge. As you know, I believe that the cure for PML lies in the genes." She pauses as if to gather her strength to continue. "At that facility we conduct research on children with the disease but it's not like here in the States. Here the parents flock to us when they are in dire need, when they realize their child will die if something isn't done. They will try anything, pay anything, to give their child one more chance. It works here. In other places, in Chad it isn't like that."

"Nancy, what are you trying to say?" Jonathon breaks in.

Nancy takes another breath and seems to steel herself. "In Chad, we pay the family. We give them a monthly stipend for every month their child lives. The parents literally sign away their rights to the child. The research, the level of the research, is beyond what would be permissible here in the U.S. or even in most Western countries." Jonathon sucks in his breath and is about to speak. Nancy cuts him off. "Let me finish, there's more. You've heard me speak about how I believe that genetically there are many carriers of the same abnormality that causes PML in a population of people that don't ever get the disease. Something in their genomes fights off the onset of the disease so it never takes hold of them. The answer to the cure would best be found in subjects that are not sick at all. In short, in healthy subjects."

Jonathon cannot sit still. He leaps from his seat and renews pacing. "Nancy, are you saying you conduct research on healthy kids? We? We conduct research on healthy kids like they're monkeys in a lab? My god, what were you thinking?" Nancy's eyes had begun to water while she was speaking, but Jonathon's outburst brings them streaming down her cheeks.

"I know. I know it sounds terrible."

"Sounds terrible! Are you kidding? I can't even believe it. So the parents, the parents let you do this to their kids? They do it for the money?" Nancy only nods as she sits and sobs in her chair.

"Good God," slips unconsciously from Clarence William's mouth.

Jonathon paces ever more quickly. He stops and looks down at her. "Nancy, Nancy, how could you do this?" It's the look and tone he uses that hurts her more than the words themselves.

"Jonathon, you don't understand. I didn't do it for me. I never wanted to do this. My hand was forced. I had no other choice."

"Of course you did," he shouts over her. "You always have a choice."

"No, no, Jonathon you don't understand. I did it for Hope."

A puzzled look appears on Jonathon's face. "What do you mean?"

"I did it for Hope." Nancy repeats. "I did it for my Hope. My daughter, Hope."

The puzzled look turns to disbelief. "Your Hope? Your daughter, Hope?" he repeats. "You have a daughter? Why didn't you ever tell me?" The look in his eyes makes Nancy understand his hurt.

As if the releasing of the secret she had been keeping, like a confession, unburdens her, her tears stop and she sits numb. It didn't matter anymore what Jonathon Weiss thought about her. It didn't matter that she had been duped by Harry. She didn't care what Clarence Williams or Homeland Security thought. She couldn't carry it any more. She is broken.

"Yes, I have a daughter. Her name is Hope. She has PML. She's at the Center. She is why the Center exists. The disease is in its final stage. Hope is being kept alive in a medically induced coma. . . while I work to find a way to save her."

The room is silent. The three of them drained of emotion and embarrassed by what they know.

Chapter 24

It is late in the day, Ted is tidying up his workspace so that he wouldn't come in tomorrow to an unorganized mess. He is surprised to see his boss pop his head into his office, it was not usual for him to still be here this late. "Hey, Ted," he says, "you have visitors downstairs, two guys from Homeland Security. They want to meet with you. Something up? You working on anything I should know about?"

Ted hesitates to think before answering, "No nothing out of the ordinary." Then thinking about the time, "They want to meet now – at 4:45?" he says with disgust.

"Yeah, right," his boss agrees, "like it couldn't wait until tomorrow? They said they want to talk to just you, so . . . I'm going to go. Catch me up in the morning – OK?"

"Sure, take off, I'll deal with them," he says with naïve confidence.

Ted finishes shutting down his computer, takes a quick look around makes sure the files that need to be locked away are put into a secure drawer – can't leave anything around that the cleaning crew could get their hands on – picks up his coat, hat, and briefcase and heads for the stairs. No sense having to come back up he thinks to himself. Hopefully this will be quick and I'll be able to get home on time.

The two agents are seated and casually chatting when he opens the door to the conference room. Ted steps toward the table and they stand, each extending their hand in turn as he introduces himself by simply stating his name. They exchange business cards. Ted leaves theirs on the table top, one to the left lined up with its owner and the same for the one on the right. He has a mind for numbers, not names.

His card has Ted Randolph printed on it, because that is what he is called, not Theodore, not Theodore Randolph II, just Ted. Homeland Security is a bit more formal, he assumes, Thomas is called Tom and William is called Bill, but their cards have their formal names. He glances down at their e-mail addresses, same darn thing, why would someone e-mail William.Agee@HomelandS.gov when you know the guy as Bill?

"What can I do for you gentlemen?" Ted opens the conversation.

"Mr. Randolph we are hoping you can help us with an investigation."

"OK, I'll try. Shoot."

"Have you done an investigation on a Nancy Glacieux?" Ted swallows hard before responding.

"Can you tell me what this is about?" which is more of a stall tactic than a real question, but the agents seemed willing to go with the flow.

"We can't reveal the nature of our investigation Mr. Randolph, however, suffice it to say we are interested in Ms. Glacieux and as your name came up in discussions with her. We naturally assumed that you had some dealings with her, perhaps audited her tax returns, might have found something out of the ordinary?"

"Well, I don't know why my name would have come up," Ted responds, loosening his now too tight collar, "To my knowledge the department hasn't done a formal investigation of Dr. Glacieux. Although we are a large organization, I can't speak for the whole department."

"So, then you are acquainted with her?" says agent Agee, "We didn't say she was a Doctor," said with a questioning and intimidating look. Ted notices for the first time how warm the room is and feels a drop of sweat drip down his side.

"Well, uh, yeah, I know Nancy Glacieux. She's my son's doctor. She has a facility over on Third" he admits nervously, "How did my name come up? Why are you guys investigating her? What is this about?" Ted had never opened up an 'official' investigation into Nancy's tax returns, as a matter of fact he had not even accessed her records since that one time months ago. Everything has been going fine. Christopher was getting great care. He was responding to the treatments. He has been better than he has been in ages. Ceci called him earlier in the day and said he could come home for Christmas.

"So, Randolph," the one called Tom says unpleasantly "you checking out your kid's doctor? I thought you guys had rules against that kind of thing?"

"Hey, hey, just wait now. Don't be jumping to any conclusions here. You guys came to see me, 'to help' your investigation, this ain't about me. Like I said, there is no investigation into Dr. Glacieux's taxes that I am aware of." Ted feels another drop of sweat slide down the side of his torso and then another in quick succession. His heart is now beating in his chest and he worries his blood pressure is going through the roof. Homeland Security, shit, he is thinking, what do these assholes want? This gets to his boss his ass is toast. He can feel his face flushing.

"Relax Randolph," Bill tries to calm him, "You're right, this isn't about you." He wants to make sure Ted doesn't just clam up on them. "We're interested in Glacieux, not you. And I don't give a rat's ass how you found out about her finances. We just need to know what you did find out."

"Is she in some kind of trouble?" Ted asks, finally realizing that he keeps asking questions that the agents don't answer. Homeland Security, this must be serious. What could she have done? What if they lock her up? What would happen to Chris? He wasn't giving these two sons of a bitch's anything.

"Look, Randolph," says Tom, "We can't tell you anything about our investigation. We would if we could," he lies, "But we can't. Now, why don't you protect yourself and tell us what you know. You don't want us coming back here with a warrant or having to subpoena you and making this into a big mess. Do you?"

"No, No, of course not," Ted chooses his words carefully. He is now thinking like Ted normally would, with self-preservation and a slyness that can get a guy in trouble. But he is not giving up Dr.

Glacieux, no way, no how, even if it cost him his job. "I'm not saying I did review her records. But I'm pretty sure you guys are here for a good reason. I mean, who would show up at five o'clock and poke around some Doctor's finances if there wasn't a good reason – right?" and he tries to coax them in with a laugh as if they are in cahoots. "But I've got to tell you, a doctor like her, again I wouldn't know for sure, but doctors like her, professionals, they get some fat-ass accounting firm to do their taxes, those babies are squeaky clean. We don't find anything on those. My guess is, she used one of the big boys to do her taxes, and there ain't a thing the Internal Revenue Service can do about it. Maybe if you guys find out something you can let us know," and he laughs again.

The agents give each other a knowing glance. They are done. They pushed Randolph, and if this weak, over-weight bureaucrat had any information he would have cracked. "Thank you for your time Mr. Randolph," Tom says as they rise in unison, shake his hand and head for the door.

Ted sits back down in the empty room. He clasps his hands and realizes that they are moist. The agents would have picked up on that. They probably figure he is guilty of something. What if they come back tomorrow he thinks? Rather than being relieved that they left, he is now more worried about what might happen. I'll go back upstairs, I'll call one of the IT guys, tell them I have a computer problem, get them to erase the memory. They will never be able to prove I accessed Glacieux's record. He glances at his watch, it's 5:20pm. No chance to catch one of them now. He continues to sit there while his mind goes through the various ways in which this could play out. His conscience takes this minor incident and blows it up to imagine major consequences. Guilt is like that, it stays with a person, eats at them, absorbs their thoughts and their time, makes them powerless. He continues to perspire and think about the ways in which he could cover his tracks. He could lie. It would be her word against his. No, no, he can't take that approach, he needs, we need Glacieux. Chris is doing well. I gotta keep her safe. What would happen to Chris if she can't continue the work at the Center? What then? 5:40 pm, cripes, I should have been home already. I can't do nothing tonight, the IT guys are gone. Let me get out of here. He picks up his stuff, shuts the light and heads out the lobby door. The wind whips his coat open and the stiff, cold breeze hits his body and a chill goes through him. He trots to car, throws the bag in and starts it. Not waiting for it to warm up, he puts it into gear and pulls out.

He drove for about a mile, still caught in his own deceit. Crap, I didn't call Ceci to tell her I would be late. She'll have dinner ready and would be expecting me. All she asks is that I call if I'm going to be late.

It is a tense evening at the Randolph residence. From the time he stomps into the house, Ted is a distracted mess. After the initial apology to Ceci and eating his warmed up dinner alone in the kitchen, he remains sullen and distant. Ceci has seen her husband in such a state before. She attributes it to an overworked, stressful day. Ted responds to her inquiries and the normal banter couples engage in with an abruptness sometimes sharp with sarcasm. Eventually, seeing that he is in his own world and considering the mood that he is in, she leaves him sitting alone in front of the TV and goes to bed.

Ted sits and continues to look blankly at the screen - neither watching nor listening he picks up the remote and searches for something that will capture his interest. He is glad Ceci went to bed. He realizes how inconsiderate he has treated her this evening. He is not himself, his conscience troubled, he took it out on her. He has recognized this tendency in the past. When unhappy with himself, he lashes out at her or even the boys, such a strange but human reaction to internal feelings. He is sure the psychologists have some arcane term they apply to it but he knows what it is. He gets up, goes to the cabinet where he keeps a bottle of bourbon and pours a half inch into his empty coffee cup, swirls it, then swallows it down in one long gulp, pours another half inch into the cup and heads back to the recliner. It is a guilty conscience, plain and simple. He is not happy with how he's treated her. It isn't her fault. She can't do anything to fix what he is dealing with but she received the brunt of his animosity because of it. I owe her an apology he thinks as he picks up the remote and finds a basketball game to watch until he can fall asleep.

Chapter 25

It is late morning by the time Clarence arrives back at the offices of Homeland Security. He had picked up a newspaper on the way, and although he had hoped for at least a day of preparation before the media onslaught, he is not entirely surprised that the story had leaked. A tag line on the front page ran - 'Terrorist Plot Uncovered – Suspect Being Held.' On page four, in a small quarter page story, they went ahead and printed whatever rumor or innuendo they could pry from their informants in law enforcement and wrote it in such a way as to entice their readers with hints of a major plot, even though they didn't have any concrete information. There were no quotes only vague 'sources confirm' type statements. Thankfully, they only indicated that Nancy's house was reported to having been broken into and that the village police turned the investigation over to Homeland Security. They will be on this like vultures today, he thinks to himself.

His fears are confirmed as he turns the corner and sees a handful of news vans lined along the curb on either side of the street near the Homeland Security office. He pulls his hat a bit tighter over his head in an attempt to shield his face and puts the newspaper up close to his eyes mimicking the look of one distracted, reading and walking simultaneously. He heads up the steps to the entrance careful to avoid eye contact with the roving media mob. He is nearly at the door when he hears someone call out, "That's Clarence Williams." There is a rush of movement tight about the entranceway, and for fear of being trampled, he cannot resist a furtive quick look to the right and left. Cameras are rolling and he hears a question called out just as he is at the door, "Mr. Williams, are you representing the terrorist?" With that unanswered question hanging in the air, he whisks through the turnstile and nods to the guard that is keeping the horde out.

He approaches the desk, signs in, and asks for Morris. Morris appears at the door that leads to the inner sanctum and calls out, "Counselor, I've been waiting for you. Banker's hours today?" smiles and waves him in.

"Late night," Williams mutters. "Anything new today?"

Morris looks down at his shoes. "No, we're still investigating."

"You're running out of time, my friend. Are you going to charge my client or release her?"

Morris leads the lawyer back to the same room he interviewed Nancy in last night, closes the door behind them and the two men stand and look at each other, both with the tired expression of men that have been doing their job for too long.

"You know how it is," he says. "We can't just let her go. This is a federal case. The boys in London have been on the phone all morning. I never said this, but as you can imagine there are political and social implications in this case." Clarence looks into Morris' eyes, sees the lines of stress in his face. Sees the same tiredness that he felt when he woke up this morning. "The Attorney General will be putting together a grand jury today. He's seeking an indictment."

"All right. Thanks for being straight. Can a guy get a cup of coffee around here?"

"Sure, how do you take it?" Morris responds.

"Light and sweet . . . like me," Williams responds with a grin. Morris laughs out loud.

"I'll have someone bring it. Give me a few minutes. I'll get your client too."

Clarence is glad to have a few minutes to collect his thoughts prior to seeing Nancy. The news from Morris is not totally unexpected. For that matter, it's mostly good news; he can tell from the way Morris explained that they have not found anything more that they can build a stronger case against Nancy with. Things remain as they were when he left last night.

The door opens and a bustling female enters balancing a steaming cup of coffee in one hand and working the door with the other, a few drops hang from the bottom of the Styrofoam. Obviously never been a waitress, Williams deduces. He wonders why, in real life, the women in law enforcement are never quite like the caricature that is portrayed on television. Every crime series, and there are many given society's fascination with crime and violence, have a team that invariably is either led by or consists of one or two females that look as if they could have been runway models but instead became strong, streetwise, hot, crime fighters. He can't recall one in real life that could have played that role.

"Mr. Williams," she says, "your coffee," and she places it on the table in front of him.

"Thank you," he says and she turns and quickly leaves.

Still, his mind now back on the case, there is enough for them to justify their actions. There had been only a slim hope that they would release her. They will bring what they have to a grand jury. She'll be indicted and likely charged with the broadly defined 'conspiracy to' catch-all. Legal blackmail is how he refers to such charges. He takes another sip, holds the cup and reaches down into his briefcase and fishes out a small creased napkin, flattens it and places it on the ring his cup made on the worn table, and sets the cup down on top. His thoughts shift to his client and he once more goes through what has become to him a plausible explanation of what happened; credible if she's telling the truth, the whole truth. A jury, if it goes that far, would be sympathetic to a mother with a dying child. Of everything, that one fact, the fact that there exists a real child that is near death, he believes would turn this case for them. The AG would play the tapes, incriminating yes, but we are not denying the fact that money was sent overseas. We purposely raised money with the intent to send it overseas, Nancy would have to admit to that. There is no reason to believe Nancy would have known that her ex, Hanif Nasrallah, a man that the government is closely watching, recruited young mercenaries for his cause. He did it without her knowledge. Actually, Clarence is impressed; this Nasrallah character played both sides against the middle. He got the money he needed to help pry the young zealots away from their families, ironically from rich Americans, and he got research subjects to help Nancy and his own daughter to boot, everyone was happy. Humph, he was even earning his way to heaven, if you can believe that. Yes, it would not be too hard to make him the bad guy in all this. The government's own surveillance would prove it.

The door opens again and Nancy steps in. She is now wearing the standard issue prisoner garb. In any other setting but this one she would still look good. The matching pants and long-sleeve pullover shirt, open around the neck, with a little imagination could pass for pajamas. It is as if she had just rolled over, yawned, and stepped out of bed. Clarence tells the female attendant to remove the cuffs which have her hands pinned together. Released, he gives Nancy a wink and asks for another coffee and water with two glasses to be brought to them.

"Mr. Williams, they will bring you coffee?" she asks. "Jonathon was right, you are a good lawyer." Clarence laughs. "How is Jonathon?" she follows up with before he can think to say anything.

"We talked for a while last night after we left you. Actually, stopped and had a few drinks. He'll be OK. As you could tell, he was upset, felt used. He'll come around. He admires you greatly. He's your friend," and after a short pause he repeats to reassure her. "He'll come around. How are you? Did you sleep some? I suppose they fed you?"

"I didn't sleep much. You know, the sheets here are a little light on the thread count." They both laugh at her attempt at humor. "And the coffee, well, it's better than nothing, but surely no reason to stay around. What do you think is going to happen now?" she asks.

Clarence takes the time to explain what he expects to happen, and indicates she will likely have another full day behind bars before they get to go before the judge and request bail. Bail could be tricky, it might be substantial. A lot will depend on which judge is given the case. He further explains that he expects the government will push the case against her for all it is worth. While he believes that she had no knowledge of the training that went on at the facility in Chad, and that a jury would agree as well, the government will not just drop the charges against her. They will have to fight this. "We'll win," he says confidently, "but we will have to fight. I don't think this is going away. On top of that, we have the media to deal with. They are going to be all over this. There was a crowd outside this morning. And here look," he passes her the paper, open to page four. "I've got to think about this a bit more. We'll have to manage the media very carefully."

Nancy sits contemplating everything he told her. The door opens again and a man who looks like a custodian brings in a pitcher of water and two glasses. He is followed immediately by the same female officer who places the additional coffee on the table, nearer to Clarence, and they leave together. Clarence passes the coffee over to Nancy, who begins sipping it immediately.

"So," she says, still holding the cup up in both hands, near her mouth, "Even though the money was being used for something I had no control over, they will still charge me with conspiracy? Conspiracy to commit terrorism?" Clarence nods. "That's bullshit. Total bullshit," she lashes out, not hiding her anger. A weaker woman would have been crying at this point but not Nancy. She's done crying. Now she's fighting back.

"OK Clarence, let's win this thing," she says. "Is there any way we can keep out the fact that we used healthy subjects in Chad; that and about Hope. Can we keep her out of this?"

Clarence gives her a grimace. "That's not going to be easy," he says. "Concerning Hope, you don't get off without bringing her into the mix. It..." and here he hesitates before continuing, "It speaks to motive. There has to be a reason for your actions that makes sense to the judge and potentially to a jury. I don't think you get off without her."

"I've never used her, Clarence. In all the time the research has been going on. I never used the fact that I had a sick child to gain sympathy or guilt people into giving money. Never."

"I understand. That speaks well to your character, but the game has changed. It's your only defense." Clarence responds. "Now concerning the healthy subjects, it's possible, but if we don't bring it up ourselves, if we don't tell the whole truth, we run the risk of being asked outright and then it looks like we are hiding something. I wouldn't recommend it."

"But what about the work?" she pleads. "Clarence, this will destroy the work. No one will donate. I won't be able to do more research. I won't, I won't even be able to keep the Center open here in the city. I have to figure out a way to keep Hope alive." Clarence finds and hands over his handkerchief and she blots her teary eyes with it.

"Right now, we have to think about getting you exonerated. We don't have a lot of options, Nancy. Our backs are to the wall. Besides, the truth is important. You know the old saying, 'the truth will set you free.' We need to go with the truth. The rest will work itself out."

Chapter 26

It is well after noon by the time they have discussed everything they needed to. Not only did they discuss the case, but how to handle the media, what to say and what not to say, and the more subtle aspects of a high profile case as well, her clothes, how she should wear her hair, make-up. In a word - image. Clarence ordered and had delivered two sandwiches from a nearby deli. They eat lunch in the small conference room and stop strategizing long enough to finish the impromptu meal.

As they stuff the wrappers and remains into the paper deliver bag Clarence outlines his plans to go to the Center. Nancy gives him a message for her assistant. She tells him Karl is someone he can trust. Clarence let's her know he will be speaking to the head nurse and will address the staff, answer questions, essentially reassure everyone. When they come to take Nancy back to her cell she turns toward him and gives him a heartfelt 'thank you,' a quick peck on the cheek, and a polite hug, the kind you might expect if you saw an old friend of the opposite sex or someone you knew from church. He liked that, not the kiss per se, but the warm friendliness. It is a bit odd for him to feel so comfortable so quickly with someone he hardly knows. As she approaches the door she turns toward him and says, "Oh, Clarence, find out how my mom is doing – please."

"Sure. I've got to make a few calls before I get going. If there is anything new, I'll leave you word." She smiles in thanks as she goes.

He speaks to Morris before he leaves, checking to see if there is any new information. There is none. The grand jury has been assembled downtown and the Attorney General is going to begin presenting information within the hour. "Thanks," Clarence says. "How can I get out of here without using the front door?" Morris nods, knowing what is waiting for Williams outside and willing to assist him in avoiding the clamoring scene.

"Follow me," he says. "This will bring you out onto the side street."

"Great, I appreciate that." The two men walk silently through the halls, down a set of emergency stairwells and with a key that silences the alarm, Morris opens a door that lets Clarence out directly onto the sidewalk. The two men part with nothing further.

He arrives at the Center for Hope and is surprised to see a uniformed security guard outside. As he approaches, the guard walks forward to meet him and asks his name and the nature of his visit. A polite, "Thank you, sir," and he steps aside to allow Clarence to continue toward the door. "You'll need to sign in and show identification at the door," is the forewarning; he reaches for his walkie-talkie.

A second guard is stationed just inside the entranceway. Clarence is greeted with, "Good afternoon, Mr. Williams. If I could just see your identification and have you sign in please, sir."

As he complies, he hears Jonathon's voice call out, "Clarence." Near the front desk, wearing a sheepish grin and what looks like yesterday's evening clothes, is his friend waving him over. He approaches and Jonathon moves to greet him. "I hope you don't mind. I knew you would be tied up this morning with Nancy. I took the liberty of arranging for some security for the Center, you know, to keep the vultures out." While surprised, Clarence is glad - one less thing for him to do today. Besides, if he made the call it probably wouldn't have been until tomorrow that someone would have shown up and he would have thought to get only one guard, not two.

"No. No, Jonathon. This is great. We need security here," he says.

"The feds were here this morning. Luckily, we got here a few minutes before they did. I woke up Thomas Moore, one of the staff guys from my office. Again, I hope you don't mind, it would have been havoc if they just marched right in."

191

"No, you're right. Having Tom here must have been a great help." Clarence says. He knew Tom; a competent, levelheaded guy.

"Yeah, it sure was. He held them up a bit. Set them up in a conference room out of the way. Brought files to them instead of having them just walk all over the place – it's just another normal day at the Center as far as the kids are concerned."

"Great Jonathon, thank you. You OK? Didn't get a chance to change?"

Jonathon laughs. "Let's keep that between us. I didn't sleep. I've been up all night and once I got my mind moving in the right direction I knew there were some things I could help with this morning. So, here I am, security guards and lawyer in tow." He laughs again. "How is she? What is happening?"

"She's fine. The AG is presenting to a grand jury as we speak. They will indict her. They won't have their act together before the end of the day, so it looks like bail will be set until tomorrow."

"What do you think of their case? Jonathon asks.

"They'll use the broad 'conspiracy to' doctrine. It's all they've got. Still, it's serious. I think we'll win but it isn't a cakewalk. The AG will dig his heals in. I'm sure of that. A lot will depend on which judge we draw, some of them can be real S.O.B.'s."

"Well, be sure to let me know who it is, as soon as you know. Agreed?"

"Yeah, sure thing. Jonathon, why don't you go catch a few winks? I'll take over here now. I'll call you later."

"OK, I could use a nap, I'm pretty shot." Before Jonathon turns to go he says, "Thank you, Clarence. Really. I appreciate you taking the case, old buddy."

"No problem, but you may not be so happy when you see my bill." He gives him a playful shot to the arm. "Go get some sleep. I'll call you when I know something."

Clarence looks for, and finds, the head nurse, Ms. Clement. She had spoken to Jonathon earlier and is already filling the role of spokesperson/morale builder. The staff is very loyal, and will act in the best interest of the children, Nancy, and the organization, Ms. Clement is sure of that. He asks to address the small team there now and inquires about the shift change and requests her to set-up that meeting as well. They part and she directs him through the medical staff doors and into the office area.

He finds Karl at his desk, looking distracted and worried. After greetings and introductions they move to Nancy's office and speak in hushed tones. Clarence makes sure Karl understands the seriousness of the situation and that he is a friend and ally to Nancy. Above all, he stresses that as her lawyer, he needs the full and complete truth to be able to represent her well. Karl expresses his desire to help in any way he can and encourages Clarence to call on him at any time if he needs anything from anyone at the center.

Formalities aside, Clarence asks Karl a few questions to see how forthcoming he would be and attempts to verify that Nancy is indeed telling the whole truth. Karl is candid and direct. Clarence is surprised that Karl seems to completely understand the operation there. Nancy is right, he is loyal; he is not afraid to take the stand if that becomes necessary and Clarence surmises he would be a good witness. His obvious dislike and mistrust of Harry seem to be well founded and he can relate the change he has seen in Harry and can recite a number of odd, potentially inflammatory things he had said over the phone in the recent past. Yes, Karl will be a good witness. He knows all the intimate details of the research operation, knows some of the recruits in Chad are healthy and arguably would have known if Nancy had any alternative motives as well. Now sure of what he is dealing with, Clarence gives Karl his first mission. He is to go to Nancy's home and get what she needs to dress for court tomorrow. He passes Karl the list, which he looks once over and then promptly puts away. Clarence thinks it a bit odd that this young fellow would not flinch over picking up his bosses' outfit or that Nancy would be as comfortable as she seems to be with it too. She had even written down accessories, jewelry, make-up, and handbag. She had confidence that Karl would know which items she was referring to. He passes Karl his card with instructions to contact him immediately if there is any problem.

Karl says, "You can count on me, Mr. Williams." Then he comes to a slack military attention and snaps him an informal salute before he spins on his heels and is out the door like a soldier on a mission.

"Oh, Karl," Clarence calls out before he can get away, "Tell Nancy there is nothing new on her mother. She's still in the hospital, but resting comfortably."

"Yes, sir," he says, and he is gone.

Clarence calls Morris and informs him about Karl needing access to the house. Before he gets off the phone he asks, "Anything new?"

"Yeah," Morris says. "It's conspiracy. Conspiracy to aid and abet terrorism."

"Just the one charge?"

"Yep, just the one. The AG is going to make a statement in time to catch the evening news."

"OK, what about the judge? Who's going to get it?"

"Hudson. He's a hard liner," Morris says.

"Got it, thanks." Clarence hangs up and immediately calls Jonathon, who picks up on the first ring. From the sound of his voice Clarence can tell he had been sleeping.

Clarence just has time to meet with the second shift staff that is coming on and get back to the offices of Homeland Security. He will need to make a statement counteracting the AG's and be available for questions from the media.

Chapter 27

Now weary, Clarence forces himself to focus on preparing his statement to the press. He knows the cameras will be rolling - he will need to give them a useable sound bite - something that takes the spotlight off Nancy. The public needs to doubt the truth of the Attorney General's accusation.

He is glad to walk the two blocks in the stiff breeze from the parking garage. As he nears the building he sets his face to brave the onslaught. He approaches the long set of steps and the media spots him. The horde heads his way. They dart for position, some with microphones in hand, others supporting cameras equipped with lights on their shoulders. They swarm about him like yellow jackets on a can of soda set out in the sun. He isn't about to stop now; that would be a mistake. He plans to make his statement after the AG. He puts his hand out in front of him, a running back preparing to stiff arm a tackler and keeps his legs moving. "No comment," he shouts above the hurled questions that come from several mouth pieces. "No comment." The crowd moves with him as he ascends the steps and nears the door. Just before he steps through he turns and hesitates. "I'll comment after we hear what the Attorney General has to say." This is important to get out. He doesn't want them running off without getting a chance to get his version of the story told.

As he enters, he can tell that preparations are being made for the Attorney General's statement. There are a number of uniformed officers and plain clothed agents mulling about the lobby. He spies Morris by the door that leads into the inner offices and catches his eye. He's waved in.

"Boy, this is some circus," Williams says as way of greeting.

"I've seen worse," Morris rejoins. "He should be out in a few minutes. They're just making him pretty for the cameras."

"Yep, the defense is always at a disadvantage. I don't suppose they would put some make-up on this old face?" he jokes.

"You don't look so bad," Morris responds cheerfully, as he makes like he is giving him the once over.

The Attorney General approaches the doorway with an entourage. His blue pin-striped suit is tailored to fit, with a stiff white collared shirt. His tie is held in place by a gold tie bar. He walks with a sense of confidence. His jet black hair, surprising because he is about Clarence's age, is combed neatly off his forehead and sprayed stiff to circumvent the wind outside. If he didn't know better, Clarence would have thought some 1920's gangster was approaching. All that's missing is a pair of black and white spats and a guy holding an ill-shaped guitar case. Morris whispers, "Show time."

The uniformed officers go first, followed by the appropriately jacketed agents. They establish a cleared semi-circle out on the entranceway. The combined lighting from the assortment of shoulder held cameras give the appearance of a Hollywood award show. The Attorney General steps forward into the spotlight. One microphone is set up to amplify his voice so that all can hear him. As the crowd settles in anticipation, he removes a prepared statement from his breast pocket.

"Today I am pleased to announce that we have in custody Nancy Glacieux, a U.S. citizen and New York resident that will be charged with conspiracy to aid and abet terrorism." This information causes a deeper hush to come over the crowd. Clarence knows it's due to the unexpected residency and citizenship of his client – no one expects to hear such things about one of their own. The AG goes on uninterrupted. "While I am not at liberty to provide specific details of the case, we have confirmed information obtained from a terrorist captured just prior to exploding a bomb in London that Dr. Glacieux is materially involved. It appears she provided funds to a terrorist training camp under the ruse of doing medical research. She will officially be indicted and charged tomorrow morning." Although he goes on for a minute or two more, offering gratuitous comments about the NYPD, Homeland Security, and the international cooperation between nations, he really has nothing of substance to say. He doesn't take any questions, thanks them and turns to exit, followed by the agents and uniformed personnel.

Clarence immediately steps into the void. The crowd, no longer held back, and with the amplifier cut, thrust forward, jockeying once again for position. He wouldn't have been able to hold his ground except for the support he feels from behind. Morris quickly steps around and with just enough violent force and a menacing look, pushes back those that had surrounded Clarence.

"Step back!" he shouts above the din of questions. "Step back, I say!" and they obey, giving up some ground to the agent. Clarence, relieved, takes the initiative now that there is a quick moment of quiet and stillness.

"Doctor Nancy Glacieux is guilty of no such thing," he says loudly into the nearest microphone. "This is America where people are innocent until proven guilty. Dr. Glacieux is victim of an ambitious Attorney General that seeks headlines above the truth."

A question shoots out, "Mr. Williams, are you saying the Attorney General is lying?"

"That's for you folks to decide. All I'm saying is Dr. Glacieux is innocent of these charges. Of this I am sure."

"Mr. Williams, how can you be sure? Do you have any evidence?"

"Well, I'm not about to give information away to the AG. But you in the news media know what I stand for. I'm not about to let someone's civil rights get trampled by an overzealous bunch of law enforcement officers and bureaucrats. Mark my words. This is completely trumped up – sensationalism, that's what it is – sensationalism - pure and simple. Thank you folks for your time, I've got a case to prepare for."

Clarence turns and heads directly for the door, Morris at his back. "Thank you, Hank. I wasn't talking about you back there. That got a little scary," he says to Morris as they enter. "Thank you."

Morris wasn't even sure that Williams knew his first name. "No problem, Clarence. Someone could have gotten hurt. Just doing my overzealous job." He slaps him on the back and laughs out loud as he leaves him in the lobby, calling out over his shoulder, "I'll have them get your girl. It'll take a few minutes."

Clarence is again relieved to have a few moments to collect his thoughts. He can see out the lobby window in the dimming lights the various news agencies conducting their 'wrap-up' reports with the 'on-the-scene' reporter. He calls the office and his wife picks up. "Honey, be sure to catch the six o'clock news. I need to know how this is being played out in the media." He is under no delusion. The terrorism arrest, especially right here in New York City, will draw top billing.

"Mr. Williams," he is being called from the desk agent.

"I gotta go," he says into the phone. "Love you. Talk to you tonight. I shouldn't be too late," and he slips the phone in his jacket pocket as he goes to see his client.

Nancy is seated at the opposite side of the table. She's lost the disheveled, pajama look. Hair brushed, her skin tone restored, a little color around the eyes. It's no wonder that Jonathon is taken with her. "Nancy, are you OK?" he says and sits opposite her.

"Oh, just fine, all things considered, Mr. Williams," is her response. "Karl came by with some of my things. Thank you for arranging that. What is going on?"

Clarence explains all that transpired from the time he left her earlier today, this culminating in the staged announcement for the benefit of the media. Nancy takes it all in, asking only a few brief questions about the circumstances at the Center. He has barely finished when she asks, "So, what's our next step?"

"We'll appear before the federal judge tomorrow, I expect around 11 am. It's just the arraignment. The thing in question is going to be bail. I'll petition for a release on your own recognizance, but I'm not sure the judge will go along with that. The Attorney General will ask for something large. I really don't know how it will go." He hesitates at this point and takes a breath. "How are you situated? I mean, if bail is set, how much cash can you get your hands on right away? I don't mean to pry, it's just that . . . if we have a target in mind I can try to . . ."

"It's OK. I've thought about this. I don't have a lot of cash. Most of what I had went into getting the research center up and running. The house is mortgaged out. I had to, there was no choice, but if I liquidate a retirement account I've held onto, I could come up with a hundred, a hundred thousand. Do you think that will be sufficient?"

"Let's hope so," Clarence responds. "Who else could help, your folks?"

"They're retired, Clarence," Nancy says. "They would give whatever they have but they were always working-class people. I can't imagine there is much savings. They live mostly on whatever social security they get, you know?"

"Yes, I see," Clarence answers. "What about Jonathon?" She just shakes her head side to side. "I could ask him for you," he offers.

"No. I can't ask Jonathon for money. It wouldn't be right. Besides, he has his reputation to consider. How would it look? It's bad enough he helped me raise money for the Center, and now he puts up bail for an accused terrorist? No, he needs to distance himself from me Clarence. You tell him I said so." There's such finality and conviction in her voice that he does not brooch the subject again.

"I understand," he says, "Well then, let's hope for the best. So, do you have any other questions? Are you OK for tomorrow? Karl brought you everything you need?" Having received the assurances he sought from his client, he stands to leave and looks directly at her. "It's going to be OK. Try not to worry. Get some sleep. I'll see you tomorrow in court."

She smiles softly. "Thank you, Clarence."

Again outside, the wind having cleared out all evidence of the prior media event, Clarence is glad he does not have to deal with any additional prying questions or have another camera thrust in his face. He waits until he arrives at the garage and closes himself in his car, shutting out the noise of the wind, to check his messages. There is one from Jonathon, so he calls back.

"How are you holding up?" Jonathon answers cheerfully.

"Fine. Thanks for asking. Did you see the AG's press conference?" Clarence asks.

"Yes, he's quite a showman," Jonathon responds.

"I spoke to the group after he cleared out. Did we get any air?"

"Not a word my friend. I caught two of the networks, not a word on either."

"Damn them," Clarence mutters. "Unfair bastards. All they care about is a good headline."

"Well, don't be too hard on them, Clarence. They have ratings to worry about. I'm guessing the eleven o'clock news will be more of the same." He takes a breath before asking, "Are you up for a few short interviews? I know some people in the media biz. I'm sure we could get a few lines in the morning papers."

"Sure thing, if you think it will work. Give them my cell number. I'll keep it handy all night," Clarence responds.

"OK, expect a call or two. What is going to happen tomorrow?" Clarence goes through what he expects, the uncertainty of the bail situation and is able to work in Nancy's concern that Jonathon create some distance between him and her work.

"That's just like her," Jonathon says. "Worried about someone else before herself. She does make some sense though doesn't she Clarence?"

"Yes, Jonathon. She sure does."

"OK, well, I have a few calls to make. Let me know if there is something else I can do."

"Right, I'll talk to you soon." Clarence sets the phone down on the seat next to him in case of a call.

By the time he arrives home it is nearly eight. His wife meets him at the door, gives him a kiss, and helps him off with his coat and scarf.

He can tell from her look that she has bad news for him. "I know. I know. We didn't get any air time" he says to her.

"Sorry, honey. I'm sure you did the best you could. You can't force them to give both sides," she answers. "Come. I have some dinner saved for you."

As they walk arm in arm toward the kitchen, his cell phone rings. "Dinner is going to have to wait, sweetie," he says to her. "I've got to take this call."

Chapter 28

Morning comes too quickly for Clarence Williams. He wakes to the sound of his wife clattering about the kitchen. That means two things: one - that he slept too late; and two - she's making breakfast. She is a good woman. After some thirty odd years he loves her more today than the day they got married. He has grown comfortable with who she is, choosing to overlook the inevitable annoying habits that surface over a lifetime, focusing instead on what makes her special. He is fortunate; her goodness displays itself in many ways and makes her easy to love. He sometimes wonders why she chose to love him and why she still does? A bigger noise comes from the kitchen and he rises with a tired body but with a smile on his face.

"Good morning, honey," he says and he sneaks close to her to give her a soft peck on the cheek and she turns toward him with a warm smile.

"Coffees' ready. Do you want toast or an English muffin with your eggs?"

"English muffin please," he answers while pouring himself a cup. He shuffles to the kitchen table, sits in his usual place, and reaches for the newspaper.

Terror Suspect Being Held
Local Doctor Funding Muslim Terrorists

Clarence reads each word of the short, page one, lead in with the blaring headline and quickly turns to where it is continued on page five. Fairly predictable, it has no facts, just conjecture and a few quotes, one from the Attorney General, one from an unnamed source within Homeland Security, and one from the local Village office that had originally responded to Nancy's call about the break-in at her home. There is a picture of the AG giving his statement at last night's press conference, another smaller one of Nancy, apparently clipped from some society page gala. Just below is another smaller headline.

Civil Rights Attorney to Defend Suspected Terrorist

There is a head shot of him, taken quite a few years ago, with his name printed underneath along with a pretty fair rendition of the points he made during his phone interview last night. "Well, what do you know?" he says aloud. "That son of a bitch wasn't kidding."

Bonnie Williams turns around at that comment and says, "Watch your mouth now. Who wasn't kidding?"

"Jonathon. He set up those phone interviews last night and look," he turns the page toward her so she can see the proof. "We got some print in the Times." Clarence laughs out loud with childish glee.

"Jonathon is a powerful man in this city Clarence and as you well know - a good man. You shouldn't talk about him like that. Here, eat this," she says as she slides a plate with eggs, hash browns, and sausage in front on him.

Clarence, still grinning ear to ear, continues scanning the newspaper and says without looking up, "Thank you, honey. This looks good."

An hour later, showered, dressed, goatee trimmed, he settles behind the desk of his home office. He is happy. Bonnie had run out and picked up the other two city newspapers, and although a bit more sensational than the relatively staid Times, they too, added his comments about the proceeding. It appears the Attorney General may have ruffled a few feathers along the way to power. His suggestion that the AG was simply using this for self-promotion was given adequate notice. One article dug up two older cases in which the AG similarly announced charges with grand flair only to see the accused go free once the facts were brought to light.

"Clarence!" Bonnie calls out from the den. A morning news show is splashed across the screen, "You're on TV!" He scrambles to get there and is just in time to catch the end of the video clip of him answering questions on the steps of the Homeland Security building; video the nightly newscasts had ignored. 'Son of a bitch,' he thinks to himself. "Well, I'll be," he utters out loud for the benefit of his wife as he heads back to the office to prepare for this morning's arraignment.

****

It is a packed house. It's the largest courtroom of the federal complex and still there isn't a seat to be had. Clarence had arrived about twenty minutes prior, milled about outside the courtroom rubbing elbows and killing time with the lawyers and court employees that he knows, entering the court room a mere five minutes before the judge is scheduled to begin the hearing. He doesn't like the sitting around and the bland small talk that's required between adversaries, and as such, he generally stays outside until just before the action begins. Judge Hudson commences the proceeding precisely at 11:00 a.m., gives a stern warning to the assembled crowd, and asks the bailiff to bring in the defendant.

Clarence generally likes Judge Hudson. He is a no-nonsense kind of guy, direct but polite, firm but fair. He has a good grasp of the law and as such doesn't care for the tinkering, demonstrativeness, and delaying tactics that often goes on within the hallowed halls of justice. Nancy is escorted in and a hush overwhelms the crowded courtroom. She walks with head erect, not smiling but with a serene expression. She does not look around as if scared or inquisitive. Clarence watches her intently as she enters. Nancy exudes a sort of clean sophistication in the way she carries herself, the way her hair is arranged and how the minimal make-up masks any appearance of distress or worry. She casts a furtive glance at Clarence who, when their eyes meet, notes an almost imperceptible upturn of the corners of her mouth in recognition. She is more the doctor than the prisoner, surely not the look of an accused terrorist, only the setting and the handcuffs mar her entrance.

Hudson strikes the gavel in the still and quiet courtroom to get the attention focused back on the proceeding. "Bailiff, read the charge against the defendant."

"Nancy Glacieux, you are hereby charged with conspiracy to aid and abet terrorism."

Hudson follows up with a terse, "How do you plead?"

"I am not guilty," rings out clear and distinct from Nancy, right on top of Clarence's, "Not guilty, Your Honor."

The crowd hears her clear declaration. Judge Hudson smiles at the confusion, and directing his attention to Clarence says, "Well, Counselor, I'm glad you and your client agree on the plea." Clarence continues to face the judge but his eyes slip toward Nancy who cringes in an apologetic manner. "There is the question of bail. The prosecution has made the case that Ms. Glacieux is a flight risk. She has the means and it appears a known accomplice has been able to circumvent apprehension and is believed to have left the country. I'm inclined to agree with that assessment. Therefore, bail is set at one million dollars cash, two million dollars bond." Nancy makes an audible gasp. Clarence, while taken back by the severe amount, is ready to appeal.

"Your Honor," he begins, "the defense would ask you to reconsider. We petition the court to release Dr. Glacieux on her own recognizance. She is an upstanding member of the local community, has family and home here in the city. She is in charge of a major research center that cares for a number of seriously ill children that depend on her. Furthermore, if that isn't enough, she is innocent of these charges and looks forward to being vindicated by this court."

The judge keeps his eyes on Clarence but does not immediately respond, the appearance of which indicates that he is giving the matter serious thought. After what appears to be an eternity, but in reality is less than a minute, he simply responds, "Motion denied," strikes the gavel to quiet the murmuring and says, "The defendant will be held until such time as bail is posted."

For the first time that morning Nancy looks around at the assembly. The mass appear as faceless forms to her mind, she searches only for recognition amongst the crowd. Her eyes rest briefly on Karl's face, then to the extreme left she sees her brother moving across the first row and toward where Clarence is standing.   He gets the attention of a guard, pointing toward Clarence's back as he moves forward.   He holds a piece of paper in his outstretched hand. She expected to see her father but he doesn't appear to be in the courtroom. The guard takes the paper from David, taps Clarence on the shoulder to get his attention, and passes him the note. Clarence opens the folded sheet and quickly skims the contents. Nancy sees his eyebrows rise and with a queer look he addresses Judge Hudson.

"Your Honor, may I approach the bench?"

Upon receiving a quizzical nod of the head from the judge he quickly skirts around the table and rushes up, paper in hand which he passes up, directly to the jurist. Judge Hudson takes considerable more time to review the document, at one point placing his tongue to one side of his mouth like a small boy deciding what to say to his mother's query, so much so that a bulge appears on his cheek. The murmur in the crowded courtroom rises to the point of bother. He strikes the gavel and says, "Settle down." Looking up at the prosecution table he doggedly admits, "It appears bail has been made."

"Your Honor," the prosecution begins to complain.

Judge Hudson merely holds up his hand to stop and the prosecutor holds his tongue. The courtroom is abuzz again. He strikes the gavel. "Settle down. Mr. Williams, you may return to your table." When all is settled he looks over the courtroom and focuses on the adversaries, Clarence at one table, the prosecution, a trio of the best men the Attorney General could muster, at the other. "Gentlemen," he begins, "On the one hand, this is a serious case. Yet from what I see of the evidence presented to the grand jury, simple on the other. There is no need to prolong the period in which we bring this to a conclusion. I have another case that is being mediated and will reach settlement in the next day or two and have room on my docket. Therefore, this court will hear your arguments against this defendant," and at this point he appears to be looking down at a calendar. "One week from today."

Both sides begin to raise objection.   Judge Hudson once again raises his hand motioning to stop; his look betrays his mood and inflexibility on this point. "Serious, but simple, counselors. If you can't pull it together in a week just throw your law degrees into the fire. This courtroom is dismissed." He strikes the gavel once more, stands and walks out quickly without further discussion.

Chapter 29

A few days pass. It's the weekend. Nancy feels as if she is under house arrest. Photographers and reporters lurk everywhere. The TV is filled with news that pretends to have a unique angle on what has happened. Late night specials, early morning chatter, talk show jibes; her life has become a spectacle. It's early morning, snow is falling, and if not for the circumstance she finds herself in, it would be peaceful. Today it only makes her feel more separated from the world, more shut in.

She had been to see her mom in the hospital and had visited the Center to speak to the staff. Jonathon and Clarence saw that she was protected on these jaunts. A car with a driver was provided for her. She was met at each location by a pair of burly bodyguards; no one got into her circle. There are still four days to go; they need to be back in court Wednesday morning.

She thinks about the visit to the hospital, her mother awake and aware but weak, thinner, and aged in the short few days that have passed. Her father sat by the bed, at her side, his presence comforting to them both. Nancy could not stay long and although they did not speak of the case, each not wanting to be a burden to her mother, her father rose and walked her to the door as she was leaving.

"Dad, I can't thank you enough," she said to him. He only smiled. "How did you ever come up with that kind of bail?"

He smiled again, "Let's just say your mother must have prayed and an angel was sent to watch over you. Let's leave it at that. Don't you worry, just help Mr. Williams clear this mess up. We'll put this behind us. You'll put this behind you. Trust me, this will pass," and with that gave her a gentle kiss on her forehead before he turned back to sit at his wife's bedside.

****

Saturday evening, on the other side of town, the rich and the powerful gather at Lincoln Center. It's a benefit concert, by invitation only, the black tie and designer gown crowd. Judge Stanley Hudson was pleasantly surprised the day before when his colleague, Judge Brian Devereux, visited him and handed him an invitation, urging him to attend. He said the ticket was already paid for; a ticket intended for his brother, who unfortunately, had been called away on business. It would go to waste.

As Judge Hudson strolls through the reception area, he is keenly aware of the scattered conversations taking place around him. Frequently, he overhears bits and pieces of what can only be chatter about his case.

"It's ridiculous. How could she not know what was going on?"

"I heard William gave her a sizable contribution."

"Jonathon Weiss must be mortified."

Truth is, Stanley Hudson is a bit out of his element. He is a modest person, conducts his life simply. He is not ostentatious. Since his divorce he doesn't go out much, choosing to throw himself into his work. He continues to stroll through the crowd, martini in one hand, occasionally picking up a delectable snack being circulated by very young ladies with very tight shirts, each with exactly two buttons open and fairly short skirts, dressed all in black. He has to remind himself that any one of these young women could be a friend of his daughter's. Worse than that, she is away at school and does a bit of part-time catering work for pocket money herself. She could be here, dressed like this too. There is something unsettling about the whole thing.

Judge Hudson wants to be sure to thank Brian for his kindness and is glad to see his friend walking towards him.

"Stan, good to see you. Glad you could make it."

"Brian, thank you so much for the ticket. I very much enjoyed the initial set, and the food is fine, my martini just right." He raises the glass and strikes it against his colleague's in a mock toast.

"My pleasure, partner. We bachelors have to stick together. You'll notice there is a bit of the old 'eye candy' about. It's worth getting all dussied up in these monkey suits just for a bit of that, aye?" Both men smile in agreement. "Ah, look old friend, at three o'clock, in the shimmering blue dress." Stanley shifts his eyes to the proper clock position and picks out the tall, thin blond seemingly headed their way. He can't help but think about the old song with the refrain, 'Devil with the blue dress, blue dress on . . .'.

Brian calls her over, waving his arm and raising his voice above the din. "Monica, Monica, over here." As she approaches he continues, "How are you dear? You get more beautiful every time I see you." Then turning towards Stan, "This is my friend, Stanley, Judge Stanley Hudson. Stan, this is Monica Moore." They exchange an appraising look with a weak handshake, accompanied with the polite,

"How do you do?"

"Pleasure to meet you."

Stanley can't help but have his eyes drawn to the long necklace gently swaying between her breasts. "Judge Hudson, I've seen your picture in the paper. So, you're the man that is going to keep our city safe from the terrorists," she says.

Stanley doesn't know quite how to respond but after a second decides to just be playful and says, "Well, someone has to do it."

"Yes, underneath that tuxedo he has a big S on his chest," Brian chirps in.

With that, the lights flicker indicating the second half of the program is about to begin. Brian excuses himself to run to the rest room. Monica stays with Stanley, takes his arm and chats gaily as they follow the flow of the crowd back towards the auditorium. They take seats next to each other and Stanley finds himself glad to have this attentive and attractive creature so near.

Throughout the rest of the program they whisper together as newly introduced friends might. He is in unfamiliar territory. When she turns to speak to him she is quite near. He can smell her perfume and feel her warm breath on his ear as they make every effort to be polite to those around them. When it is his turn to speak he does the same, the advantage of this being he can look at her without meeting her eyes. More than once, she touches the side of his arm with her hand as she speaks. She has her legs crossed as she sits, her stocking leg exposed, her foot bobbing up and down with her shoe dangling loose off her heel, held in place only by the toe hold. Normally an ardent listener of fine classical music, he barely hears the notes, his thoughts turn from the music to his new friend.

When the program ends they remain seated and let the bulk of the crowd worm its way out before they stir. She ropes her arm through his as they walk out of the venue. Again feeling awkward, Stanley does not know exactly what to do or say; he is too polite a man to assume too much. After all, they just met. He searches his mind for the right words. What do girls today expect, he ponders? They had already established that they both had a car in the parking garage, so there would be no need to share a ride home. Unsure of himself but not wanting the night to end, he makes a desperate suggestion as they near the door. "How about a nightcap?"

She makes a mock look of surprise and says, "I thought you'd never ask. Perhaps just one. I know of a nice place, quite nearby. Follow me, Your Honor."

They make a left out the door and walk about a block before they come to an upscale bar, the kind one would expect in this neighborhood. It is dimly lit, the outer edge of the room made up of small, two-person booths and the occasional circular one designed to handle a small group. The bar is across the room, busy. Two bartenders work feverishly to keep up, literally all the chairs are taken and other patrons stand behind them either in conversation or crowding in, seeking a drink. They take a small booth. Stanley looks around the room as they settle in. It appears to be full with guests from the show, many of the ladies are dressed for the event and the men, still in black tie. He half hopes someone he knows will notice him. Monica makes a stunning appearance. He thinks wouldn't it be grand if one of his ex-wife's friends saw him? He continues to scan the faces even as he gives her the attention she demands. Unfortunately, most of the crowd is a bit blurry. Still vain, he isn't wearing his glasses; sitting this close to her they aren't necessary. He is beginning to feel conscious of his age, hairline receding, graying. He often thinks that perhaps his time has passed. It's not fair really, he deals with women surely older than he every day and they have an advantage. They use make-up to appear younger, that and the fact that they retain their hair, along with spending money on keeping the gray out, it surely isn't fair; even an old barn looks better with a fresh coat of paint. Sitting here with Monica makes him feel like a younger man. Yes, it would be great if someone he knew saw him here with her.

The waitress comes around and he realizes he hadn't thought about what to drink. Gladly, she turns to Monica first who orders an Irish Coffee. Perfect, he thinks, this one knows just what she wants. "I'll have what the lady is having," he says. They banter a bit, friendly, playful, and the drinks soon come.

He feels flush. The hot coffee laced with the strong liquor goes down warm and easy. Monica sips hers with an even pace. When it came she held it aloft in both hands keeping it near her mouth. The cream staying on her upper lip as she indulged. Stan is able to watch her closely as they sit across from each other, separated only by a few feet in the concave booth. He is conscious of looking at her too much and attempts to divert his gaze but inevitably his eyes come back to her. Monica's gown is open at the neck revealing a delicate yet seductive frame. The neckline plunges but the dress hangs in place as if by magic just above what might be considered too revealing. Stan shifts uncomfortably in his seat.

"So, Judge Hudson," she says in mock adoration. "What can you tell me about this 'terror plot,' is it safe for a girl to walk about the city?" He smiles. He likes the idea that people think him endued with some knowledge or power beyond what he actually has. Loosed by the alcohol and encouraged by her presence he maintains the playfulness when he normally would have been ill at ease.

"I don't know if it is ever safe for a woman to walk in the city. Especially one as charming as yourself."

Now it is her turn to watch him closely. He feels her eyes looking directly into his and diverts his gaze. He loses track of his thoughts, then collects himself and continues. "The case is really not a difficult one. I can't really talk about it, you know." Still her eyes bore into his and he looks away again, down at his hands which hold the nearly drained mug. She seems to expect more and he is willing to give it to her. "Monica, you realize you must be discreet?"

"Stan," she replies, as she leans forward, the dress popping open just a bit more as she presses against the edge of the table to move closer and strokes the back of his now trembling hand. "You never met a girl as discreet as I can be."

He smiles back at her. "Yes, I'm sure. As I said, it's not a difficult case, really. The papers have pretty much printed all that is relevant. It all hinges on what the government can actually prove. Not conjecture. Not supposition. But proof, my dear. Concrete, relevant proof. That said, this case has 'political considerations.' The city needs to show the populace that it is making it safe for . . . 'a girl to walk the streets' to use your phrase and the government needs to prove that all the money it is spending on anti-terrorism is bearing some fruit. And the people, the people want someone to pay for what was done in the past and to hopefully deter what might be planned for the future. Essentially, someone has to pay." Here he hesitates before continuing. "So, while the case itself, or rather the facts of the case, appear straightforward on the surface, how it all works out is not so simple."

"Interesting. That's almost *exactly* what my brother said. I believe he used the same term you did, 'political considerations.' Here she sits back, appears to think, and shakes her head in a worried fashion. She leans forward again and continues, almost whispering. "Stan, I can't imagine being in your shoes."

"What do you mean?"

"Screw the political considerations, from what I read in the papers it doesn't appear this woman doctor running these clinics would have any reason to send money to terrorists. In your shoes, I'd be more worried about the 'personal considerations.' Jesus, Stanley, she is supported by a list of who's who in this city. Jonathon Weiss helped her raise money. If she goes down how do you think he will look? Stanley, a man like that, he has connections everywhere. Listen Stan, I know people who are connected to Jonathon Weiss. He has a way of taking care of people that take care of him. You are going to get tired of being a federal judge someday and you talked about your daughter and your son, both in college. Having a guy like Jonathon Weiss on your side would be a great thing."

"Monica, do you know Jonathon Weiss?" he asks.

She arches her pencil thin eyebrows as if to convince him, and says, "Let's just say, that I've worked on a number of projects with Jonathon."

Innocently, he says, "Monica, I couldn't do anything unethical."

"Stan, I'm not saying that. You said yourself it comes down to what the government can actually prove. But if I was in your shoes, I would use my discretion. Jonathon Weiss doesn't have to tap you on the shoulder himself and ask for a favor. He doesn't work like that. But if I'm in your position, I would just do my job and if it happens to all work out . . ." and here she shrugs a bit, "and he thinks you're a friend. What harm could come of that?"

Stanley sits back and begins to think through all the implications of this night and what Monica has said. He must have stayed too long in this muted stage because he hears her say, "Listen, we both have to drive. I can't possibly have another drink and drive home after that. You're going to be so busy until this terrorism case is wrapped up. Let's see how it goes, and call me." She reaches into her purse and hands him a card. "If it all works out I'm sure I could be available, perhaps if the conditions are right we could spend more time together." With that she snaps the purse closed, squeezes his hand which still holds her card, and quickly leaves. He watches her go, the shimmering blue dress catching the muted lights of the bar as she sways. He shifts in his seat, reminded of his desire.

Chapter 30

The days move slowly to Nancy as she waits for her day of judgment. There are distractions of course, but she is accustomed to a routine that keeps her with little time for quiet reflection. Things happen that are out of her control and that makes her anxious. She is in near constant communication with Clarence as he works feverishly to put together her defense. Amazingly, the Center functions in her absence. Hope and the other children are being cared for. She has Jonathon to thank for that. He took on the role of overseer, spoke to her about the need for an Acting Director that would maintain the day-to-day operation, provide a cushion, a degree of separation from her, and convinced her it was the prudent thing to do. On Monday they had named William Hart, MD, the former head of Mercy Hospital to fill the role. Nancy knows Billy Hart, likes him. He is smart and competent. He left Mercy mostly due to the politics of health care. Caught between the government and the insurance industry he had been tired of wasting his days in bureaucracy. His resignation had made quite a splash in the profession and was picked up by the media. It was reported that he has a book deal in the works. This is a good match, Jonathon picked the right person and even though Nancy balked at the idea of giving up the control she had of the Center, even she concedes that the circumstances demand a change if the Center is going to survive. Billy joining the organization actually gives it a chance to not only survive, but to move forward, to continue the work. Who knows, maybe even get it to where Nancy had always dreamed it would go – to find a cure.

She and Jonathon speak several times each day. He is conscious of her need to know what is happening. He relays things to her in a matter-of-fact manner, objective, without emotion. He solicits her input, but maybe for the first time in her life, she allows herself to be led. In a sense, she feels as if she is dying to self and willingly turning over her future to someone that seems to know better than her what she needs. In a strange way Nancy feels a peace about the future coupled with a calm that things will work out. Even through the turmoil of the past week, there are already signs that the worst of the storm has passed. There has been the inevitable upheaval among the patients, or rather among the parents of the patients. Little Sammy's folks, the Robinson's, opted to remove her from the program. She had been progressively sliding backward, her last set of blood work indicated a full relapse is imminent. Although the dad proclaimed their decision was based on the incompetence of the administration, an administration that allowed money, their money, to be siphoned off to support terrorism, Nancy doubted if they would have been so vocal or determined to leave if Sammy had been doing better. There are two others that pulled their child from the Center. It's the newer clients she worried the most about. Christopher Randolph is doing splendidly; he is due to be released to go home for the Christmas holiday. The odd thing is, Christopher's father, Ted, has become a staunch supporter. She had been told how Ted argued openly with the Robinson's and other parents about how she and the Center should be given time, that they are innocent until proven guilty. Mr. Randolph had called Clarence, offering whatever support he might need, proposing even to verify that there is nothing in her tax record that indicates anything illegal. Nancy laughs to herself - funny how things have turned around.

It is Jonathon's report that surprises her most of all. Her biggest fear was not for herself but for the work and how it would be able to continue amidst the circus of this publicity. Jonathon is receiving a half-dozen calls a day from people all over the world inquiring on how they might get a loved one admitted for treatment. Not only that, but there is an even greater number of calls with offers of donations to keep the Center open. Checks, large and small, are pouring in from all over. They talked about this at some length, amazed at the generosity of strangers, dissecting the rationale behind this behavior. It appears people believe that she has done nothing intentionally wrong. There is a contingent of letter writers and donors that express enthusiasm for the Center's treatment philosophy, that believe in how they are going about resisting the disease. A third group, smaller in number, are from parents, grand-parents, and relatives that had lost a young one, some with PML, that simply want to show their support and express how they wish their loved one had such an opportunity.

Beyond that, there are pockets of people in the medical community from all over the world who are aligned with their cause. Jonathon is creating a database of those that have done or are still doing related research. While Jonathon could not talk to their medical competence or their research methodology, Billy Hart told him some of those folks seem to be on the right track. While only a small few had the audacity to put in writing that the concept of testing healthy, genetically disposed human subjects is the best and quickest way to discover a way to stop disease, Nancy secretly suspects the real number is much larger. Jonathon showed her a handful of the e-mails and letters. She can't help but wonder exactly what someone means when they write, "I believe in what Dr. Glacieux is doing."

All in all, through this odd series of events, Nancy finds her spirit rising within her, feels fortified by the belief that she is not alone, that 'the light at the end of the tunnel' is not an impending train.

Still, in the quiet of her own mind she questions if she can really be free from Hanif's influence over her life.

Chapter 31

The morning of the trial Nancy wakes from a restless sleep and moves about as if her actions are as scripted as her words are to be later. Filled with apprehension she readies herself and waits impatiently for the car to arrive. She hears it pull into the driveway and is at the door as Clarence approaches.

"Morning," he says. "Are you ready?"

"I guess."

Throughout the drive she is nearly silent. Clarence talks sporadically, primarily to remind her of something they discussed, of how he wants her to act or respond to certain questions. He warns her for what she feels is the hundredth time to not let the prosecutor bait her, to answer only the question asked and no more. She can tell, he is absorbed with the case, is living it in a similar state as she.

They pull up near the courthouse and the pack of media wolves they expected prowl the sidewalk. Clarence and Nancy wait as two burly bodyguards exit the car and prepare for the walk through the crowd and up the steps. As the door opens, Clarence turns to her and says, "Remember, stay close to me and keep moving." Then he steps out of the car first. Nancy follows. There is sound and movement all around but she focuses on the two broad backs that walk ahead of them that create a wedge for her and Clarence to walk through. He holds her left elbow and shelters her side while a third bodyguard immediately steps into the void on her right. A fourth comes up behind and the six of them walk in unison through the crowd and up the steps. She hears Clarence call out, "No Comment," to some question she cannot make out distinctly over the clamor.

Inside, they go directly to the courtroom. She is escorted up the aisle and takes her place at the table set for them. A wave of nausea hits her, her guts swell and heave and she would have fallen off the chair if Clarence hadn't noticed and steadied her. "Nancy," Clarence calls out. Reacting to her name, pulling her eyes off the ground and focusing in the direction of the call, Clarence's face comes into focus. "It's O.K. Look at me. It's O.K." When she looks into his eyes it is as if the fog begins to clear and she senses the safety of a sailor upon seeing the shore after being in a tempest.

Judge Hudson does not keep the crowd waiting long. He is announced and enters the courtroom. He gives terse instructions to the jurors, a stern warning to the spectators, and they are under way.

Finally in control of her quivering insides, Nancy's exterior is composed; however, she cannot shake the impression that she is outside herself, watching the proceeding from a perch above the table where she sits, being talked about but not really part of what is happening.

The opening statements are deplorable. One side paints the dark side, the evil Nancy Glacieux, and the other the pure white version.

The dark Nancy is related to the one she sometimes sees in the mirror. The one that questions her own motives and methods, concerned for nothing but her own convictions.

The light Nancy is the too good version. Saint Nancy. Walk on water Nancy. She knows that neither is true but today that isn't even relevant. What will the jury think? Is she a good witch or a bad witch?

The prosecutor begins by calling a member of London's elite Scotland Yard, an Inspector Maurice Thoroughgood. He summarizes the main events of the discovery, apprehension, and interrogation of the terrorist nabbed in London. The tediousness and the pace in which he tells the story, and in how the prosecutor asks minute follow-up questions, makes her want to scream, "Get to the point, already!" When the prosecutor is done, Clarence rises and greets the Inspector warmly, thanking him for taking the time to come to the United States to testify. This seems to unsettle him a bit and he looks, Nancy thinks, suspiciously at her lawyer. Clarence is brief, focusing on just one aspect of the testimony. "Inspector, it appears Scotland Yard did a bang-up job with the scoundrel – eh?"

"Why yes, I believe we did, sir," the Inspector responds warily.

"I imagine, from the way you tell it, your folks interrogated him thoroughly?"

"Yes, thoroughly sir," the Inspector agrees.

"Can you tell us how many hours he was in custody before calls were made to the States letting us know?"

The Inspector stops and thinks a bit, clearly trying to be accurate, and he begins by explaining how he arrives at the number he eventually gives. "Well sir, as I said previously, he was apprehended at right about 7 o'clock in the morning, just before the commuter rush hour was about to begin. At the Piccadilly Circus station, sir, caught right in the tube. We were diligent, as I said. We wouldn't have wanted to get you folks all worked up without being sure we had good information, you know?" Clarence nods to keep him moving. "So, it wasn't until the next day, around two p.m. London time, nine o'clock a.m. on this side of the pond that our Director made a call to your Homeland Security."

"OK," Clarence begins, "by your estimation he was in custody 31 hours? From seven a.m. to two p.m. the next day. Is that right?"

"Yes sir. That's right."

"And Inspector, were you personally there the entire time, actually conducting the interrogation, in the very room with the suspect the entire time?"

"Why no, sir," the baffled Inspector responds. "Why would I be? I went home in the evening. Not till after 8 pm," in an attempt to prove his diligence. He continues with, "Others were involved. I don't want to give the impression that it was my work alone. I slept, came back early the next day."

"Thank you, Inspector. No further questions." Clarence turns and sits back down to the dismay and confusion of Inspector Thoroughgood.

Next, the NYC Homeland Security team leader who is in charge of investigating Hanif Nasrallah is called, Agent Frank McCarthy. The prosecutor again asks a series of questions in an attempt to show the jury how thorough and complete their suspicions and processes are in the case. Agent McCarthy had been aware of Nasrallah for the last twelve months, initially because of calls that were being monitored going to locations that are on the department's watch list. It is disclosed that due to 'confirmed suspicions' they had stepped up surveillance of Nasrallah ten months ago. The prosecutor walks Agent McCarthy through another series of questions, the gist of which is to expose the contents of the tape recordings in which Nancy was on the phone with Hanif. The prosecutor takes this opportunity to present two statements, both from a few months ago. He reads wherein Hanif complains about the currency rate and needing additional money to keep the camp open; Nancy is identified and her response is that she will wire money to him.

The second is even more damaging. The prosecutor has Agent McCarthy read the transcript:

> Nasrallah: Well, we can't expect too much too soon. These things take time.
> Glacieux: Yeah. By the way, I'll arrange for another wire tomorrow, enough for the rest of this   month, and next.
> Nasrallah: Good, we can't move forward without funds.
> Glacieux: I've been thinking though. Wouldn't it be good if we could enlist more girls? I   mean, having more females could be beneficial in the long run. Don't you agree?

Nancy sits and listens, remembering the conversation and thinks to herself, Oh God, help me. They are going to send me to jail.

Clarence approaches this witness in a different fashion than the fellow from London. He does not attempt to appear friendly, rather his measured approach, tone and pace give the entire courtroom the impression he is suspicious of Agent McCarthy.

"Agent McCarthy can you tell the court why you were listening to these phone calls?" he asks.

"Hanif Nasrallah was the subject of an on-going Homeland Security investigation. Our protocol is to monitor all calls either to or from individuals suspected of being involved in terrorist activities. It's how we keep our citizens safe," says the agent.

"And you said earlier in your testimony that your department had been watching Hanif Nasrallah more closely for the past ten months. Isn't that right, Agent McCarthy?"

"Yes, that's right. Ten months."

"And does that mean that you have been monitoring his calls for that entire time as well?"

"Yes sir, for the entire time."

"Can you tell the court how many hours of Mr. Nasrallah's conversation you have monitored in that ten months? Approximately."

"Well, I can't say exactly today. I could find out, but we generally see four hours of activity on a light month and eight hours on a heavy month, so approximately. . . 60 hours in that timeframe."

"Ten months. Approximately 60 hours. Is it fair to say that in that timeframe there were a quantity of calls between Dr. Glacieux and her ex-husband, after all, this case aside, they are parents and like most divorced parents still maintain some communication.

"Yes sir, there have been a quantity of calls between the two parties."

"Can you estimate, again for the court please, the quantity or frequency of these calls."

The agent gives this question some thought, "I'd say on average about two or three. They didn't speak frequently, but some months twice, a few times as much as three."

"That's fine, Agent McCarthy. We're only looking for an estimate from you. Ten months, an average of two and half calls per month. Is twenty-five calls a fair estimate in that timeframe?"

Then with almost a begrudging tone, as he begins to see where Clarence is going with this, he says, "Yes, Mr. Williams. I'd say that's a fair estimate."

Here Clarence takes some time, surveys both the judge and the jurors in his gaze as he fashions his next question. "So, Agent McCarthy, the prosecution read one statement and had you read one from all the calls made between the two parties. Please tell the court were either of those statements that you read into evidence is the full and complete transcript of the call?"

"No, sir. We read only what is relevant to this case."

"OK, so neither call was the complete transcript. The second example you read into evidence, that wasn't full and complete either?"

"No, sir. It was not."

"Agent McCarthy, I have here," Clarence returns to his table and scoops up a pile of papers and waves them with a flourish, "the full transcript. Would you mind reading the portion of the conversation that was conveniently left out by the prosecution? I have it highlighted in yellow, there." He points to a highlighted portion as he hands over the stack of papers to Agent McCarthy, who looks up to the judge for direction. Clarence continues to speak, this time addressing the jury, "You'll notice Dr. Glacieux *starts* the conversation, a fact that the prosecution purposely deleted."

Judge Hudson nods his head in response to Agent McCarthy's look indicating that he should read the transcript as directed.

> Glacieux: Hi, Hanif. I'm reviewing this month's report. I've been going over it since this morning. There doesn't seem to be anything that moves us forward.
> Nasrallah: Well, we can't expect too much too soon. These things take time.
> Glacieux: Yeah. By the way, I'll arrange for another wire tomorrow, enough for the rest of this month, and next.
> Nasrallah: Good, we can't move forward without funds.

Glacieux: I've been thinking though. Wouldn't it be good if we could enlist more girls? I mean, having more females could be beneficial in the long run. Don't you agree?

Nasrallah: I hear you, but it's not that simple. There are strong customs and traditions that encourage families to consider the males more worthy, more able. Women don't hold the same place in our society.

Glacieux: Yeah, but still. There has to some families that are progressive thinkers, some that want their daughters to attain the same goals as their sons? Maybe we can increase the stipend? You know, provide a good old capitalist incentive program?

Nasrallah: You might be on to something there Nancy. I'll have my people work on that.

Glacieux: OK, anything else? I gotta go.

"Thank you Agent McCarthy. That's a *much* different conversation. Dr. Glacieux is clearly stating she is concerned for the lives and welfare of the female research subjects. Wouldn't you agree?"

"Objection!" The federal prosecutor rings out. "Counselor is clearly leading the witness."

"Withdrawn," Clarence responds, his point made with the jury. "No further questions, Your Honor." He takes the transcript right out of the agent's hand and returns to his seat beside a relieved Nancy. Judge Hudson takes this opportunity to call a quick recess.

****

The courtroom nearly empties but Nancy and Clarence stay in their seats. He informs her that the prosecutor will call her next. She cannot sit still while they wait out the short recess. Her fingers tap the tabletop and she realizes her legs are involuntarily going apart and together repeatedly while she sits. She gets up and paces in the small space between their seats and the railing behind them, feels her pulse quickening, sits back down and prays simply, "Lord, help me. Help me please."

As the crowd begins to come back in and re-take their seats, she can hear the guards out in the hall ordering the stragglers to make their way back into the courtroom. Judge Hudson re-enters and instructs the prosecution to call their next witness. Nancy walks slowly up to the witness box, stands and answers affirmatively to the administered oath. The prosecutor goes through the preliminary questioning and after about twenty minutes, finally gets to the questions about the raising of funds. He attempts to paint a picture of someone that is more concerned with raising money than helping children. He tries to trap her into saying something incriminating. Nancy responds well to each temptation. Clarence prepared her well. Her answers are short and to the point. Each time there is an opportunity she directs the jurors back to the fact that she is a doctor and that she always has her patient's best interest at heart. Her testimony is unwavering, and at one point, the prosecutor becomes exasperated, literally crying out a taunt, "Ms. Glacieux, do you really expect this court to believe that you knew nothing of what your blatantly, fanatical, Muslim husband was doing with all the money you were sending him?"

Nancy takes the high road in her response. "Mr. Clark, Hanif was raised a Muslim from the time he was a child. And while I don't understand the reason why he seemed to have renewed faith as an adult, I surely could not have been expected to assume he had become a terrorist. After all, the vast majority of Muslims are sincere, kind, loving people. So, yes, I do expect the court to believe me when I say I knew nothing of any plan to siphon money intended for our work to find a cure to a dreadful disease to any other purpose." She looks toward the jury. "Because it's the truth."

In the end, it became a tiring joust; the prosecutor asking different versions of the same questions, vainly trying to catch her in a contradiction. Occasionally, Clarence would object. "Asked and answered," he would call out. Later, pleading with the judge, "Objection, Your Honor. Where is the prosecution going with this endless parade of questions?" He knows he doesn't have to do too much. He can tell the jury is just as annoyed as everyone else in the room. Thankfully, at long last, the prosecutor gives up the floor.

"No further questions, Your Honor. Your witness, Mr. Williams."

Clarence stands displaying the weariness that they are all feeling. Nancy sits in the witness box and again admires how her lawyer works the jurors with his subtle movement and the intonation of his voice. "Your Honor, I'll be brief. Dr. Glacieux, would you like a glass of water?"

"No thank you, Mr. Williams."

"Fine. Nancy, can you tell the court how it is that you were able to start up the Center for Hope."

"Sure, I took what savings I had and I was able to get a loan against my home. We started in a much smaller place, of course, and we had only a handful of staff members. Some of the people that I had worked with previously, nurses and doctors, volunteered their time to help us cover a full schedule."

"And yourself, Dr. Glacieux, what kind of work schedule do you personally maintain."

"In the beginning, for a period of about seven or eight months, I worked seven days a week. Generally from seven in the morning until ten, or eleven o'clock at night."

"Dr. Glacieux, Nancy, tell the court why you began the Center, why you mortgaged your livelihood, your home, why you worked so incessantly."

"It was for Hope," and here her eyes water, and she hesitates, seemingly struggling for words. Clarence reaches into his pocket and hands her a handkerchief with which she pats the corner of each eye before continuing. "My daughter, Hope, suffers from PML. She is at the Center now. She's one of seventeen patients we currently care for. I started the Center, for Hope."

"Thank you, Nancy. I have only one more question for you. A lot has been made by the prosecution of the amount of money that kind and compassionate donors have given to your organization over the past few years. But tell me, that mortgage you took against your house, how much of that do you still owe?"

Nancy gives a soft chuckle. "Nearly all, Mr. Williams." At this point she looks toward the jury. "Like most people I make the monthly payment but most of that goes to the interest. The principle amount owed is only a few thousand dollars less than when I took the loan three years ago."

"Thank You, Dr. Glacieux. I have no further questions, Your Honor." The prosecutor declines the option to ask any follow-up questions.

The summary statement from each party follows. The prosecutor rehashes the portions of the case that indicate Nancy's involvement with Hanif, and what she knew, or should have known about where the money was being spent.

Clarence does not speak long, but Nancy feels he's effective. He focuses on three main things, each of which puts her in favorable light and are designed to place doubt in the mind of each juror. He attacks the government's case, reminding the jurors of how the prosecution tried to 'trick them' into believing the small portions of the recorded conversations were full and accurate; that Nancy was clearly concerned for the welfare of the girls that became part of the research. If she had known Hanif Nasrallah was training terrorist destined to die for their cause would she have been interested in the possibility of bettering their lives? He questions London's handling of the accused terrorist, who by Inspector Thoroughgood's own testimony, admitted that he wasn't present during the course of the entire interrogation. That while he slept the accused was likely denied sleep and he hinted at the possibility that at some time during the thirty-one hours of interrogation, perhaps in the middle of the night, someone may have tortured or even water-boarded the accused to force him to make an accusation, any accusation, that both governments were desperate to make stick.

Finally, he speaks of Nancy's child, and what a devoted mother she must be to lay everything aside, to mortgage everything she has, in the faint possibility that she can discover a cure for her child.

****

Judge Hudson addresses the jury, gives them directions on what the law says and what latitude they have or don't have in considering a verdict. Nancy thinks he goes out of his way to ensure they understand the difference between conjecture and fact. At one point he intimates, with an example of something the prosecution had said, about the difference. Nancy feels thankful that she has a friend like Jonathon Weiss, a lawyer like Clarence Williams, and a family that believes in her and what she is doing. As the jury leaves the room, she places her face in her hands and rubs her now throbbing temples. Clarence gently massages her shoulder and whispers to her, "Not to worry, Nancy. This is nearly over. Not to worry."

****

The jury is back in forty minutes. Nancy has freshened up and the pain reliever she took has taken away the edge from her headache. Judge Hudson comes back to the chair, bangs the courtroom into order. "Has the jury reached a verdict?" he asks.

The jury foreman stands and announces, "We have, Your Honor."

"The jury foreman will read the verdict," the judge says.

"We the jury find the defendant, Nancy Glacieux, not guilty." The noise in the courtroom obliterates the rest of his statement. Nancy jumps up and gives Clarence a bear hug that nearly knocks the wind out of him. Judge Hudson bangs the gavel and there is movement and excited chatter throughout the packed courtroom.

"Order! Order!" The bailiffs work through the crowd until all are seated again and the room is nearly quiet. Judge Hudson bangs the gavel one more time, thanks the jury for their service, looks toward Nancy and says, "The defendant is free to go." He stands quickly and leaves the courtroom, which erupts a second time.

Epilogue – 32

Outside the courthouse there is a bedlam of lights, motion, and a frantic clatter of voices. Although the bodyguards are still nearby in case they are needed, Clarence has them allow the media to encircle Nancy and him. This is their opportunity to give the sound bite that all the news outlets will broadcast. As they move to get themselves into position on the top step they are bumped and jostled by the crowd as if it is New Year's Eve in Times Square. Finally, they are in position and the media has no choice but to stand on the steps below in order to face them, get their statement and the picture for the evening news. A question shoots out distinctly above the noise, "Mr. Williams, what do you have to say to the Attorney General?"

Clarence smiles. "The Attorney General and I are colleagues. He knows I have no animosity towards him. Sometimes you win and sometimes you lose. Today, justice was served."

"Dr. Glacieux, how do you feel?"

"Tired. Relieved, but tired. I knew I was innocent but it's a relief to see the jury agree."

"Dr. Glacieux, what's next? Will you be continuing your work?"

"The Center is in very competent hands. Dr. William Hart is a top physician and administrator. So the important thing, that the work continues, is already happening. While I won't be involved in the day-to-day operation of the Center, I will not abandon my daughter. In some way, in whatever way I can, I will continue to work on a cure."

"Dr. Glacieux, what will happen to the research center in Chad?"

Clarence steps in with the same authority he displayed in the courtroom. "That's enough for today folks. Thank you." He nods to the guards. They step forward and usher Nancy and him down the steps and into the waiting car.

Inside, they both sit back and take a moment to relax. Nancy slides her hand across the seat and takes his. "Thank you, Clarence. You were wonderful. I can't thank you enough."

"My pleasure, Nancy. We were fortunate. Everything went as planned. There were no surprises."

The car pulls into her driveway and comes to a stop near the walkway. She turns to him, "I'm going to have a celebratory drink. Do you want to join me?"

"Thank you, Nancy, but no, it's been a long few days. I just need to go home. I'll toast you from there. Some other time."

"I understand. Definitely, some other time. Thank you again, Clarence." She leans over and gives him a kiss on his cheek. "We'll talk soon," she says as the driver opens her door and she steps out into the chilly air. The wind had died down but it is still cold. As she goes up the walkway she puts her hands into her coat pockets in an effort to keep herself warm without bothering to do the zipper. One pocket holds a small lip balm and a tissue, the other a cell phone. That's odd she thinks to herself as she goes up and hits the code on the alarm. She opens her pocketbook, grabs the keys and notices her cell phone sitting there where she thought it would be. Once inside, she takes the phone from her pocket and stares at it in wonder. "This isn't my phone," she says out loud. "What the hell?" Still wondering how someone else's phone could have gotten into her coat pocket she places it on the kitchen table and goes about satisfying her desire for a drink. She puts some ice in a glass but is unnerved when the odd cell phone rings. She goes to it and looks to check the number before answering. It is only a notification. 'You have a new message,' is displayed on the screen. Well, that's useless she thinks. Her curiosity aroused, she goes through the steps to see if she can identify the owner's number or if there are contacts she can call who might know who this belongs to. There is nothing. It is a cheap phone. It looks like one of those pay-as-you-go throwaways. How did this get in my coat pocket, she wonders for a second time. My coat was with me the whole time. Either I was wearing it or it was near me in the courtroom. Outside? In the rush and confusion on the steps? Could someone have slipped this into my pocket? A wave of anxiety comes over her as she once again goes through the steps to see if there is any information that can be found on the phone itself. Nothing.

The message envelope is the only discerning feature. "What the hell?" she says out loud in the empty room, and pushes the button to check messages. The phone speaks back, "You have one new message. Enter your password and hit the pound key." She puts in the month, day, and year of Hope's birth, the same code she uses for the security system. Nancy is startled by the sound of a muffled voice. "Need to talk. Come alone to Momentums. Sit in the back booth, expect a call." Nancy stands immovable, trying to get her head around what this all means. It has to be Harry. No one else would guess the security code they've used. No one else would remember or care that Momentums was the sports bar where she and Harry first went out together. Clarence told her that the feds were certain Hanif had left the country. How could he have gotten this phone to her? What could he be up to and why did he want to talk to her? Should she talk to him? Could this be some kind of trick? Were they setting her up?

Despite her misgivings she downs the drink, changes into jeans and heads out. As she drives she thinks how silly it is. There was no time given. She has no appointment and will probably end up sitting by herself and waiting to no avail. How would he even know she is there? He is probably half-way around the world? The parking lot is nearly empty on this wintry afternoon as she pulls in. Entering, she recalls the first time they came in together. They visited a few times after that, quiet dates, when they were together. There are only two people sitting at the bar. They don't even turn to see who entered, transfixed to the event on each screen above the bar. Nancy walks toward the back, past a number of empty booths, and sits by herself in the corner. This place hasn't changed. The same stuff on the walls, a pair of entwined lacrosse sticks and a full size canoe perched off the ceiling. The old fashioned phone booth, the kind with the accordion door that you can slide closed to block out the noise of the room is just to her left on the back wall. Music is piped through the speakers that hang strategically at various angles along the upper edge of the wall. Eventually, the barmaid makes her way back. She is doing double-duty, no waitress on a slow time like this. She is young. Nancy thinks she's annoyed that she had walked by all the empty booths to take this one in the rear.

"What can I get cha?" she calls out from a few feet away, mouth open, chewing a wad of gum.

Nancy waits until she's closer. She doesn't even have the strength to raise her voice. "A beer. Whatever you have on tap – light, please."

"You gonna want to order somethin' from the kitchen?"

"Yes, I think so, but just bring the beer for now. I'm . . . I'm kind of waiting for someone."

"Sure thing." She turns to walk back to the bar.

"Wait," Nancy calls out, and the barmaid turns and looks back. "Did anyone call? I mean, did anyone call and leave a message? My name is Nancy."

"Sorry, honey. No messages. Not yet anyway. Let me get you that beer. I'm sure he'll call and if that s.o.b. don't, both of the guys at the bar are nice guys." She tilts her head toward the bar and gives Nancy an exaggerated wink before she goes.

Despite herself, Nancy laughs. What would Jonathon think if he found her here? She picks up a menu, not expecting anything beyond what was there a few years ago. Turkey club. That's not too bad, she thinks as she scans the appetizers and burger platter specials. She waits with the mysterious cell phone sitting in front of her on the table, drinks the beer and tries to figure out exactly why she came here. It isn't that Harry has some uncanny pull on her. No, it isn't that at all. But they do share something, something that binds them together even through their differences. Harry cares for Hope, Nancy is sure of that. Her illness, it may have been worse for him than for her. Even through the pain Nancy could rationalize illness. It happens. Harry didn't feel the same way. To Harry it was a sentence, a clear sign that God had turned His back on them. He felt Hope was innocent, the victim, but he, they, were responsible.

The blond, wearing skimpy tight shorts makes her way back with the soup and the turkey club Nancy ordered. She carries a second beer as well.

"This one's on me, honey," she says as she places each item down in front of Nancy. "Can I get cha anything else?"

"No. No thank you. This is fine. Thanks."

"Sure thing. Enjoy."

Nancy almost forgets why she is there. The drink at home, the two beers, the familiar setting, the food, not too bad for a bar, it all worked to take her away from her trouble. She hadn't realized how hungry she is. Between bites of the club and washing it down with swigs of the beer, both are nearly done. Over the sounds of the bar and her own musing she finally realizes that a phone is ringing in the background. The cell is quiet. Is it coming from the bar? She peers up and sees the two men and the girl. They make no attempt to pick it up, as if they don't hear it. It continues to ring. Is that the fourth ring or the fifth? How many did I miss, she wonders? Then it dawns on her. She bolts for the public phone in the booth on the back wall. She scoops the handle up quickly and slides into the seat.

"Hello. Hello," is all she can think of to say.

"Who is this?" a man's voice says from the other side.

"Who is this?" she counters.

"Never mind, I must have the wrong number," says the man.

"It's Nancy" she blurts out, not wanting to risk making a mistake. "I'm at the Momentum Sports Bar. Who is this?"

From the laughter she can tell it's him. "Woman," he says, "it's good to hear your voice. I see they let you out of prison," and again he laughs.

"You bastard," she can't refrain from answering. "It was your ass they were after."

Again, a hearty laugh. "Allah has preserved me. I wouldn't be much good in jail, would I?"

"Perhaps not, but that's where you belong. What the hell is this about? Why did you call me?"

"Nancy, relax, please. I don't want any trouble with you. We only have a minute, I can't stay on the phone, you understand?"

"Yeah, I understand. So talk – what do you want?"

"Nancy, I can still help. We can still find subjects for the research."

"You're crazy. Do you realize what happened here? The feds are looking all over for you. I can't risk getting caught talking to you."

"Don't worry. I will get in contact with you. There are ways. I must go. Just tell me you won't give up. I'll take care of everything here. Tell me you won't give up!"

Nancy is crying, tears streaming down her face. She doesn't know what to say. The barmaid is at the door peering in at her and puts her face into the opening and mouths the words, "Are you OK?" while handing her a tissue.

"Yes, I'm OK," Nancy says to the blond.

"Good. It's settled then," comes the answer from the other end of the phone. Hanif Nasrallah hangs up.

Nancy sits with the phone still up to her ear and all the ramifications of what just transpired hits her right between the eyes.

Acknowledgement

A special thanks to friend and editor, Lee Mandel. Her selfless devotion, keen insight, and faith in me to write this story made all the difference.

A reading group guide to *Hope-A Story of Devotion* is available from the author. E-mail: Hopeanovel@gmail.com
Visit – www.hopeanovel.com